This is a work of fiction. Names, characters, places and incidents either are the product of the author's imagination or are used fictitiously. Any resemblance to actual persons, living or dead, events, or locales is entirely coincidental.

ISBN: 9780578331638

Book design by Impress Design
www.I-D.design

www.JackMcDaniel.net

Printed in the United States of America

POET OF THE MOON

a novel by

Jack McDaniel

Published by

BOOKS BY JACK MCDANIEL

Agents Of The Undertow (Book 1 Pan21 Series)

Agents Of Hope (Book 2 Pan21 Series)

Agents Of Change (Book 3 Pan21 Series)

Purple Hearted Man

For Madison

POET OF THE MOON

PROLOGUE

I became the Poet Of The Moon because of Edward Burgess—not because he gave me the name, or because The Oligoi celebrated me, but because he provided the platform where a few words and actions made gods tumble and fall from the sky, made crows rise and resist, and demanded the average man on the street look up and take note. Legends and revolutions are like that; they grow from simple deeds that take on a life of their own. Behind the myth that developed and unfolded was rage and blood and mayhem, accompanied, as always, by human grief.

The idea of a poet doesn't immediately conjure up a killer, a mass murderer and terrorist, but times changed, the earth changed, and with those changes society became something different from the past. It's a messy, imperfect thing—being human. Events unfolded and played out in linear progression, but after, when the story began to be told and repeated, the events came to life in a new way: meaning was added. In the moment there was too much to consider to understand how or why a shift in the winds, in the form of a few words, seized a people and captured their spirit. In the moment, I only wanted to survive.

"Just passing by, friend," he said, and extended a hand for me to shake, as if all the while we had been negotiating safe passage. He was nervous, almost trembling as he reached out his hand for me to take.

There are two types of men who might have done this in my experience. The devious who only want a chance to get at you before you could have a go at them, and idiots who thought that friends and allies could be made there and that such a thing as trust and that a fair fight existed. This man, I could tell, was the latter. Never harbored a violent thought in his life. How did he get here, I wondered? How did one so timid and . . . *hopeful* . . . come to be here?

This, I thought as I looked at him, is the wrong reality for you. We were a full kilometer into Great Cavern, which was itself two kilometers long and almost as wide. I sighed and bowed my head, ever wary, but determined to toss aside any social inclinations I might have had, to bury my humanity, harden my heart and become what was necessary. As I reached to shake his hand I manufactured a smile, an attempt to conceal the coldness in my heart. I reached to his elbow instead of his hand and pulled him down and into me, unbalancing him. I dropped my rock-chipped knife from concealment into my left hand and thrust it deep into his side, then ripped hard up toward his heart, the force lifting him from the ground a slight bit. The density of rock in Great Cavern varied: not so the human body. My makeshift knife did its job.

The man fell in a heap, dead before he hit the ground. I looked up from his fallen body and did a 360 check—rocks and the sound of water burbling nearby, nothing that raised an alarm. I bent over him. He had little of value: the standard issue shirt, pants and shoes, some manufactured rope around his waist I could use. His clothes were torn and worn a minor amount—otherwise a typical recruit not long in residence. I wiped the blood off my knife on his shirt and took everything from the man and folded it up and put it in my bag. I could use it all.

Few men ever re-make themselves, re-invent who they are. Any of us, at any time, can walk out the door, disappear into the world and re-emerge wholly new in some other location and circumstance. You only have to be willing to leave everything behind, say goodbye to the things and habits and people you love and go. But few ever take that step, ever pass through that door, no matter how miserable their lives are. Most never make that decision, regardless of the numerous fantasies and idle thoughts whose gaze is cast in that direction. We are creatures of habit, us humans. We like comfort, routine, the uneventful, like a child clinging to its favorite blanket or toy. We invite it. We become slaves of the mundane. We are far less the complex creatures we believe we are, tied to our social moorings like a boat to a pier.

I took that step, left it all behind and re-invented myself. But not out of desire. I was forced.

Occasionally, events press themselves upon us and force us to become something other, to re-make all that we perceive that defines us. Those on the front lines of war understand. They've experienced it. But war is different. Soldiers have causes. They take allies and friends into battle, fight by their sides and for the memories of those they are protecting back home. Not so here: there is no cause or social network to prop you up. Many are incapable of changing under these circumstances, too many material or spiritual attachments to their pasts. They perish quickly, especially on this hard and unforgiving rock. Even when faced with death most could not become that thing that was necessary to survive, so they didn't. Survive, that is. Others, a select few, if truth is to be told, embraced the change because to live, to be alive, was all there was. For those who made that decision and embraced the new, to die with the false honor of not doing harm to another was to allow the system a victory, to maintain the status quo, to simply become lost in the machinations of others.

I didn't believe there were any moral victories to be found in dying because you could not find it within yourself to kill. Nature doesn't distinguish between honor and dishonor. That is a human construct, and one that is often misplaced. Ethics and morality can be situational. They live in the grey, between the facade that we are our culture and manners on one side, and the razor sharp blade of reality on the other. Dying because you believe it is wrong to kill another does not mean your purchase in heaven—or nirvana, or Valhalla—is confirmed, that St. Peter or any other gatekeeper is going to smile upon your arrival. It simply means you are dead. All of the evidence for God in the entire universe—any God—still adds up to a lot of conjecture and loads of pretending. What is moral and immoral when facing death? And does it really matter or change if we are the only ones—us humans—to witness and judge it?

At a very core level we lead dishonest lives. Forget for a moment the question of God and his complete lack of involvement in the human experiment (despite all of the claims to the contrary). Consider instead the perception we have of ourselves. We believe we are different from the other animals on the planet. We believe we are not part of the same processes that created them, or that spur them on. We believe with a great deal of arrogance that we make the rules in the circle of life, even after the spillover pandemics and the climate-change that fueled earth's insurgency and killed so much of the human race. Of course we are smarter and we are the only animal capable of organizing on such a large scale. We are creative and self-aware. We manipulate technology like it is a magic that flows from the font of our big brains. But we also breathe and defecate and screw and eat, and not out of choice but of necessity. Still animals, each and every one of us. Our disconnect from this fact, I believe, is what led us down the rabbit hole of haves and have-nots and delusion. It was the reason I was trapped on that rock and why my metamorphosis mattered.

I stood over one such man—a non-animal incapable of changing who he was, even to survive. I could have easily been him, I realized. I refused to believe that I was different from the rest of humanity. I had simply made a choice and decided I could live with it.

I bundled up the man's clothes and meager belongings. I rolled him off to the side of the path. I didn't make any attempt to hide him. I didn't need to. Besides, a maintenance bot would be along soon enough and collect him. In all likelihood, everything that had happened was on camera. I squatted down by the body and looked at the man for a moment. Somewhere loved ones might have been grieving for him, but I had my doubts. No one got on that rock by chance. To some degree, we all earned our places, even me. I looked up and listened intently. Still no signs of anyone else nearby, no danger. I raised up and grinned then for the cameras and hummed a little ditty from long lost days and began walking back to the Crow's Nest, my home.

I was a killer, a mass murderer. I made no apologies for it and I bent no truths in justification of that fact. If anyone wanted to understand that place, that time—and me—then I would have to start from the beginning and tell my story as honestly as possible. As should be obvious by now, it wasn't all pretty. But it was mine. And it is at least an honest story.

My name is Clay, Clay Alexander. I ruled that rock for a short while. But that home was only temporary. I was just passing through. I was going to get back to The Edge, at any cost, and when I did I was going to have my revenge.

1

THE MERIT ANALYSIS

"Tell me, how does a man smile while betraying his god?"

"I'm sorry, I don't understand."

"Let's at least be honest with ourselves, father, if we're going to do this. Or is it only fealty you desire, and not honesty?"

"How is it you think I betrayed God?"

"In one respect, that's nearly impossible, as you know. Your god painted His moral landscape with a wide and very conflicted brush. Don't you think?"

"I can't imagine how you could say that."

"So, it is fealty. Definitely not honesty, anyway."

"God has given us a moral framework, but we cannot know God's plan entirely. That is beyond us."

"I've never understood that line of thought. It's utter nonsense, to be honest. But it's also beside the point. We have his words, no?

When He says that slavery is fine then surely it must be. When He orders you to murder anyone who believes in another god then we must comply. Except there is that commandment where He tells you not to murder. Which do we choose? Or, as your lot are so fond of doing, should we lie and act as if there is no conflict, that somehow God's words mean something different?"

"Sometimes God is literal, others His teaching is more subtle, more nuanced."

"But then there is Deuteronomy 4:2. 'You shall not add to the word that I command you, nor take from it.' How do you explain that? All of that schizophrenic nonsense and things that can't possibly coexist, that's way beyond *subtle*."

The priest just stared down at the table, unmoving.

"Don't tax your brain too much. That's not the betrayal I'm speaking of. Your test is a sham, an offense to your god, and His creation."

"How do you mean?"

"Your test measures compliance, obedience and docility. It looks for those who accept the status quo and never question the realities of the world we live in. Huge chunks of our population live in The Edge, or someplace just like it, amid poverty with little to look forward to. If yours is a loving god how could He accept that? How can you, as His emissary, be a part of it?"

"The Merit Analysis determines one's worthiness before God."

"Does it now? Sounds like a lot of marketing drivel to me, no different from the holo ads when you go shopping."

"But of course. We know what God desires above all else; our loyalty, love and obedience. The test simply measures these things."

"And you believe you—the church—to be the best judge of this?"

"Not me or the church—God's will."

"The same god who said that we shouldn't judge one another? You believe in this instance He has no qualms with you passing judgement on us all? Somehow, after 2,000 years of racist, xenophobic bigotry, the church is now more enlightened and capable of discerning God's truth, as you would put. In other words, if we're being honest, now you *are* God."

The priest started to make comment but halted, an anguished look as he contemplated.

The test—the Merit Analysis—was the only method for most to move from what was essentially the others, the poor, and become Cleric. The Cleric class had all of the advantages of wealth minus the power. The Oligoi reserved that for themselves. Being Cleric meant a job and good wages. It meant status and it was a way out of The Edge, assuming one desired to leave.

"So, as God you denounce free will and individuality. You desire only to coddle the like-minded and those who forgo critical thought to mindlessly acquiesce to your wishes. In other words, after 2,000 years, your primary goal is still repression."

"The church has always been more than that, as you know."

"Of course, it has. You comfort those in need. You provide a centralized form of community. But you also prey on the poor and you are in the business of oppression. Those are your primary modes of operation, now, just as they always have been. Never has the church made an effort to elevate the poor, to educate them, to eliminate hunger and poverty. Not really. As you know, the church's profits from a single year alone could virtually end all suffering by providing the tools and teachings necessary to make all humanity independent and self-sufficient. But then, when people have enough food and work and they needn't beg for sustenance what need do they have for the church?"

"You have a very dim view of our work, Mr. Alexander."

"It's not opinion, just simple observation based upon history."

The test, the Merit Analysis, measured many things. It was a personality test that classified each individual based upon the answers given to a series of questions. But it was far more than that. It had an artificial intelligence component to it that measured eye movement, posture, response time, perspiration and heart rate and other variables that were put through its program to determine how truthful the responses were to the questions. It was said to be impossible to fool.

"Tell me something, father, how often is the test updated, the program that runs it, that is?"

"Every quarter an updated version is rolled out. We are constantly changing it, making it better."

"So, by your own admission, God—the church—is flawed and your test is lacking. If it can't be trusted to provide accurate information can you really claim it to be the will of God? And what sort of judge are you if your test can't be trusted and has to be updated regularly?"

The priest swallowed hard, eyes stared out though focused inward.

"Let me ask you a theoretical question, then. Why, if I don't believe in your god, or if I believe your view of God is warped and twisted, should I be forced to live by these rules?"

"You aren't. You can stay where you are and believe what you will. That has never been forced upon anyone. We simply seek to elevate those who are deserving."

"Right, to not believe means I am forced into a life of poverty and reduced to living in a shack. How is that fair?"

"This is our society."

"About that, and back to my original question—How does a man smile while betraying his god?—you must know you have made a deal with the devil. Doesn't it bother you to be in bed with our Oligoi overlords? You betray your god with such nonchalance. I find it difficult to believe you sleep well at night. Unless you are one of those who is happy because you got yours, and all of its comforts and perks, to hell with the masses."

Again, the far-off stare from the priest.

Finally, after some time, he said, "Do you wish to take the test, or not?"

"I have no hope for passing it, as you know. Your recommendation, along with your AI's, will be that I fail, regardless of the test scores. Has your AI been observing and recording this entire conversation?"

The priest confirmed it had.

"Well, then, by all means, let's get on with it."

2

THE EDGE

"Would you look at that," said one police to the other. "What's he doing going into The Edge?"

I was only a few feet away, in easy ear-shot as I crossed their paths, but like many Clerics they had no issue speaking about me as if I wasn't there, just a lower-class *enfant terrible* in their eyes.

They stopped walking and watched the man dressed in his nice clothing with his neatly cut hair and nice shoes—me—as he stepped across an imaginary threshold and entered The Edge. "Poor fucker," one said, "couldn't pass the test."

"Sad, that," said the other.

They chuckled.

I didn't look up, just ambled on. What would have been the point? We all had crosses to bear, burdens to shoulder, and wrongs we carried that couldn't be righted. Why draw attention and give added weight to them? Why give them the slivers of dignity I possessed? Besides, I knew the truth. Underneath the facade and the surface-level pretensions they were no different from me. In truth, they were less than me in some important ways. They lacked knowledge, critical thinking skills and curiosity about the world. Their station in life made them slaves to a system that rewarded subservience and demanded individuality be discarded.

I was also aware that humans are social animals, and society, however ruined it was, defined our truths to a greater degree than I would have liked to admit. Individuals are slaves to its systems and rules. You played the game well and succeeded. Or you got overrun, or passed-over, or forgotten. Sometimes, you were the wrong person at the wrong time. Then there were those like me who asked too many questions and expected answers.

People like the police I had passed weren't philosophically bent. They were simple-minded and too guarded of their place to ask the questions I wanted to ask. Still, if I could force them to think, to really consider, there's only one question I would have asked, only one I would have wanted to know the answer to. My guess was they wouldn't have been able to conjure an answer, any answer, other than the one dictated by their social status and standing.

I stopped on the other side of the street and looked back at the police. They had moved on. I was something they had already forgotten, just an odd part of their patrol beat.

"What's up, Clay?"

Tab Sinclair, eleven or twelve year old neighborhood kid, appeared beside me. Her face and hands were dirty, her gray t-shirt had the blue streaks of something spilled on it, but she wore a toothy grin composed of big teeth and mischief and eyes that sparkled to highlight it all. Tab was a good kid but she struggled under the delusion that most in The Edge did; that one day she would escape, become a Cleric, or maybe even an Oligoi.

I smiled. We began walking deeper into The Edge, toward my home.

"How was it today, out in the world?"

Same as every other day, Tabitha. What have you been doing to get so dirty?"

"Oh, you know, just stuff."

"Break any rules today? Get in trouble?"

"Clay!"

"Come on, kid. You have to push the limits to really experience life."

"I'd never become Cleric if I did. Then my parents would kill me." She rolled her eyes, skipped a step, and looked down the road.

The Edge was 3-D printed homes and other buildings, a prefabbed board game designed by someone in an office whose only goal was to cram as many people into a small space as cost-effectively as possible. They had statistics and rows of data and study results that determined the minimum amount of square footage needed for families of various sizes. Tab's family was one of the statistically convenient pieces to that puzzle. The five of them lived under the roof of a 1,400 square foot gray box, a basic kitchen with a small family room and three bedrooms, boxes all with small windows. The windows were wasted, ornamental: the view from any of them was more gray, square boxes.

When the earth re-invented society—after the oceans rose and the Oligoi Wars ended—communities like The Edge showed up outside all the new cities and urban areas. They became the home to the *other*, the masses of humanity who couldn't qualify as Cleric and weren't Oligoi. They became home to the poor and many of the former independent thinkers of the land.

"Life is about more than becoming Cleric, Tab."

"Of course it is. But it's a big deal to my parents. You have to do well in school and pass the test just to qualify. If I get into trouble I wouldn't even be considered. You know?"

"Uh-huh," I answered, but I wasn't paying attention, besides, we'd had the same conversation several times. Down the street a small crowd had gathered. I could hear their laughter and feel their energy from where we were. "What's up down there, do you suppose?"

"Oh, that's Sarah. Came to see her mom and dad. They're finally going to be moving out of The Edge."

"Sarah? The one who married some big-wig?"

"See, Clay, it can happen." Tab made big eyes at me and displayed that toothy grin again.

"Tab, you're too smart to think along those lines. Quit assuming this is the way the world should be and start thinking about how to change it."

Sarah, I thought, nice name. It had a nice sound to it. She'd been around before. I'd said hello once, in passing. She was beautiful, to be sure, but there seemed to be more to her than that, as I recall. I saw a hunger in her eyes I recognized, felt myself. A restlessness was there that could only barely be contained.

"Tab, didn't that happen a long time ago?"

"You mean her getting married?"

I nodded.

"Over a year ago, I think."

"Took a while for them to move out," I said.

The crowd bothered me. Why would they act like that? She was a neighborhood woman who had married into money. That was all.

Yet, they prized her as if she were something special, worshipped her. Nothing against her, Sarah, but the crowd were so swayed by the shiny thing dangled before them it seemed wrong.

"Idiots," I muttered.

"They're just happy for her, Clay."

"No, they want to be her. They won't make something of their own lives. They want someone to pick them out of a crowd and make them special instead of working to become it."

We stopped walking and watched as the crowd began to disperse. They were jovial and content to have seen something special, someone who had made it.

"I need some milk."

We turned into the cheaply printed and brightly lit convenience store. Dom was behind the register, looking down at his PED, smiling. He nodded a hello and kept watching. Tab wandered through the aisles, looking at the packages and fancy advertising. The holo ads recognized her as a child and began showing her all kinds of printed algae gel treats laced with sugar. It was illegal to recognize her directly because she was a minor, not the same for me, though. Despite the highest privacy settings possible, I was immediately recognized and suggestions were lobbed at me by the AI data algorithms, all based upon my past purchases. I did my best to ignore them, pushed right through and grabbed a pint of milk.

"Clay," said one of the holo ads, an older, gray-haired man, "did you forget cereal? I see you haven't purchased any in a while. Your favorite wheat and oat combo is one row over to your left, on the top shelf."

"You never respond to those things," said Tab, who waited at the end of the aisle as I walked toward her.

"And yet, they still persist. Want anything?"

"No, I'm good."

I put the milk on the counter and pressed my thumb onto the digital window that opened next to the milk carton.

Dom looked up. "Seen the newest from Fugitive Theater, Clay?"

"No, Dom. Not interested in watching that drivel."

The machine beeped and I held my wrist over the digital window and let it scan my bank info.

"It's fun, man, crazy shit. Bag?"

"I'm sure it is. Yes, please."

"Enjoy," I said as Dom handed the bag to me.

We stepped outside the store and looked back up the street where we had come from earlier. Two guys were shouting up the street, early twenties, shoved each other and got up in each other's faces. The Edge gangs were always trying to mark their territories, someone wanted to expand, someone else wanted to push them back. It would get violent soon. It always did, a never-ending loop until someone died.

"I'm going to head home, Clay."

"Good idea, kid. Don't go near that mess." I indicated the two young guys up the street.

"I won't."

"Hey," I called to her as she crossed the street, "you're a good kid, Tabitha. I just want you to make the most of life. I'm proud of you for doing things and getting dirty. Better than being on your PED all day."

She smiled, waved, and took off up the street. I went the opposite way from Tab. My place was a little over a block away.

The previous evening I had been reading *The Oligoi Wars* and it got me wondering about life before the changes—before the Wars and before the seas rose and nature was doling out punishment to the monkeys with the big brains and short-sighted tendencies. Somewhere between forty and eighty percent of humanity lived within fifty miles or so of coastline back then, and that might still be true. There had been a lot of argument over the number and how to properly measure things. But the only thing they should have been focused on was the number of people displaced when the oceans rose. It was a lot.

Of course, the coastlines of the past were vastly different from today's. They were places of great beauty and access to abundant resources before the changes. Shipping and fishing were big industry. Vacationers often made their way to a coast. Places like The Edge didn't yet exist. There had been poor people, sure. But, as far as I could ascertain, the last time anything like The Edge existed was in the Hoover era, whenever that was. The historians in *The Oligoi Wars* weren't too clear on that.

On an emotional level The Edge was difficult to describe. The places—homes, schools and businesses—were cheap, incredibly cheap. The Oligoi and the corporations that created The Edge, and other places like it, touted their humanity and beneficence for all that they gave to the *Others*, including our meager guaranteed living wage, designed to keep us on the edge of poverty. But it felt more like a way to lock people—the masses—into a way of viewing the world, and another way to encourage and enforce conformity. *You are not special or unique, not you. You are stamped out and cheaply produced and utilitarian, like the place you live,* they seemed to say. That's what it felt like to me.

I reached the end of the block on my way home and rounded the corner and almost stopped dead in my tracks. She strode confidently toward me, head held high, not in arrogance, almost defiant. She was casual in manner, yet guarded.

"Hello, again," I said.

Her eyes lit up and it was there again, that hunger, or something I couldn't quite get a handle on. It wasn't sexual, though that portion of her was hard to deny. Something more was there.

"I'm Clay."

"I remember. Sarah, Sarah Burgess. We met once before, I believe. You live near here?"

I raised my head and pointed my chin. "Just over there."

"The old warehouse?"

I smiled.

"Huh," said Sarah. "I'd like to see that sometime. I don't know anyone who lives in an old warehouse."

"Any time. Open invitation."

She looked at me oddly, head to toe. "Why do you live here, Clay?"

I shrugged. "I'm not Cleric and there isn't much else for a man like me. Is there?" I looked around. "Besides, I like the people, most of them, anyway."

She was quiet, thinking.

"I thought you just got home," I said, "visiting your parents, I believe. Why are you walking out here?"

"I've been here for a few hours, actually. Slipped out the back a while ago. The crowds just left, finally, so I'm going back to say goodbye." She shrugged. "You know how it is."

"Can't say I do."

She frowned. "What do your friends think of you?"

"What do you mean?"

"Well, you aren't Cleric, but you obviously have a nice job, that's odd. I'm guessing you're one of those who can't pass the test."

"That might be why I don't really have any friends, unless an eleven year old girl from the neighborhood qualifies."

"What about at work?"

I sighed. "I'm not really part of that world. There's a stigma attached to me and my situation. No one wants to be seen with me, not at work nor here. I drag them down at work if they associate with me. And here," I looked around, "well, their focus is higher than what I represent."

Sarah looked around. I could tell she was actually seeing The Edge and everything it represented. "Not focus, Clay. Hope. They have hope."

"Yes, nothing more tragic than hope among the hopeless."

I saw pain pass behind those blue eyes of hers. She knew what I meant and what I was thinking. I was impressed by that. We hadn't become a nuisance to her, yet, trivial little things to be minimally tolerated. She still cared. I felt like a heel then.

"I didn't mean to imply," I said, "that you—"

"Of course you did." She looked directly into my eyes. I tried to block out how captivating she was, how alluring. Just be present, I chided myself. "And you weren't wrong," she continued. "I know they point to me as an example, that I fuel their hopes and dreams. They treat me like I've done something special, like I am special. Some days, I'm not sure if I should hate myself, or them."

She stared off into the distance for a few beats.

"Well," she finally said, "I have to go. It was nice talking with you, Clay. I hope we can do it again."

"Like I said, open invitation."

I half expected the milk to be spoiled as I climbed the stairs to the second floor of the warehouse. My chat with Sarah had been intense, and with the thoughts swimming in my head, I thought the milk would curdle. Stupid thought, I knew. Still, I reached into the bag as I climbed the stairs and felt the sweaty coolness of the outside of the carton, just to be sure. Then I laughed, went through the security protocols and entered the place.

Just inside the door I removed my jacket and tossed it onto a chair. Then I slapped the wall and activated the local EMP to kill any bugs or tracers I might have picked up. It was a bit paranoid, but I preferred the safety and my privacy.

Miyamoto strolled over and looked at me. He was a huge cat, athletic, mostly siamese, but something else that came through. He had longer, scraggily hair that made him look like a wild animal, sprouting out and up around his ears and whiskers. I named him after the great Japanese samurai warrior, Miyamoto Musashi, who never lost a battle and rarely suffered injury, even though he fought in six wars and several scores of life or death duals. He was a great samurai. The name seemed to fit. Miyamoto, the cat, kept the place clean. He was as effective as the samurai had been. I poured him a bit of milk into a saucer and sat down.

"I don't know what to think about that," I said to the cat. "She's beautiful and pretty smart, I believe."

Then I remembered the last name, Burgess. That got me thinking. I had seen the name in *The Oligoi Wars*. I was certain of it. I got up and grabbed an algae-based dinner—steak and potatoes, though I wouldn't know if it was steak, or not, never had it in the real—and popped it in the microwave. Under the window next to a chair and table I pulled off the cover to the hidden compartment, unlocked the safe within, and pulled out my copy of *The Oligoi Wars*. It was an actual printed book. It was illegal to own, of course. A last gift from my mother after she died, and something of a complete surprise to me. I found it in some of her things before I became a ward of the state, buried it in the one bag I was allowed to take with me and guarded it with my life ever since. It was a huge volume printed on really fine paper, like an old Bible, because the book was over 2,000 pages long. It purported to be the true history of the Oligoi—or the aristocrats, oligarchs, titans and lords, as they used to be known at various stages throughout history. They became known as the Oligoi during the Wars, some journalist made it up and it stuck.

The microwave pinged. I closed and locked the safe and replaced the cover. Then I grabbed my dinner and climbed the back steps to the roof. I had built a small area on the roof to sit and watch what was happening in the neighborhood and to enjoy the sun or the stars in peace. It was well hidden from the immediate area around the warehouse. Distantly, I could see the towers of The Edge's low-rent apartments.

There was still an hour or more of good sunlight left in the day, then the blues and reds and greens would drain away and conceal the open wound that was The Edge, to be defined then more by its sounds. At night it would become an audible ooze of violence, shouted arguments and, eventually, a tenuous quiet, until morning when the veil of darkness would lift and the open wounds would be exposed in the sunlight.

I took a bite of dinner and looked up the Burgess family in the book. Sarah hadn't just married into money. She had been wedded into history. Now, she was history, or historical, anyway. The Burgess family line traced back to medieval times. They had topped the food chain for centuries. Edward Burgess, her husband, was head of Burgess Entertainment and Media, and he was on the board of several other corporations.

The Burgess family had done well in the Oligoi Wars. They survived when several others hadn't. That made sense. According to some of the history I browsed, they had played an integral part in constructing the world before the changes. I sat there for a while and read more about them and their place in the past.

Finally, darkness descended and the night settled in. I closed my eyes for a few moments and she was there, beautiful and dangerous—Sarah. I shook myself, fended off the cooling temperature, and looked upon the bright glow of an area known as Skin. The Edge was large, a several hundred thousand lost souls made it home, like an anthill or beehive, small and full of hustle and bustle. Skin, maybe a third of a mile away, was one area where the hookers, whores and transvestites plied their trades. The dealers dealt and the junkies looked away from the world, toward more hellish inner demons they couldn't escape. Two fast-food joints were on opposite sides of a large shared parking lot, brightly lit for the duration of the night. It was where most of the action took place. Police sirens blared and their loudspeakers squawked. It was a statistical certainty that multiple someones would die tonight in The Edge, lending credence to the thought that its inhabitants were somehow less human than those made Cleric. Never mind the packed-like-sardines qualifiers and the volatile certainty that type of closeness and poverty dictates.

A large full moon, white that evening, hung low in the sky and signaled a busy night for the purveyors of misery and their victims.

Were we the right creatures, I wondered, to evolve to this level on the planet? We are wasteful and violent beings no matter how those are measured. We kill each other at unprecedented rates in nature, unlike any other species. We are short-sighted and egocentric. We could have ended hunger around the world over a century and a half ago. And poverty, too. These things we choose to allow. On some level maybe we need them. I couldn't say. I only knew them to be persistent, even if unnecessary.

Violence and hope, I decided, were the songs of The Edge. One forced. The other misplaced.

A siren blared in the distance. The Police. Earlier, when I was returning home, I wanted to ask a question of the police. One I would like to ask of the Edward Burgesses of the world, as well, and of many others, too. A question I wanted an answer to, especially given our proclivities for violence and misery, and given the realities of The Edge: Is this what it means to be human?

3

SARAH

"So, you're the guy who is supposed to know how to fix things. Can I trust you alone in my factory?"

Tompkins, my boss, and actually a pretty nice guy, sent me to one of our affiliate companies to help out. Seemed one of their printers was malfunctioning and the self-diagnostics and the drone maintenance bots couldn't make the repairs. So they called me. That was my ticket into their world. I could piece together the puzzles, find the frailties and bottlenecks, and keep the machine running. Often the issues were physical, parts broken or worn out, things jammed that even the maintenance bots didn't see. But I knew where to look. Other times, more often than I would have guessed, a software update would kill the system and I would have to write a patch or figure out a way to re-align the machine. Sometimes the machine was too old for the updates. It was good to have a wide range of knowledge and skills. It kept me employed.

This guy, the production manager, which meant he was little more than a watchman with a staff of fewer than ten or twelve in this huge facility, was a short, fat man who believed with all his heart that he was my better. He knew my story. It must have chewed at his bloated sense of prestige to need my help.

"Meyers, do you want my help, or not?"

"The powers that be say I have to, so—" He waved a disdainful hand, palm up, toward the shop. "Aisle 17, third in line."

"Not going to hold my hand? What happened to your lack of trust? Buried under years of apathy?"

He scowled.

I chuckled. "Don't even want to know what the issue is, do you?"

"Just fix the damn thing. Quit being mouthy with me."

Meyers wasn't any different from most of the managers I dealt with. He spent his days in the control room, watching the screens for any alerts and dispatching a repair bot. When a real issue arose, like this one, he didn't cope well. My guess, based upon the few minutes of interaction I'd had with him, he hadn't spent much time, if any, on the production floor in a long while. He wasn't the sort to get dirty or down on his knees, if needed.

This facility was 200,000 square feet in total. Only 50,000 of that was designated for inventory, though the inventory was stacked at least a hundred feet up. Things shipped out of here fast. This was one of the places where they printed algae based protein bars. That meant the job, my puzzle, could be messy. The machines were efficient and sturdy, but when things went wrong, well, biomass isn't always contained like plastics or steel. Without the proper enzymes and proteins the substance can become unstable and liquify. It all depends on the set-up, timing and what is being produced. Injecting the proteins and enzymes into the algae gel at the proper time caused it to solidify. It varied based upon the flavors or goals for the product. Some products, like mashed potatoes, were purposely liquified. When microwaved they develop their consistency. I hadn't seen much of those issues, but I knew what to look for. With printers it's always software, parts failure, or something blocking a path.

Sure enough, maintenance bots were cleaning the floor around the printer when I approached. I stopped and observed the production floor for a moment. It was like a beehive with all the movement and action. Maintenance bots, feeder bots, transporters, cleaners, quality control testers, you name it. No people. Not one. This was why the wonderfully and oxymoronically named Guaranteed Living Wage existed. After all these years, we figured out a way to put ourselves out of work. The problem was we made certain those same unemployed monkeys with the big brains were also poor, a recipe for something other than utopia, you can be sure.

While I worked on the problem I thought again of Sarah. It had been several days since we ran into each other in The Edge. I still couldn't get her out of my mind. I knew it was wistful fantasy, but the days were long and boring and normally uneventful. Don't misunderstand, I liked my work, but it wasn't as challenging as one might expect, which made me wonder why they needed me. It also made me believe that my view of the world wasn't all wrong; worker bees and drones aren't good at coloring outside the lines, or thinking through problems. They are followers. I may have been on the outside looking in, but that was meaningless and overlooked when that red light stayed on and help was needed. Even guys like Meyers would yield to his own misgivings when production goals were on the line.

The answer, at least partly, to that look I saw in Sarah's eyes, part of her hunger, was a counterintuitive revelation. I couldn't figure out why I believed it true, but I did. She missed The Edge. She longed for something there—the people, sights, sounds, smells, who knew. Why would the chosen one be so unhappy? I wondered. But that's the other thing I knew to be true: she was unhappy.

Of course, I could have been completely off base.

The issue with the printer took most of the day. It was a typical combo of industrial mass production machine and the protein bio printer. It was older than most of the other machines in the area.

Meyers never once came down. At one point, I walked to the inventory shelves and took a protein bar for my lunch. It had three soft divided sections that tasted of chicken, beans and some dessert, strawberries, maybe. It was the standard 1,000 calorie meal.

I figured out the issue sometime after lunch. Software glitch. The most recent update broke the system and a patch wouldn't work. Glad I'd seen that before. I found the previous version on their system, installed it over top of the new version and then hardened the machine so it couldn't accept any more updates. It was an older machine and nearing the end of its life. I didn't see any others like it, but the place was big and I didn't feel like looking around. Meyers could do his own work.

I posted my report and documented everything, including all the processes needed for my fix. If they had any enterprising employees they could effect the fix pretty easily on any of the other machines. Most likely, I'd be called back someday soon. These machines weren't on the same update schedules. They were all independent, probably due to the age of the broken machine and a desire to not have the entire floor down at the same time if an issue came up.

"Good to go, Meyers," I said, as I entered his office. He startled and sat up.

"Got it fixed, good. What was it?"

"I posted my report. You can read it. You might want to check to see if you have any other similar machines."

"Fine. So, you're leaving?"

"And I didn't even ruin your factory. I did take a protein bar, though."

"Whatever, get out of here. I need things to crank up again."

"Calm down. It's running now. I have to know it's fixed before I leave. That means it has to be producing."

I didn't want to hang around. There'd be a positionally compelled lecture if I did. Guys like Meyers were like that. They got nervous around me, had to make certain the social status and hierarchy was understood. It was late afternoon and I decided to go home. No need to return to the office. Meyers just glanced at me, not even a thanks.

I took the light-rail a few stops until I came to The Edge. As I was getting off my PED pinged. I exited and pulled it out of my pocket. I had been sent a notice; I failed the test again.

I sat down at a nearby bench. The notice was disturbing and I wasn't certain why. I knew it was coming. You got two shots at becoming Cleric, no more. So, I was done. I didn't really care. I didn't like most of them. They were a bunch of guys just like Meyers. And yet, sitting there just outside The Edge, my heart beat faster, my stomach was in knots and my mind wouldn't quiet.

It wasn't failing the test itself that worried me, though. I doubted I could pass even if I had wanted. It was the finality of it all. I'd never get another chance. What that meant, what anguished me, was that I would be forever between two worlds. I'm a loner, but at some level I needed to belong, especially when individuality wasn't appreciated and only barely tolerated amongst the Others.

I had wondered what would change for me when I didn't pass. I knew I could still work. They might try to cut me out after a while from the big corporate jobs, but people needed my skills and knowledge at all levels of business. At worse, I could freelance. That made me wonder. Not passing wouldn't have a big impact on me. Things would continue as normal. But *passing* the test would have meant big changes. If I had passed I would have been expected to live accordingly, within the system and according to the rules of the class. I wasn't sure I could do that.

Conflicted and troubled, I walked to my place. The Edge exposed itself; its impermanence documented in cheaply printed buildings and the lack of history that helps root people to a place, and its dirt and grime and graffiti, the signs of crime and poverty. Spillover zoonotic diseases flourished here once they got started. That was always a danger, even with the advanced research to understand them. But given the choice, I preferred to stay versus living amongst the Clerics and well-to-do. I'd be a fraud there.

Something was different as I climbed the stairs inside the warehouse. A feint aroma lingered, something new, fresh. Sitting at the top of the steps, just outside the door, was Sarah.

"Took a gamble you might be home soon." She smiled.

"I did say the invitation was open. Glad you're here."

She stood up and I went through my security protocols, which seemed more important given her presence and the recent news I'd been given. I fumbled about a bit, nervous to be so close to her, in my home.

"Got a PED?"

"Sure," she answered.

I held out my hand, asking for it. I put both of our devices in a small Faraday bag and hit the local EMP switch by the door. The EMP shouldn't have been able to fry the systems of our PEDs, but it would disrupt and disable them for a while. There was always the chance they could be damaged, so the Faraday bag eliminated that possibility. Keeping the PEDs in the bag would hide them from the network, too.

"Paranoid much?"

I smiled. "The people you associate with like to think they own others' privacy. You know what I did?"

"I'm not stupid. Have there ever been any drones or spy bots?"

"There have, once or twice. Nature of my job and who I am."

"And just who is Clay Alexander?"

"Not much to him, really. I'm the guy they call when they can't figure out an issue with one of the printers. They don't want to waste time waiting for a manufacturer's rep. It's more cost effective to keep me on staff than to lose production time, especially given the number of machines in service. Also, I'm better than the manufacturer's reps. I have a wider range of skills and knowledge. But they don't like that they need me. Not Cleric, you know. Sometimes my boss, who I like, is ordered to keep tabs on me."

"He told you that?"

I shook my head. "He hasn't, but, you know."

"They don't complain when you kill their bugs?"

"They would have to admit to using them, then. Not that they would really care about that, but it wouldn't look good. As you know, they care a lot about how things look."

A thin smile and acknowledgment that she understood.

"Wow," she said, looking around, "you really do live in a warehouse."

I looked the place over. It wasn't a large area, all things considered. It was neat and orderly, but no one could deny the dried wooden floorboards, or the brick walls. I had built a makeshift wall between my living area and the bedroom and bathroom. The place was big enough and well-lit. I even had some abstract art that I was fond of on the walls.

"Too much for you?"

"No! I love it. It's almost like something out of an old magazine."

"Oh! Nice." She surprised me. I didn't think the place would be refined enough for her, given her position in the scheme of things.

"Aren't you worried," I asked, "about being here?"

"I don't think he keeps me under that close a watch."

She could see my skepticism and shrugged.

"You've killed the surveillance and he knows I come to The Edge to see friends and my parents. He doesn't like it—appearances, you know—but I can't just forget my former life."

"I thought your parents were out of here."

"They are, mostly. They still have a few things at the old place. They'll be gone completely this week."

"Didn't you grow up here?"

"I did," she said. "I always thought the greatest thing ever would be to get out of The Edge, but—"

"The good life not all it's cracked up to be?"

Sarah didn't answer right away. She walked to one of the windows and looked out. "There isn't a lot to like about this place, Clay. Everyone can list the reasons why, and there are many of them. But that doesn't mean it is better outside, either."

"You sound lonely, like you miss a lot of things here, and too few that attract you on the other side."

She kept staring out the window, arms crossed over her chest. "I'm guessing you understand that."

"I explained before, I don't have many friends. I'm shunned in The Edge and at the office I'm not good enough for anyone to be friends with me, in their eyes. But I'm okay alone most of the time."

"Are you really?"

"It's not easy, I admit. I find I have become a creature of habit and routine. Maybe it masks how I feel. I don't know."

"What does it all mean?" Sarah kept staring out the window. She leaned against its frame for support.

"Of the two of us, I would have thought you could answer that better than I could."

"I'm not so sure of that." She turned and looked at me. "I shouldn't be speaking to you about these things. We don't even know each other. I'm sorry. You're right, I really shouldn't be here."

"No one is listening, remember? I'm curious, why do it?"

"What, marry Edward?"

I gave a slight confirmation and cocked my head.

"I thought I was helping my family. It was all a dream and he was quite romantic and caring for a time."

"Well, your family must be happy."

"Perhaps, I'm not certain. My dad passed the test and Edward got him a job. But I don't think my dad likes it very much. I'm not even certain he cares to move. But not my mom, she won't shut up about how wonderful it all is."

"She must be very proud," I said, knowing it wouldn't make her feel any better.

"I didn't accomplish anything, Clay. In truth, now I'm not *sup-*

posed to accomplish anything, except give him an heir."

"You had something else in mind?"

"I'm pretty smart and I have things I would like to pursue."

"And that's not possible now, with all the resources at your disposal?"

She looked at me for a long while, deciding how much more to say.

"Let me ask you something. Why do things have to be this way? So many poor and the few with so much?"

"Human nature, I think. Despite all our technology and abilities," I said, "despite our big brains and grand ideas, we always need others who have it worse than we do. When you build a world, a society, based on greed, opportunity will never be parceled out evenly, nor will the riches, whatever those are."

"And why do so many accept this?"

"Beats me, Sarah."

I considered where we were, The Edge. I had wrestled earlier with the consequences of becoming Cleric, or not. But I never considered that I would be unhappy, especially when I failed the test. It all seemed so meaningless. When do we cross the line where helpful illusion becomes delusion? When—*why?*—do the little lies we tell ourselves become absolute truths? Her previous question wouldn't vacate my mind: *Why do so many accept things as they are?* We live by so many illusions. That's part of what society is. Currency has value because we agree, as a society, that it does. But the universe doesn't care. An old twenty dollar bill is no different from a five. They both were printed on cotton and linen paper with some green ink. Neither was worth anything in the grander scheme. Only society assigns them value. The same for the damn test.

And what about the Oligoi? Do the Oligoi believe they are different from the rest of us? Has that illusion become delusion with them and the masses? Are they no longer flesh and blood like we are?

Sarah turned and walked from the window and plopped down on a chair. "Do you have family?"

"Mother died when I was twelve in an accident. Grew up an orphan after that. We didn't have any other relatives I could live with."

"I'm sorry. That must have been hard."

"She taught me to be independent early on. That helped a lot after she died."

In all the years since her death, Sarah was the first to ask about my family, my mother. She looked so comfortable the way she had relaxed into the chair. She had let down her guard completely then. She made me feel good. I liked talking to her. Her concerns and perspective weren't too different from mine.

"Thanks," I said, "for asking about my family. No one has ever asked before."

"Ever?"

I shook my head. "Not really."

"Thanks for letting me talk. But I should be going."

"Are you sure?"

"Edward will get suspicious if I'm gone much longer."

We both stood. For an awkward moment we faced each other silently, then began walking toward the door. I didn't want it to end.

"I probably shouldn't come back Clay. It could get us both in trouble."

I reached into the Faraday bag and pulled out her PED. "The invitation stands open. Thank you for coming by."

As I opened the door, I asked, "Why do you miss The Edge?"

She shrugged and thought about it for a few seconds. "I'm not certain. For me, it's real."

"Well, come back when you need more real."

4

SUBDUCTION ZONE

Edward Burgess pinched the bridge of his nose, breathed deeply and bit his tongue so as to avoid making the comment that begged to come forth: *impatient idiots the lot of them*. Seven opinionated Burgess Media and Entertainment board members were seated around the conference table in the company headquarters. Three of the seven had concerns over the performance of their new flagship reality show, Fugitive Theatre. But their concerns, Burgess felt certain, were misplaced, the disquieted nerves of the faithless. The show would come around and find an audience, and a huge one at that. They just needed time to reach more people to get them hooked, and he had a plan for that.

It was an ongoing issue with the Board, always grave concerns over one issue or another due to their lack of industry experience, and the perception that every new fad had to be pounced on immediately. His family had been the purveyors of media and entertainment for *centuries*, for God's sake, tracing their roots to Gutenberg and the printing press. He had grown up in the industry. It was, literally by now, in his blood. And yet, they quibbled and questioned as if the empire would collapse if the new venture failed. It—Fugitive Theatre—wouldn't fail, he knew. And neither would the empire falter.

Tilda Hogue, whose family had built their fortune in real estate decades before and never ventured outside of that market avenue, was an alarmist, the type who tried to draw everyone into her views. She said, "Shouldn't the numbers by now look better? That's all I'm asking. This is a huge investment of resources and at a great cost to the family."

The family, as everyone seated at the table understood, were the ultra-wealthy ruling class who had, after the Wars, bounded together to pursue the common interest of leading humanity along the desired path, toward a future dictated by themselves. It had been Tilda's father, Stanley Hogue, who had suggested the Merit Analysis and the incorporation of the church as partners into their long-term plans. Burgess understood it to be a stroke of genius. Stanley Hogue had also suggested the creation of cities like The Edge and the Guaranteed Living Wage as they took the land and resources from the poor and lower middle classes, a generation or more ago, to build their new cities due to the encroaching seas.

"Tilda," said Burgess, "we need to exercise patience. I've seen this before many times. Shows like Fugitive Theatre can take time to build an audience. Besides, what cost is it really to the family? As everyone here knows, the moon base was a dormant white elephant before my proposal."

To understand the colossal development of the moon base is

to descend into earlier times, the realities and the fragile mindset, when chaos and fear waltzed hand-in-hand down every street, where change ignored its slow march through time and became an insistent and ever present and immediate nightmare. The world had unravelled in a gradual and clock-like manner for decades, small increments of sea rise and change that disguised their impact under the veil of time. But once it neared its transformative end and began to find equilibrium again, things shifted, only this time to be played out nearly in real-time, like some cheap cinema thriller. The hulking nature of the changes made every day appear one tick closer to some vague termination-clock, an almost inevitable conclusion. The final changes to the landscape weren't played out over glacial time periods or even decades, as they had been proceeding for nearly a hundred years. They came in a rapid-fire staccato.

The oceans rose faster as the Greenland ice sheet disappeared. The additional water caused changes in the tectonic plate subduction zone of the Mid Atlantic Ridge, thousands of feet under the ocean surface, and caused the release of billions of tons of water from under the earth's crust. The oceans rose at unprecedented rates, then, and land simply disappeared. Florida was entirely under water, as was most of the old eastern coast of North America. The ultra-wealthy had long understood the most valuable thing on the planet was land and the most valuable land had always been along coastal waters. Most of the world's great cities were built on those coasts. When the waters rose a different and unique war began. The ultra-wealthy, soon to be known as the Oligoi, began to take—not acquire—the new coastlines.

But the consequences of the rising oceans reached far beyond real estate. Humans became more densely packed with less land mass available. Conditions were less sanitary for a time. Infrastructure couldn't keep up with the rate of change. Next to the closer and more densely grouped human populations were the wild animals who had been kept at distance in the past, something no longer possible as humanity had no choice but to retreat into their wilderness and claim more of the wild. The frequency of spillover zoonotic diseases skyrocketed. Some of the old diseases came back with a vengeance—Hendra, Ebola, Avian Flu, to name a few. And several new diseases, especially those built around mutated versions of the H5N1 virus, spilled over into human and animal populations. Identifying the virus and creating a vaccine looked like a temporary measure, at best, most of the time, as the rate of new diseases outstripped the ability to identify them and then fabricate treatments.

Burgess took a long look at Tilda Hogue. He knew the truth behind much of her fear. Her father had died on the near-earth orbital Olympia. Like many, Stanley Hogue had thought himself and his family safe by making Olympia their home for a while when the worst of the viruses were spreading across the planet. But Olympia wasn't self-sustaining. It needed supplies—supplies from the surface. A virus, never identified, found its way to the station and most of the souls onboard died. No one could escape from the closed environment and few were immune, Tilda being one of them. The elder man died as his daughter looked on.

Once things settled a bit, the families decided to launch the grandest of long-term projects, something to guarantee their safety if, or when, times became unpredictable again. They built an underground city on the moon. Burgess understood how the moon base could seem like a refuge for her if things went sideways again. He understood her fear. But she was one of the few who now felt that way. Most were ambivalent, at best, preferring to ignore it more often than not.

Men like Stanley Hogue and Burgess' grandfather were visionaries. To allow the moon base to rot from disuse would be to dishonor the men who put so much into making it possible. It was, in many respects, the greatest achievement in human history. But the moon base shouldn't just sit and be sustained by its robotic staff. It needed people using it, interacting with and adding to its ecological systems. Besides, something as remarkable as the moon base needed an audience. Burgess told himself a degree of family pride wasn't misplaced in how he felt toward the moon base, but more than anything he wanted Fugitive Theatre to work. He needed it to for reasons he didn't quite understand. It was perhaps, he felt, his chance to make his mark on the world.

A generation, or slightly longer, was a long time to build something. And what mattered to the previous generation wasn't always of concern to the current. Science had put an end to most of the zoonotic diseases as the moon base became functional, and those that did occur were usually contained to places like The Edge. The new generation found the trip to the moon too long and uncomfortable. They complained there wasn't enough to do once on the base. It bored them and it wasn't their project. The generation gap was a distance too far for most. And many of those who made it happen were dead or too old to care.

Burgess could see he had hurt the woman's feelings. "Tilda," he said, softly, "if things don't turn, if we can't make Fugitive Theatre profitable, we can always go back to its intended purpose."

He saw her soften somewhat at that. "This idea just seems crazy to me, Edward."

"What? Fugitive Theatre?"

"Yes."

He smiled, then asked himself, *What will they think when I un-*

veil the changes? "The numbers are trending in the correct direction. Each week ratings inch up. We are becoming really popular with the younger audience, a key segment for us. And you know how they are. They like to talk about things they like."

He pulled out a PED and tapped the screen. The large overhead displays, one at each end of the conference room, showed the statistics to back up his claims.

"Look at the last two weeks," he said, highlighting the areas on the screen. "We've had big spikes across all the social networks. We are building some good momentum."

"It's not just the numbers, Edward," said Jonathan Sterling. Sterling's family had made its fortune in shipping. "There's some concern over what we're doing. It could cause long-term damage to the company, to the brand."

"Yes," said Tilda, "I mean, criminals killing each other as entertainment isn't exactly high society. Some of them are very creative, I admit, but it's just so brutal sometimes. I'm still surprised we have as many viewers as we do."

"The gladiators of ancient Rome were no different from our Fugitive Theatre. I'm not worried about perception. Besides, I wouldn't expect anyone in this room to like the show. It's not for us, is it? This is for the masses. If they believe it is too violent they won't watch. But I think it is the perfect entertainment to distract them. They like knowing others have it worse than they do. Besides, these are the worst of the worst criminals. All are sentenced to be executed."

"I understand that," said Sterling, "but I think you have an inherent problem keeping the show from becoming bigger—namely, the lack of a star. How long does the average man survive on Fugitive Theatre?"

"Eleven days. I am addressing that issue, by the way. We are looking throughout the penal system for just the person who can capture the attention of the public. And then we have this," Burgess paused and smiled at each. "Beginning next week, we are airing a new show to address some of what you are saying. It's called The Lottery. The show is thirty minutes long and the audience plays a key role."

"The Lottery?" Tilda looked confused.

Edward nodded. "Each week we will introduce a new set of criminals with their biographies and the list of crimes they've committed. The audience will vote for the ones they want on the show. My hope is that it will give them someone to cheer for. In addition, we are launching the Fugitive Fantasy League. To start, the audience can pick three from the Lottery for their team. If any of them die during the week they get to replace them with the next week's crop, or from those still surviving. A player on Fugitive Theatre who survives week to week gets bonus points for extraordinary kills, creative escapes, for tactics and for longevity."

Mouths were agape, some looked confused. Edward continued. "My goal with this isn't to just create stars and heroes on Fugitive Theatre, or even super villains, but in the fantasy league, as well. I want to celebrate the local guy who is great at predicting who will perform well and who won't."

Burgess tapped the screen on his PED again and displayed the news headlines from a couple days before. "Remember him? He murdered his neighbors and then his own family recently. He will be on The Lottery next week."

Sterling was in disbelief. On the screen was Jose Mann, The Edge Knife, as he was known. "Has he even gone to trial yet?"

"Next day or so," Burgess mused. "He's pleading guilty, so I pulled some strings and made a deal. With all the publicity around him it should jumpstart the show and the fantasy league."

"I feel . . . dirty," said Tilda.

"Nonsense," said Thomas Ulbright, impeccably dressed and tanned, one of the members of the board whose support Edward knew he had. "Edward is correct, this is about distraction and keeping the masses engaged in something other than their little lives. What do we care for any moral component? If they don't like it they won't watch, or participate in the fantasy league, and all will be forgotten soon enough. I understand your personal hesitations. But remember, as Edward noted, this isn't about us. The others—the masses—don't see the world as we do. Let's let them decide."

Edward gave a slight nod to Ulbright.

"I do like," said Ulbright, sitting up straighter, "these changes. I'm excited to see what they bring." Ulbright always seemed bloodthirsty to Edward and times like these reinforced that intuition. Edward half expected him to drool with the announcement of the Fugitive Fantasy League. He had no doubt the man would set up an account and play.

"Well, what do I know," said Tilda, "you men and your games. It's all too much for me." She smiled and raised a hand in surrender.

It wasn't an easy time for Edward Burgess, despite the backing, ultimately, of the board. He wasn't certain Fugitive Theatre would become the success he so desperately wanted. He believed it had the chance, but belief wasn't enough, he knew. But he also was short on other ideas. He was bored with his role, which his father had made certain he understood on multiple occasions before his death: His job was to manage the family's assets, manage the business and nurse it back to health. No more than that, which meant he wasn't to take too many risks or vary from his father's long-term vision. But the old man was dead some years and, besides, Edward hadn't been the one to gamble and lose so much during the Oligoi Wars. Certainly, they had come out better than many of the old families, some hadn't even survived. Still, this was about more than survival, even if profits were stagnate and the company was, across all the subsidiaries, underperforming slightly. Edward hated his role as what amounted to a night manager, a simple watchman, when it should have been his birthright to preside over nearly a thousand years of history and dominance.

Minutes after the board meeting broke up, he strode through the executive offices on the top floor of the building toward his own suite. The meeting had ended mostly positive—the board gave him more time to make Fugitive Theatre a success—but he still felt pressured. Hanging on the walls were portraits of the men who had built the companies and the family's fortunes going back hundreds of years. Men like Howard Burgess stared back at him. Howard's vision had moved the company from printing into radio and television during that era's boom. And Robert Burgess, too, looked down from that wall. He had expanded the company into real estate development during the golden era of expansion and population growth, when cities climbed toward the sky. Robert Burgess had sculpted the skylines of several of the largest cities on the old East coast. All the greats were there, all stared back. Edward wondered, were they supporting him, or mocking? Did they watch over, or judge him? He couldn't say. He only felt the burden and strain of his position and a rising sense of desperation.

What he knew, what he was absolutely certain of, was that he wouldn't be a footnote, one of the men who had occupied his position over the generations who had never done enough to be remembered, or honored. That wouldn't be his fate.

Edward's PED chimed. Sarah was in The Edge again. He sighed and continued walking to his suite. He didn't understand her or the desire to mix with that lower class of humanity. He had elevated her, pulled her from the muck and gifted her a life people in The Edge normally could only dream about. Sometimes he felt she wasn't grateful for all he had done. He also didn't believe she understood the gravity of her new situation, the expectations that came with marrying into the family. It seemed odd that her mother understood perfectly well what was expected and that her daughter didn't. And her parents had now moved. They were Cleric now and no longer members of The Edge. Edward had made that possible, too. Why go back there, ever? What was the point?

His patience was pulled taut, the pressures to make the business profitable and to move the entire enterprise forward weighed on him, intruded on his thoughts to the point that everything else became a distraction. He didn't have time to worry over these sorts of things. The last thing he needed at the moment was Sarah stepping out of line and causing issues. He was going to have to speak with her, maybe keep a closer watch on her. He sent a message to his assistant, Tom Chambers: *Are there any Dragonflies around? I need one.*

5

PONDERING THE IMPOSSIBLE

The rain glowed a blur of neon. The streets were greasy. The sounds of the neighborhood were distant and hidden under the tap, tap, tap of falling droplets, while the temperature took a nose-dive and settled somewhere just below comfortable. With each minute that passed more of the grime, dirt, angst and illusion that held The Edge together disengaged and flowed without protest down gutters and sewer lines. But the cleansing rains only exposed the cheap underside and impermanent facade—and a bare-faced truth that few wanted to admit or confront: squaller had them surrounded. With the downpour came an embarrassed quiet. No one was out and about. They hid behind curtains, blinds and paper-thin walls and lost themselves in one inane entertainment after another, preferring that tiny bit of escape to the truth just outside their front doors. Aside from me, I walked toward home, pondering the impossible.

It was strange how exposed The Edge could be, naked and vulnerable, denuded. I couldn't understand my own species then. What were we? Was humanity this stratified, categorized and ranked assortment of flesh and bones and grandiose ideals, a continuum from something base and barely elevated above the rest of the animal kingdom, to the sublime beauty of artistic expression and mathematical insight? Were we creatures still trying to slough off the muck and mud, young sentients who needed time, or were we worse—only concerned for ourselves, indifferent to all others in our fight for survival, pretenders at something greater? At times, I believed society was nothing more than an exercise in dominance, nothing but an extension of the principles of evolution. At others, I believed it was supposed to overcome our evolutionary needs, that it was meant to reflect our highest values as we searched for meaning.

It was difficult to find separation between those animal instincts and our higher values when I looked around me, perhaps too much of it ran down the gutters and sewers. The local middle school loomed on the opposite side of the street. The function of education here was contorted. They trained kids to become good citizens—conformists—but not good thinkers. It was designed to distill originality and let it run off down the drain, much as the rain chased The Edge's facade down the sewers, to quiet overactive minds and level out the range of thought to something manageable. Perhaps that had always been the case. The primary goal was to produce a herd animal, a production line citizen incapable of complaining because he couldn't know any different. No amount of rain can wash that away. The dirt and grime and angst may wash down the sewers, but under that the cheaply printed homes and buildings of the place were nothing more than exposed greed. Control the masses and turn them into good little consumers. It was a good formula. It worked. Tab was an exception, but only barely. She was constantly slipping into the way of thinking taught inside the school's walls. But her nature was to question. She was curious. She just needed a little prodding, a nudge in the correct direction.

I was aware of these things when I was in middle school. Before she died, my mother told me to be careful at school. "Don't act too smart, Clay," she had said. "Don't object too much to what they teach, even if you know it to be wrong. They don't value people who think that much. We become suspect to them."

"But why? Seems stupid," I had said.

"It sets you apart, makes you different. That isn't something they consider desirable. Just as getting the highest scores on your tests will mark you as someone to watch. It's just the world we live in right now."

My mother always believed this world we had invented was temporary, just a phase we were going through. But I had read enough history since she died to see things differently. Great growth stretched over long periods of time could be seen in our past—technical and social advances and a better understanding of the universe—but humans had been fond of taking several steps backward on multiple instances over the past few hundred years. It was more of a pattern, and not the anomaly she thought it was. It was part of our make up. This wasn't an exception, our current era. It was us being human.

But my mother had been correct about other things. I became aware, after her death, of the many ways we were corralled into believing this was how things were meant to be. It was difficult to see beyond the gloss and the corporate propaganda, beyond the teachings of the priests. I found it easiest to understand when the questions were simple, basic. But they were also the most troubling.

The rain made me think too much. I shrugged, pulled my coat tighter around me and quickened my pace.

I was putting the dishes away and toweling off my hands when a knock at the door startled me.

"Sarah, I'm . . . surprised," I said, stammering like an idiot, as I opened the door. "Come in."

I held the door and reached to take her jacket off as she passed. Her cheek was bruised. It was discolored and somewhat swollen.

"What happened?"

"Oh, nothing really, just an accident, Clay."

She was hesitant and I sensed she might be shaking some, but trying with some effort to hold things together. I reached, still standing to the side of her, and put my hand on her forearm. Her eyes glistened from some internal torment.

"Really," she said, turning to face me full on, "it was an accident."

I hung her coat on the back of an old chair. It had been a few days since I had seen her, though I had thought of her every day since. I was nervous and didn't know what I should do.

"Something to drink?"

"Just water, thanks."

"Take a seat anywhere."

I grabbed two glasses and got us both a drink. She found the same chair she had sat in before.

"How do you do it? How do you live between two worlds and still be happy? You are happy, aren't you? You seem like it."

"I don't know, Sarah." I walked to the living area and handed her the glass and took a seat. "Sometimes I am, others I'm not sure. I feel like we've missed something important, that we've lost sight of something that matters. Then I get tangled up thinking through things and I'm not so sure I know what happiness is then."

"What have we lost sight of? I mean, there are a thousand answers to that question, God knows I could come up with that many myself, but what do you think? What comes to mind at those times?"

"Sometimes I look at The Edge and think: Is this it? Is this all there is? All of these years of civilization and this is where we've got? When I go to work I'm just as appalled by what I find there in that supposedly elevated world. Big questions come to mind, usually. What is the meaning of it all? That sort of crap."

I forced a smile and sank back into my chair.

"Is there any meaning?"

Exactly, I thought. Here was this woman—the pride of The Edge—who had made it and found her way to the top and even she questioned what it was all about. We looked at each other for a long while, comfortable in the quiet, lost in our thoughts.

Finally, she said, "Meaning is invented. But what happens when that isn't enough, or you can't invent something that grabs ahold of you and creates passion? What then?"

"You can't equate our species-wide search to an individual."

"What do you mean?"

"One is invented, I think, as you said. The other is defined by purpose. Humanity has no purpose, other than to exist. But people, individuals, can find purpose."

She tightened her lips, then said. "What is it they say about the universe, we live in a clockwork machine?"

"It's a deterministic universe. There is no room for meaning.

Cause and effect. We're always trying to create a greater purpose for humanity, to conjure something up, or act like God has a plan for us. But what if all that is just fiction? I think we're not so important."

She got up and walked to the same window she had looked out on her previous visit.

"So, if we find purpose in our lives," she asked, "we can find meaning? Those who can do that are the happiest among us."

I gestured agreement. "Is that where love fits in?"

"I think so," she answered. "But let me ask you, does sacrifice count the same? Is sacrifice the same as finding purpose?"

"I couldn't begin to answer that. You sacrificed for your family, to give them a better life." I smiled. I knew that was an assumption, but I went with it. "I find it curious that you view marrying into the Oligoi as a sacrifice. Millions around the world would disagree with you and denounce you for saying that."

She stared out the window. The rain had stopped and the last rays of daylight had broken through and danced upon her face and hair, making her even more beautiful. Her face was softly lit while the rest of her remained in the dark shadows. Dust motes hung suspended in the fading light. It cast a magic spell over her, which broke when she turned and looked my way.

"What if it was a sacrifice and nothing more? Not that I ever intended that. But now, now I don't know what."

I was becoming aware just how attracted I was to her, not just her beauty and the way she moved, but to the way she thought and saw the world. She had a calm personality and examined things slowly and carefully, something I learned to do when I was young. Still, I doubted what I saw and heard, not knowing if I could trust my own feelings in the matter. I had spent too many days dreaming up conversations with her. Perhaps those imaginings clouded the reality, gave them a new look. Or, maybe that is what budding love does. I was the last person who could answer that question.

As a ward of the state I found it difficult to trust anyone. I was a product of the system. I knew I was different from the other children and I never made close friends. I didn't like groups or much social interaction. I was apart. I found solitude peaceful. My interests were unique.

I found myself in an odd position. I had never had a serious relationship before, not where I felt completely invested in it. It wasn't a lack of desire. I would have welcomed it. Things are difficult when you become a ward of the state at a young age. Trust is a risk. It's also difficult to build when others come and go quickly in your life, a revolving door of people and friendships. You get used to saying goodbye, and those goodbyes become permanent. Adopted children don't want reminders of the their past. Once they got out from under the system they only focused forward, on the future.

Those who ran the home where I lived weren't the most personable people, but in their defense, they had a lot of bodies to worry over. Time was always running out and staff too short, or turnover too high, for someone like me to make any waves that got noticed. The home was packed with kids in the same position as me. Most of them had issues adapting. Several were consistently going from one trouble to another. Their actions demanded the attention of those in charge.

When you are a quiet kid who avoids the uncomfortable phone calls or knocks on the door you blend into the woodwork, disappear off the radar. I was just so much white noise in a loud and chaotic world.

"There goes that Clay," Mrs. Cotton would say, as if I couldn't hear. "So quiet."

"Wish they was all like that," Mrs. Potter would respond.

Mrs. Cotton would make a clucking sound and watch me for a second and then get on with whatever she had been doing.

I liked being alone. At least, I wasn't uncomfortable with it. I found ways to entertain myself. Several blocks away from the home was an old library. I spent hours there lost in other worlds. It wasn't large, but when you're young that hardly matters. There was plenty to learn and keep me busy and I found the old printed books fascinating. My visits became a pattern, a habit. The librarians got used to seeing me. Occasionally, they would show me new things—books or VR sims—or even give me a piece of fruit.

A short walk away from the library was an old industrial area, small factories no longer relevant, all brick and wood and steel, analogue archives of some other era. They were dusty places with old yellowed windows, where the glass still remained, many had broken over time and stayed that way from a lack of care. A feint smell of oil pervaded, birds chirped and fluttered about, nesting up high in the rafters. They were the rightful owners of the place by then. The smells, missing glass and brick walls were ghosts of the past, a forgotten time.

Behind the row of buildings were railroad tracks. A few people lived by them, just beyond where a small wood began, their makeshift tents and homes blended in with the rest of the area. I always wondered why they didn't live in the building, but I never asked. I avoided interacting with them. I would climb to the windows up high inside one of the buildings and watch them going about their business sometimes, as I read from whatever book I had borrowed from the library on my PED. The sun would drift across the sky in the summer and the shadows stretched in small increments, their length telling me when to head back. The days had a slowness I found inviting and comforting.

The home, and all my related experiences, forged me into a loner, if I wasn't one before. In truth, I think it just solidified who I was. By the time I started high school I didn't have any real friends, nothing meaningful or long-term, anyway. I took advantage of that. I was good enough at sports to be respected by that group, and an outsider that wasn't viewed as a threat to any other groups. I did well in my classes, but I didn't try too hard. Again, just like at the home, I skated by unseen.

Years later, I stood in the old warehouse I called home and asked myself what I expected. Sarah was beautiful and I loved the way she saw the world. But where could it lead? What hope was there for the feelings I felt welling up in me?

Or did any of that matter?

Trust isn't just about the other person. At some level, you have to trust yourself. This was new territory for me and I didn't know what it meant, or how to react.

I walked to Sarah and looked out the window. The Edge was quiet, the streets wet from the rains that had stopped and the darkness encroached slowly. The clouds hovered low in the sky, though their manner not so menacing as earlier, less brooding. Lights were on everywhere, reflecting gold on the rain-slicked streets and buildings. Things were slow in the Edge, but they wouldn't stay quiet long. They never did. But in times such as those I could almost like the place.

Sarah smelled of springtime, nothing overwhelming or too strong, nothing artificial and forced, either. The small amount of space between us was electric and tense, charged. Was that just me, or did she feel it too?

"So," I said, softly, "what sort of accident?"

I stared ahead, as she was, but still observed her peripherally. She turned one corner of her mouth up and it slowly morphed into a grin.

"Edward got really upset. Something about the analytics for his new show bothered him. I think he is still under pressure from the board. One of his staff was speaking to him on his PED and he got upset because he wasn't getting the news he expected. Threw something that ricocheted off the wall and hit me. Didn't even know I was standing there."

That concerned me. I've heard the abused will often defend those who hurt them. I hoped that wasn't the case. I hoped she was being truthful. I turned to her. "And you are grinning at this?"

"Ah," she said, turning her head to look up at me, "He is mean and condescending, especially these days with all of the pressure he is under. Seeing him get angry over the performance of some damned reality show is funny. He is trying desperately to appeal to the very people he looks down his nose at." She shrugged.

"Why is he under so much pressure?"

"The show isn't going well. Afraid they might lose money, too much money from what I gather. But it's more than that. Other things have been worrying him. Who knows, really? He also desperately wants me to get pregnant to give him an heir. You would think he would treat me better under the circumstances. But after a year of marriage, I feel like a prop, something that has to be tolerated because of its necessity."

"You should be treasured," I said. It slipped out, just like that. Even I felt awkward. I've always been straight-forward, to the point. Most called me abrupt at work, when I did speak with anyone. I'm not much for small talk. I say what I mean. But even I could see this was a situation where a more delicate approach might have been better. But Sarah didn't get upset. She didn't turn and walk away. We faced each other for what felt like eternity. She was several inches shorter than me, but that didn't come across in the moment. She commanded her space.

Finally, I reached with my left hand and ran my fingers lightly over her cheek where the bruising was. I focused on that area so I didn't get caught up in her eyes and all the promises and fantasies I found in them. "Ricochet, huh?"

"I swear, Clay."

"Okay."

Then I reached my hand behind her head and pulled her to me. We embraced for a moment, my face buried in her blond hair. Now I wondered: Can a loner truly love someone? Could I give enough of myself to this woman, to any woman? I believed it possible in that moment. But would everything I had to give be enough for her? I had always been so guarded and private. This was uncharted territory for me. I supposed no one could answer that question. I could commit to it, with every fiber in my body. I could try. Only she could determine if I was worthy.

Fantasies, though, some part of my mind told me. Just damn fantasy.

Smelling her hair, my hands on her back and our bodies pressed in close, I was keenly aware of everything about her physical presence. I wanted to swallow her whole, to lose myself.

She puled her head back, her smooth cheek and soft skin on my face. Then our lips were locked and a kaleidoscope of emotions exploded in my head, an electric jolt ran through my body and all I could feel were her full lips pressed to my own. My hands dug into her back and pulled her even closer. She wrapped her arms tightly around me.

But some part of my mind refused to stop ticking over and pushed aside the frenzied emotions and reminded me just how impossible the situation was, the danger wrapped inside the lust, and I hesitated, unsure.

Sarah pulled her head back and looked at me, those blue eyes so inviting. "You okay?"

"Maybe. You sure about this?"

She squinted and let out a huge sigh. "I'm sure we can't do this—as much as I want to."

She put her forehead on my chest and I felt her shaking.

"I'm sorry," she said. "I'm so sorry. That shouldn't have happened."

"Quit apologizing." I lifted her chin. "I'm not complaining."

"I don't mean to lead you on, Clay. I got caught up in the emotion and . . . I should go."

I wrapped her in my arms for a moment. "Your eye—"

"Just an accident, Clay, I swear."

"That's not the sort of purpose I'd want to explore, you know, hell-bent on destroying the man who hurt you."

She laughed and put her hand on my chest, "Don't worry. I wouldn't let that happen. I'm too ornery and strong for that."

My gaze lingered on her for a while. I couldn't let go. I wanted to pull her to me tight and melt into her and stay that way for as long as possible. But then we broke apart and something switched off between us. Decision made.

"Sarah, you are taking a big risk coming here, to The Edge."

"Now you sound like Edward. I grew up here, remember? And I still have friends here. I can take care of myself. I know not to go near Skin and to get out of here before it's too late. Speaking of which, I should be leaving now."

"Come on, then. I'll walk you out."

Crime was a part of the fabric of The Edge. You can't squeeze that many people tightly together and expect anything less. It lurked in every neighborhood, around every corner. Sometimes, it was brazen enough to stand out openly for all to see. Walking her out was a way to make certain she got out safely—and to be near her for just a bit longer.

Outside The Edge little crime existed, though that might depend on definitions and semantics. Stealing someone's soul and awarding them for their loyalty could be considered a crime by someone like me. I'd almost prefer the physical violence of The Edge to that. But outside The Edge were public safety cameras and the occasional drone keeping watch. Everything had a camera embedded and they all recorded your actions.

The Edge was still the wild west. I believed the Oligoi liked it that way. They could justify their behavior by pointing to the statistics and shaking their heads as if they were sad at the lack of control or discipline displayed here. It played perfectly to the way they wanted to stratify the population.

"There are worse risks, I think," Sarah said. "It sounds like another outbreak of avian flu is growing."

"I'm sure they have a cure already. But they may wait before dispensing it. The masses dying from another would-be plague just reminds us that we are different."

"You are too cynical."

"Not cynical enough, I'm sure."

We exited the warehouse and walked down the street. It was still relatively quiet, The Edge was still under clouds and a wet blanket, though I could see it was clearing not far away where the sun peaked through. Something buzzed behind us as we walked, not loud, just out of place, but when I turned I couldn't see anything.

"I'm just over there, Clay."

We stopped walking and faced each other. Neither said a word for some time. Finally, I said, "The door is always open."

She flashed a smile and turned away.

I needed to move, to burn off energy and clear my head. I walked and again pondered the impossible, as I had earlier when coming home in the rain, except this time it wasn't the perverted state of the species or society. This time I pondered a future that couldn't be, that couldn't exist or be made. Still, my mind wouldn't let go, despite its impossibility. Some dreams, no matter how fantastical or long the odds of realization, are persistent and all-consuming. They tug like gravity, tenacious and single-minded. What I should have asked at the time, what I should have considered, had I been in a state of mind to think it, was just how dangerous some dreams are.

6

SPIN

Edward Burgess opened a window on his PED and pulled up the Dragonfly feed. The tiny drone was sunning itself on top of a roof in the early morning sunshine somewhere near his home. He wasn't concerned with that. He had asked the program that runs the drone to put together a montage of Sarah's movements from the previous day, focusing on her interactions with other people. He felt a moment of guilt for his actions, staring at the current view the drone was showing, but some deeply repressed anger and sense of entitlement nudged the guilt aside, and he pressed the link to the footage.

There were several interactions for the day. The first was a visit to the gym in the morning. After lunch she went to the doctor in the early afternoon, just as she had said she was doing. The next was a trip to The Edge. Edward felt a tick of anger as the drone footage showed the familiar skyline and tightly packed homes and other buildings. He was shaking his head at the sight of it. He would never understand her desire to remain connected to The Edge—to visit the place and to remain friends with the people there.

The Dragonfly, as instructed, hung back fifty yards, alighting on branches or the sides of buildings when Sarah wasn't moving. Its camera was powerful enough to zoom in and get a clear image of anyone at that distance, though the drone was struggling some with the heavy rains. He was surprised it had kept going and was able to stay airborne.

Edward recognized the woman Sarah first met, an old childhood friend he had once met, though he couldn't remember her name. The second stop puzzled him. She walked up to an old warehouse and entered. The drone stopped and rested on top of a truck parked on the street. It couldn't follow her into the warehouse without getting too close and being detected. The rain came down hard and the drone moved to a perch that was covered to keep its camera as clear as possible. And it waited.

According to the time stamp, about an hour lapsed before Sarah came out of the warehouse. The rains had stopped but obviously it was still cloudy because of the low light in the camera feed. A man walked out with her. He looked vaguely familiar, though Edward couldn't place him, probably one of her friends he had seen or met before. The drone activated and took flight. They appeared to talk for a few seconds, saying goodbye. As they parted ways the man walked off in the opposite direction.

Something nondescript unsettled Edward, nagged at him from afar. He paused the feed, zoomed in and took a still shot of the screen and the man's face and sent it to his assistant, Chambers, and asked for a full background check.

There was nothing else in the report from the drone. Sarah had returned home directly. On some level he had a sense of disquiet over his use of the drone, an invasion of Sarah's privacy that almost felt wrong. After considering things for a moment, he instructed the drone to sit tight and wait further instructions.

It was late in the day when a message from Tom Chambers popped up on Edward's PED: *Got a minute?* Chambers opened the door and quickly entered his office. He looked grim and troubled, despite the impeccable manner he was dressed and the smoothness of his movements, but that was his natural state, something Edward had learned about the man long ago.

"He works for us, one of the subsidiaries, anyway. Tech guy. His name is Clay Alexander. There are some things in his file I can't access. Your eyes only, I imagine."

Clay Alexander. Burgess took in a deep breath. He didn't recognize the name. "Can't say I know him."

"You probably wouldn't, sir. This might be something important, though." Chambers handed the tablet to Burgess and pointed to a spot on the screen. "Failed the Merit Analysis—twice. The last time was recent."

Edward tried to imagine what that meant, any ramifications that were associated with the information, but he couldn't come up with any. The photo looked more familiar now, but nothing specifically came to mind.

"Apparently," said Chambers, "he is the best we have at fixing problems on the factory floor. He knows the printers better than anyone. He gets paid pretty well for someone . . . like him. There isn't much else in the file. He keeps quiet, doesn't associate with anyone in the company, but doesn't make any waves, either."

Edward saw the red icon in the lower corner of the screen. "Thanks, Tom. Leave this with me, please."

Chambers nodded and walked out of the office.

Edward tapped the icon when Chambers had left. The device said: "Authorization code and voice print required."

Burgess went through the protocols, opened the file, and found two things of note. The first concerned his mother. The second was the recent Merit Analysis. Burgess clicked on the file regarding his mother first. Alexander's mother was considered a dissident. She had been watched by the family for years, either directly spied on—an AI search on the networks, or by association. It was believed she was a member of a resistance group that called for freedom, and the overthrow of the Family's rule and the arrest of the Family's members. There had always been a few who disagreed with the Oligoi Wars and the aftermath, but most were bought off or hushed. A few persisted. There was no direct evidence against the woman. Much of what they knew was based upon her association with certain individuals known to be in the group. She had never been arrested but she did fail an early version of the Merit Analysis. The group had been labeled terrorists, of course, a timeless spin of those in power to taint the reputation and distance the group from the average guy on the street. At some point, Edward knew, over two decades ago, the known members of the group had been hunted down and killed. The file didn't have any particulars regarding what had happened to her, but not everything was documented for obvious reasons. Her accident, he supposed, could have easily been manufactured.

Clay Alexander grew up a ward of the state from the age of twelve to eighteen. No other known family was listed. Kate Alexander had been a single mother. Alexander's school record was good, clean. He was an excellent athlete but considered a loner by most who knew him. His exit exams were off the charts, which didn't match his performance in school. Bored most likely, surmised Edward. But that fact bothered him.

Burgess looked at the image in the file. A hint of jealousy, fuzzy and amorphous, but there nonetheless, crept over him. This man had spent time alone with his wife, after all. But in an old warehouse? Edward pulled up Alexander's address. The man listed the warehouse as his home. Odd, but he was an odd guy from all Edward could see. Still—

Edward next pulled up the video of Alexander's last Merit Analysis. Clay Alexander had badgered the priest and made a mockery of the test and everything it stood for. The AI program running the test had failed him immediately, before he had even answered a question, but that was to be expected. "This man is dangerous," Edward mumbled. Then he thought again about the time Sarah had spent with him, shocked she was even friends with him. Righteous anger welled up, then.

The screen on his desk had pinged several times. He wanted to ignore it, but he knew he couldn't. The board were getting impatient. The changes in Fugitive Theatre were in place and they expected immediate results. But nothing ever changed overnight. They were going to have to wait a while, give the show time to develop, a few weeks, at least. But that wasn't their nature and it was irritating. Almost as irritating as having to deal with Clay Alexander and whatever his wife was up to.

Suddenly he wondered: Is she having an affair?

He supposed it was possible. Their relationship wasn't going too well, and for several months it had been getting worse. Could that be what was going on? Maybe that was driving the unrest he was experiencing. Maybe his intuition was trying to warn him. He looked again at the photo of Alexander and his anger focused on it, poured into it. He was shaking and clenched the tablet hard with both hands. Eventually, he slammed the tablet onto the desk, rubbed both hands over his face and leaned back in his chair. *I'm Edward Burgess,* he told himself. *No one—NO ONE—would fuck with me like that. And if they did they would pay with their life.*

Tilda Hogue's impeccable timing surfaced again. She was asking for a video link. Edward's anger got the better of him and he banged the link on the screen. "What?"

"Well, hello to you, too."

"Sorry. What do you need?"

"What do I need?" Tilda asked in a sickly sweet voice. "How about better ratings and the promise of a little profit."

"Damnit, Tilda, that's not fair! We've only just made changes to the show. Give it some time."

"Time I've got, Edward, but I'm afraid you don't. And what I'm running out of is *patience.* This experiment of yours isn't working."

"It'll work. Shows like this take time to build. And that doesn't go any faster with you badgering me all day long."

Tilda's look softened a bit and she took a moment to consider. Finally, she asked, "When does Jose Mann go on the show?"

"Next week," Burgess answered. "The Lottery announcement is this weekend. We're dedicating the entire show to him."

"Well, let's hope that does it. I'm not trying to be a bitch, Edward. Something needs to go right—that's all."

"It'll pull through."

"Let's hope." Then she nodded and cut the connection.

Ping.

Edward was exasperated.

Jonathan Sterling, another of the board's impatient members, was asking to link through. Edward leaned forward and back-handed the screen off his desk. No more distractions, he decided. "And who the fuck," he said aloud, "is Clay Alexander?"

Edward tried to get some work done but it was a futile attempt. His mind was trapped in a never-ending loop that began and ended with Clay Alexander and Sarah. Anger built like a tidal wave, slowly dredging the bottom and pulling all the muck into the swell until it rose and moved with an unstoppable force. Nothing in its path was safe. He left work early, unusual for him, and headed home.

Once in the car he told it to take him home. He pulled out the files on Alexander again. He stopped the video when Alexander and Sarah were coming out of the old place. His mind wouldn't stop searching for clues to what they had been up to, how they spent their time together. He spent ten minutes rewinding and watching the video over and over, looking for any tells, facial tics or feint gestures. He looked in the background to see if others had come or gone. If Alexander's mother had been a dissident then maybe he was, too. Maybe he was part of a group. Maybe Alexander was more dangerous than he had supposed. So he searched and searched. But he couldn't see any others enter or leave the warehouse. He chased that goose around and around attempting to uncover some plot or organization that he just couldn't find. At one point he realized the drone's view of things was limited, too limited, for what he was trying to see. It had been focused, as instructed, on Sarah. It wasn't looking for conspiracy.

His thoughts tumbled farther down the rabbit hole despite the lack of proof. Burgess convinced himself something was there.

He just couldn't see it. Yet. Nonsensical questions arose: Is Sarah a plant? Was she with him as part of some covert plan, betraying him all along? But that was nonsense, he told himself. He found her, courted her, persuaded her to become part of his world. And her background had been thoroughly vetted. It wasn't in her nature. He knew that. Still, his thoughts raced and veered and spun uncontrollably, drowning out the rational side of his brain under their weight and frenetic activity, swallowing it with their urgency. Those in the family had to be on the lookout. It was a never-ending part of membership, which was why so many had married within. Outside interests could always be pursued for fun anyway. No need to tempt fate and lay themselves open to the conniving of the underclass. But I courted her, he said to himself. While shaking his head and staring at the finely crafted dash of the vehicle, lost moments disappeared into the grain of leather and polished chrome, anxieties swelled, trouble brewed.

By the time he reached home he had morphed into something . . . *other*. He was a mountain of anger and cynicism, a hell-bent man on an undefined mission. His frustrations with work, the board and his and Sarah's relationship contrived to turn him angry and bitter, and to spin him out of control.

He was breathing hard when the car parked itself in the garage. He left his PED on the front seat of the sedan, a thin blue line pulsing along the top with a message notification, exited the car, jerked the door open to the house, trying to control his anger, but failing. The rational side of his brain was brushed aside, nothing but feint background noise. He was unfocused, confused almost. However irrational it may have been, he felt betrayed.

Inside the door he turned left down the hallway toward the study and the front of the house. Sarah came around the corner, quiet, eyes down and focused on something in her hand, just as he got there. They were two points blindly merging with perfect timing. Edward banged into her hard. She was caught off guard, spun around and fell back into the wall, sliding down it out of balance. She cried out. Edward's breath caught. Some degree of sympathy swamped through his nervous system, but just as quickly the anger fought back and took control.

"Jesus Christ! Watch where you're going, will ya?"

Sarah scowled at him, reached up and rubbed the back of her head. "How was I to know you were there? Next time I'll file an itinerary."

"You do that. Maybe next time you go to The Edge you should file one then, as well."

"What, you're tracking me now?"

"And you might want to be careful who you associate with."

"What does that mean?"

Edward was fuming. He was having trouble keeping the anger at bay. It lashed out toward freedom and release. The world was still off-kilter and spinning and off its axis. "I know about Clay Alexander, all about it."

Sarah pushed herself up off the floor, leveraging her back against the wall part of the way for support, then stood fully erect. She faced him directly. "Whatever you think you know is bullshit. Clay is a friend, that's all." Her voice was low and measured, though the subsurface anger screamed in defiance. "And I'm tired of this. I don't know what's gotten into you lately, but I don't like it."

Something in her tone or manner convinced Edward she was lying. The slight quiver in her voice, perhaps, or the way she stiffened and leaned, almost imperceptibly, toward him robbed him of any rationality.

"Don't get sassy with me," he said. "I can see to it he never works again. I don't have to tolerate his kind, you know."

"His kind?" Venom laced her voice.

"Just another damn scumbag from The Edge. Can't even pass the test."

"No one who thinks for themselves can pass that test, Edward. It's just a bullshit measure of how far they can stick their noses up your ass."

Edward sneered. "Your father did just fine."

"Fuck you!"

The anger had mounted, gained momentum with each brushback and reprisal, became a thing unto itself. Before he could stop it, before he was fully aware, Edward reached out and slapped Sarah in the face.

She cried out, not so much from the impact of the slap as at the stinging sensation of betrayal. It was a violation of the trust between two lovers. Something broke inside her and she slumped to the floor, sliding down the wall against her back, hair fallen around her face and her left hand glued to the cheek that had been struck.

Edward watched her motionlessly. Part of him, small and insignificant he discovered, wanted to reach out and hold her, to apologize. But the animal part of his brain kept him in place, lording over her. Time slowed while his thoughts raced. He felt shame for his actions, but really, he reasoned, she brought it on. He'd never have done a thing like that unwarranted before. He wasn't to blame, not entirely, not really.

"I'm sorry," he muttered, eventually, and then, breathing had as if he had just run a race, made his way to his study.

He sat for some time at his desk, glass of liquor next to him, head in shaky hands, trying to think clearly. No matter how he rearranged the events and facts, he still felt betrayed. Clay Alexander couldn't pass the Merit Analysis. He hated the system and had badgered a priest. His mother was a dissident. And most importantly, his wife spent time with him. Edward's catecholamine-addled brain spun a web of conspiracy and deceit, ensnared him in the thing of his own making and wouldn't let him go. He saw one solution to the situation, only one path he could take.

Clay Alexander had to go.

Edward couldn't let go of the thought. It clung to every neuron in his brain and was the terminus of every synaptic pathway, regardless of the direction he started off in. All thoughts led back to that singular point, that locus. It didn't take long to embrace it and then begin planning. He logged onto his cloud and pulled up the files on Alexander again, read through his background once more. Then he opened his work file. He was going to lose a good employee, sure. That was clear. But he was only an employee. Others could step in and do the job, they'd find a way to get his work done. Then he looked at Alexander's recent work history and the tasks he had been asked to perform.

Ideas swam in his head, some formed and congealed until he had the beginnings of a plan. Those thoughts gained momentum and before long he could see everything fleshed out. It was late when he finally finished, when the chemicals in his brain had died out and his head was no longer spinning, the rage dissipated and became a calculated anger, something simmering, not boiling over, something to focus him but not take over his behavior. The alcohol had help smooth things out.

He looked at his notes and smiled. It was devious and easy to execute and no one would question anything. He'd barely have to throw any weight around. Despite the hour, he sent a message to the corporate black ops team leader: could he meet some time after lunch?

7

INEVITABLE

Some actions are inevitable. Some events can't be escaped or stopped. They defy reason and logic and planning. Good intentions fade away under their appearance and momentum. They are chemical-laced and pheromone-spiced portents of change, often leading to disaster. But they are eagerly accepted, grasped with an end-of-all-things lust and ridden hard until they are spent and nothing is left to drive them forward. I wasn't thinking these things when she was pinned to the wall of the warehouse, our mouths exploring and probing with an immediate need to peel back the veneer and the layers cloaked in pretense and circumstance to reveal the other's soul. Those thoughts came later, much later, and with a great deal of harsh reflection. At that moment thinking was jettisoned and desire stepped forward and pushed all else to the wayside.

Sarah let out a low grunt as I ran my lips down the side of her neck and pulled her in tight to me. She ripped at the t-shirt I wore, pulling it over my head in as fluid a motion as humanly possible. I wrapped my arms around her and picked her up. She wrapped her legs around my waist and our lips locked together again, and I walked us toward the bed. I felt every inch of her and tried desperately to pull her inside me, to slip under her skin and let her fill me up. I wanted to absorb everything about her right then, the passion so raw and unfiltered it hurt. One of her shoes clanged onto the floor, then the other, as I walked us across the hardwood. I felt her fingers comb through my hair and I tightened my grip on her to alleviate my ache. I dropped her onto her back on the bed, pulling free her top in the process. She laughed freely, blond hair falling from her face, nothing self-conscious in the laugh at all. I leaned down on top of her, trying desperately to keep even the smallest amount of control, but found that was impossible. I pulled her pants off and tossed them behind me, ran my tongue up the inside of her right thigh, moved her panties to the side as she spread her legs and invited more.

The world disappeared then—all of it gone. The Edge fizzed away, all its warts and desaturated cheapness. The class divide between Sarah and me was gone. We were just two people, man and woman, connected, physically and psychologically, as I slid up inside her. Everything was as black as the deepest night except us. Like all great moments of love and lust and ecstasy it was a moment out of time, just the two of us, me devoted to her pleasure and she to mine. The first time she arched her back and shuddered and cried out I watched her intently and experienced it all through her, then ran my tongue over a swollen nipple and tugged at it lightly with my teeth. I ran my lips up her neck again, pulled my hand from the small of her back, up her side and over her smooth skin and cupped her head in my hand. She was lost in a post-orgasmic fugue state. I breathed her in and held onto the moment.

Sex was different with Sarah from any woman I had been with before. I was inside her head. I knew what she was thinking, what she wanted and desired. And somehow I knew it would always be that way. No matter how many times we made love that connection was locked in, a chemical bonding between us.

We spent a couple hours that way, neither speaking, just the immediacy of lust and then a post-coital fog that held us in suspension until the batteries recharged and we hungered for more.

Heads together and touching, we were both on our backs and staring at the rafters high up in the warehouse, intoxicated by our lovemaking.

"Jesus, Clay, I'm scared."

"Scared?"

"It feels like you're in my mind, like you know every thought and desire. I've never felt so naked—and so wonderful. It's kinda scary."

I rolled on top of her and stared into her eyes a few beats, those beautiful blue eyes. I brushed her hair back from her face. We were still breathing hard. I had no words to offer. It was as true for me as it was for her. I was frightened by the depth of the intimacy and the feelings that had welled up inside me. I grinned, leaned into and kissed her, relishing the fullness of her lips and the feel of her soft skin where our bodies touched.

The catalyst for this was when she had told me about being slapped by her husband a couple days before, the tears that flowed as she told me the story broke the dam within me and between us. Truth was, the sexual tension had been building from the first time we met.

Miyamoto jumped onto the foot of the bed. The oversized cat skulked up to us as if delivering a message and buried his head into Sarah's hair and then rubbed across her cheek, the bruised cheek, before sauntering off to the corner of the bed. Our private world unfolded then, our temporary reality receded like one of those Japanese fans folding back up, the design on the fan slowly becoming less coherent before disappearing and revealing another reality. What remained was stark and harsh and demanding, where and who and what we were. We stared at each other. The silence harbored the elephant in the room; neither of us wanted to confront it, nor could we deny its presence or its inevitable demands.

Sarah closed her eyes and groaned, squeezed me a little tighter. "I've done exactly what Edward accused me of."

She opened her eyes, a sad smile formed. I ran a finger along her lips. "Is that regret?"

"No, never. But what now?"

Yes, what now? I rolled onto my back and looked up to the rafters again. I wasn't certain I was in a state to figure that out. I didn't know if I was equipped for it, either. I'd never experienced these things. I just wanted to hold on to her and keep riding these feelings, this wave of transcendence. I had asked myself a short time ago if a woman like Sarah could ever love someone like me. And here we were tangled together with such ease, like we were made for it, for each other, both exposed but as comfortable with our bared souls as with our naked bodies. Still, we weren't alone and we didn't own it, not as long as she belonged to someone else. I knew that.

Sarah raised up, lifted her leg over and straddled me. "I've got to go, you know. We'll figure it out."

She bent down and kissed me, reached down between her legs and found I was nearly hard again and slid me up inside her. The ache whooshed in from wherever it had been waiting, for both of us, the urgency ratcheted up and we became a tangled and frenzied ball of passion until she came and collapsed on top of me, dead to the world for a few moments.

"I'm worried about you," I finally said.

"Don't be. I won't be caught off guard again. He won't get to hurt me like that anymore."

"It's not just that. You said he was watching, tracking you. He probably knows you're here."

"Well," she said, "you shouldn't have been inside my head so much. I wouldn't have lost track of time."

She laughed and pressed herself up and then climbed off the bed. "Oh, I'm a mess."

"A beautiful mess, at least. Jump in the shower."

She smiled, ran her hands through her hair and pulled it back as if to tie it off, then turned and walked to the bathroom. Even then, naked and spent from lovemaking, she moved with such grace I couldn't take my eyes off her as she walked away from me. I realized then I would never forget her effortless grace. It pervaded everything she did. I had noticed it during sex and it fueled my passion for her. That unexpected realization left me smiling. Her presence lingered long after she had left, the sweet memories, her smell and her love and grace still filled the space.

They came hours later when the night had crept over The Edge and I had dozed off into a deep and restful sleep. I heard the security alarms too late. They cracked the encryption with ease and pushed through the door, barking out orders as the security system brought the lights on, stun guns leveled, visors down on their helmets as they flooded into the living space. Couldn't have been police. They were too well kitted out, new state of the art weapons and nanokev clothing.

As I jumped from the bed one of the guns fired. They didn't even wait, the bastards. They had to have known I was outnumbered and unprepared. The bullet clipped my left arm and released its electrical charge. I screamed out, the electric shock coursed through my body and my left arm went numb. Lucky it wasn't a full on hit. I went down on one knee and tried to fight off the effects. Things blurred and I lost clarity for a moment. When I had recovered enough to try to stand the butt of a rifle smacked into my head. I saw it early enough to turn my head and deflect most of the blow. My face planted into the side of the bed. Adrenaline-fueled anger took over. I pushed as hard as I could from the bed toward the man. He was surprised I was still able to move after the shock and the hit on the head. His weapon wasn't in a position to be used. I raised up into his midsection and put a fist into his groin. He sprawled back into another of the intruders.

I saw then there were too many of them, at least six, weapons raised. But I wasn't going down without a fight. Another of them had been hit and knocked off balance when the man I had punched sprawled backward. The second man wasn't down, just unbalanced, but it was enough. I jumped and landed an elbow on top of his helmet before he could recover. He crumpled before of me.

I stood ready for a fight to the end. But a charge round pounded my chest and then everything went black.

I came to as two of them were dragging me down a hallway. Something hazy moved in my vision, a sprite of light that flickered, probably another of the assault team. The world was unfocused, blurry. I ached all over and my head was ringing like there were church bells inside my skull. I was nauseous and wanted to vomit, but I wasn't going to give them that.

Someone opened a door and put me in a hard chair and zip-tied my hands behind my back. I kept my eyes closed, trying desperately to gain some measure of control but mostly failing. One of them lifted my chin to see if I was awake. I tried but realized then I couldn't open my eyes. My mouth was open and I felt drool move down the right side of my chin.

"Fucking terrorist," he said, and let my head drop again.

I stayed there a long while. Slowly I came back to the world, the focus still hazy but the pain became manageable. The room was an office of some sort, emptied except for the chair I was in and an old desk. I had no idea where I was but I was certain this was no police action. This is corporate, I thought. I'd heard of these groups who operated outside the law, in the Oligoi interests: Private armies, basically. But they were only rumors, nighttime stories to scare the kids straight, urban legends designed to set limits that even the gangs wouldn't go beyond out of fear.

My nervous system was still overloaded. I tried but couldn't stay conscious. My head grew heavy and dipped, eyes wouldn't open, and then I was out again, slumped in the chair.

"Wake him," I heard someone say. It must have been awhile later. My wrists hurt from the zip-ties and my back was sore from the odd position it had been held.

One of the assault team prodded me and lifted my head up. The lights were bright through my eyelids, too bright, causing headache-like pain. My vision was more clear when I finally got my eyes open.

"Leave us," the man said.

Two of the assault team walked out the door and closed it.

"Think you can sleep with my wife and get away with it?"

"Edward fucking Burgess," I managed to get out. "How is the wife-beater tonight?"

I came around enough to see him clearly. He was grinning like someone who knew more than everyone else.

"I know your kind, Alexander. You think you're smart enough to see things more clearly than everyone else. You think you can see under the facade, behind the curtain. You believe that puts you on equal footing with me. It doesn't. We aren't even the same species, you and I. You're just an orphan from The Edge. No one will even miss you when you're gone."

"The cat might—maybe. He's pretty independent, though. So, that's up for debate." I tried to smile but it came off as more of a grimace, I'm sure.

Burgess walked around the desk and sat on the edge of it in front of me. "Let me explain your situation. You are a terrorist. Earlier this evening you bombed one of my factories. You know, the one that produces food packs for your kind, The Edge degenerates. I'm sure you remember the visit you made there a while ago."

Burgess smiled, crossed his arms over his chest and paused. It was a practiced move designed to add effect, but I was all caught up. I remembered the job perfectly.

"Too bad for me about loss of production, but that's only temporary. Hell, I get to write off the inventory and the old machinery you destroyed."

"What bomb?"

"Come on, keep up. I know how smart you are. I've seen your work records and your test scores. So, here's what's going to happen.

My crack investigative unit, the guys you met earlier, are going to trace the bomb to you and we will be able to show videotape from when you had access to the machines. Meyers, the facility manager, has already said you were obstinate and difficult to work with. He even mentioned, thankfully, that he didn't trust you, but orders were orders, he said, so he let you have access to the machines. Then there's your failure to pass the Merit Analysis for a second time. The video of you badgering the priest will be enough to convince anyone you had a grudge against our pretty little society. And the AI, well, might not even need that testimony. And we know the history of dissidence in your family. Your mother associated with some unsavory revolutionary types before her accident. Your guilt will be so well established no one will think twice about it. Misfits like you are always disrupting the system. Occasionally, one of you cracks, goes crazy and does something that hurts us all."

He smiled, uncrossed his arms and held his hands out, palms up. Fait accompli. Job done.

"You can't get away with this Burgess! It's all a lie and you know it."

"Of course it is! Some big conspiracy. But that's the way the world works—my world, anyway. I control the narrative. My family has for centuries. Your world, I'm afraid, is somewhat different. I haven't even told you the best part."

"What are you talking about?"

"You aren't going to jail. You won't even get a trial. What you did was treason, worse than simple terrorism. It won't take much to circumvent the legal system. Your punishment is far worse than a little jail time. You are going on The Lottery this week. You'll be on Fugitive Theatre a few days later and dead, I'm guessing, within a few days of arriving."

Fugitive Theatre? I had heard it before. Dom, that was it, some show he had been watching.

Burgess continued. "I am moving you as far from my wife as possible and you'll die on the moon. And when you're dead I'm going to instruct one of the maintenance bots to throw your body out an airlock. You fucked with the wrong guy. And you fucked the wrong woman."

I had no words. I wanted scream and lash out. I wanted to wring his entitled neck. But I couldn't do any of those things. My thoughts centered on Sarah and that we would never even see each other again. I was spiraling then, my life was in free fall and I couldn't see any way to stop it.

Burgess stood up and walked to the door, reached for the handle and then turned back to me.

"Here's the best part, Alexander. When you die on the moon—when someone guts you and you are writhing in agony and bleeding out nearly 250,000 miles away—my wife and I will be eating popcorn and watching it all on a big screen in our family room. It'll be glorious."

"Maybe," I said, my voice solemn and weak, "but she's still going to know you're just another wife-beater, another thug. She'll never forget that, no matter how far away you ship me. She's always going to see you for what you are. You are like every other gang member in The Edge, except you have money. You are right about one thing, we really aren't alike. You are a different species, something that hasn't yet been scrubbed from the gene pool, something primitive."

"Says the dead terrorist."

The door clicked shut behind him. His footsteps faded quickly down the hall. Then I allowed myself to weep—not for myself, but for Sarah, and for the helplessness of the situation.

8

SAYS THE DEAD MAN

I spent forty-eight hours in a holding cell. It was a small room with a cot, small chair and screen that was tuned to one of the news feeds. I was all over the feeds; video of me at the factory, my talk with the priest and that I had failed the Merit Analysis a second time. I was the troubled orphan who couldn't fit in, the angry man who wanted revenge and railed against the system. The media, fed by Burgess, no doubt, painted the perfect picture of the outsider gone bad; my poor and shady family background made me into a ticking bomb just waiting to explode.

At one point, early in the afternoon of the first day, they interviewed Meyers, the factory manager.

"Did you notice anything odd when the terrorist was here? Was there anything out of order?"

"Nothing I could report. I mean, the guy was rude, you know, confrontational. But he got the work done and the machine was functioning properly when he left. I checked that, you know. I made sure it was running. But I didn't see anything when he was here that would make me question what he had done."

"We're told," said the journalist, "that you never trusted this man, the bomber?"

"Well, yeah. Look, I mean, he wasn't Cleric, was he? Kind of hard trust someone like that when they aren't Cleric. It's an important job, what we do. We feed people. Disrupting production is gonna be hard on some people. But in the end, you know, the guys higher up had sent him, so I didn't think too long about it. It's a shame, really," Meyers looked away from the camera, probably at the mess I had supposedly created, "everyone here loves what we do. We contribute. We make things better, you know."

They never called me by my name after the first couple hours. I was always "the terrorist" or "the bomber," the threat was more removed that way and they could peddle basic fear.

Meyers, in the background after the reporter had thanked him and turned away, was shouting instructions and pointing. Hilarious, that. I remembered Meyers as too lazy to walk the factory floor when I was there. Now he was acting like the man in charge.

The injustice hit me hard the first time the segment cycled through. I was guilty of a few things, bad judgement for one. But I wasn't some psycho so angry at the system he would blow up a factory. But the third and fourth times the segment played I was just bitter and tired of it all.

Then they added a new wrinkle, later in the day. Someone got the priest from the Merit Analysis test in the studio. He was a pompous prick on air. "We need to feel for people like this. We need to pray for them," he said. "Clearly this man became unhinged after he failed the test a second time. He said such horrific things about the church and our society, all baseless, of course."

I saw the way his eyes twitched and the quick sideways glance: The priest didn't believe what he was saying. He was lying. Of course he was lying.

"I feel a little blame for what happened. Maybe I should have picked up on it and brought it to someone's attention." The priest breathed deeply and exhaled. "Who can say? In the end, some things are difficult to predict or prevent. Thankfully," he smiled, "nobody got hurt, just machinery and the building, and those things can be repaired or replaced."

Well, I thought, never rely on the religious to be honest.

By the next morning I was old history, except for the loonies and conspiracy theorists who sprouted up like weeds after rain. They had in the studio some joker claiming there might be a connection between me, the bombing, and a radical group of terrorists, an organization under deep cover trying to ruin our way of life. The man spoke about it as if it were a certainty. His name was irrelevant. His message, baseless with no facts offered up, was all about fear, of the unknown, of others. Who knew? I was pretty certain that part about the others was a dog-whistle signal to raise the hackles of those who wanted to sterilize The Edge, or make it go away entirely. They were a loud and persistent part of the Clerics, hardliners for purification.

"What we need to focus on here," he said, "is just what are we doing to prevent these sorts of organizations from getting a foothold. What steps are we taking to prevent them from forming at all? Look, this is a difficult time. We all feel uneasy and vulnerable, but we have to address these issues. Maybe now is the time to look past our current laws to something that will protect our freedoms better."

"What do you mean by that?" The studio host, a perky brunette with bright white teeth, asked.

"We allow these people to exist freely in places like The Edge, where this terrorist was from. We allow them to believe as they like—any god or no god at all. My God, look how hateful he was toward the church! Maybe that needs to end. We need to cleanse the land, so to speak. These non-christian types can be our undoing if we aren't careful. To protect all our freedoms we need to crack down on these people, get them in line. If it turns out he was part of some subversive group, like his mother was, then we need to take a hard line. We have to have the guts to stand up to them and do what is necessary. And that means giving the church more power to work in our behalf. We have to take off the gloves and the shackles and put these dogs down, and I mean now."

On and on it went after that. It was about the conspiracy, then, the radicals among us, not about me, not the fake bombing, and not any of the truths I had spoken of to the priest.

In the evenings I chewed on my situation, swallowed each detail, spit out philosophical angles, broke them down and examined them. I chided myself for the subsurface guilt I didn't deserve. You slept with a woman whose husband had hit her, I reminded myself. That's the worst thing I had done. That was ethically challenged, sure. But I didn't deserve all this. Granted, I'd pissed off one of the few guys capable of pulling this off, but that didn't make it any more right or justified.

Eventually, the doubt and second-guessing, the guilt, reshaped itself in my head and vectored toward anger. I sat at the edge of the cot and reached for the nearby chair and stood up. Holding it by one of the legs, I hurled it into the screen on the wall. The chair shattered, the screen too, then both collapsed to the floor.

But it didn't stop there. Anger wasn't enough. I wanted revenge, vengeance. I wanted Burgess dead. And I wanted Sarah.

Says the dead man.

Dead? Not yet. And as long as I was breathing I had one goal, one purpose. All I had to do was figure out how. I could do that. I was always good at solving puzzles. It's what I did.

The next morning they roused me from bed, threw me in a shower and then handed me some basic clothes; jeans, a t-shirt and socks and shoes. While dressing I noticed how badly bruised I was in spots. I was stiff and sore, but there wasn't any time to worry over the wounds. They marched me out of the holding rooms and down the hall to the other side of the building. The hallway was dark, the lighting low, and deserted. It felt as though we were underground, but I wasn't certain. I had no clue what was happening.

"Where are we going?"

Someone belted me between the shoulders from behind. I fell forward into the two guards that paced us down the hallway. "We don't speak to terrorists. Don't open your mouth again."

It was a long walk with a couple turns then finally we stopped and they unlocked and opened another door and shoved me inside. I was pushed hard through the opening and stumbled right into Jose Mann, The Edge Knife.

Mann had a greasy smile that was almost childish. He wasn't what I expected. He was short and thin, scraggly dark hair with streaks of gray throughout, wavy in front. He looked like the kind of guy who pushed a broom all day, cleaning up other people's messes. Not the mass murderer and evil thing the press had turned him into. The press had portrayed him as large and menacing.

"Sorry," I said, and straightened up and backed off. I was a good eight inches taller than him. The man was puny and anything but menacing. Still, I reminded myself, this man murdered his own family and his neighbors with a knife.

There were three other men in the small room. No one said a word. They barely looked up or took notice. They were hard men, all tatted up and thick, prison weights, I guessed. That, and the presence of Mann, meant this had to have something to do with The Lottery. Wished I had spoken more with Dom, back at the store in The Edge. He could explain it all.

So, no trial for me, and no attorney, either, that was certain. I had been railroaded. Burgess was going all out. No one should have that kind of power.

Some time later the door opened and the security team took us one at a time into the hall, cuffed our feet and hands, then walked us down the hall and held us outside a set of double doors. One by one we were marched through the doors. Each time they opened I could hear the muffled sounds of an audience. It took about five minutes for each man, then the doors would open and they would grab the next. Finally, it was just me and Mann in the hallway outside the doors. He had that child-like smile on his face, beaming energy. I was a nervous wreck, but Mann was calm and quiet, almost enjoying himself. The doors opened and one of the security guys grabbed me and jerked me through. At least they didn't save me for last.

They marched me up to the stage. There were a dozen guys like me standing at the back, side by side. Flashy graphics were all around, dropdown screens, holograms, and floor graphics all told the story of how I had blown up the factory. Clips played of my tirade at the priest and the interviews with Meyers and others were playing. Bright lights beamed down on me. A studio audience booed and jeered at me. Something struck my temple and deflected away. The security guy prodded me from behind to the center of the stage. A black and white image of me hovered overhead. It looked like a mug shot. Beneath it the caption read: Clay Alexander, Terrorist.

The music that was playing as background to the videos and my march to the center of the stage died out and the host said from somewhere I couldn't see: "No need to explain this one. Is there?"

The crowd roared and screamed. The guard jerked me by the back of my shirt and pulled me to the back of the stage with the others. The theater went dark and loud music was piped in through the speakers again. The doors cracked open, a slice of light cut the darkness and Jose Mann walked in. No security detail for Mann. He was by himself, like the star of the show entering stage right. He raised his zip-tied hands above his head and smiled and moved to the center of the stage.

A few tenuous jeers from the crowd. Then someone cheered. Someone else yelled, "Fuck yeah! That's what I'm talkin' 'bout!" Everyone joined in then.

The announcer said something, but I couldn't hear. I wasn't listening, anyway. Questions raced around in my head. What was that? They asked. Why would anyone cheer for the man? Are these people insane? Most likely it was planned by Burgess and his production team, audience plants, trying excite the viewers watching on screens or their PEDs.

It took a few moments for the noise to die down. They showed the gory details of the Jose Mann story, the brutal deaths and coroner bags and blood spattered walls. They detailed the kills, each one of them. They spoke of the great futures robbed from the victims, the brutal nature of their deaths, and the man behind it all. It was surreal. Mann stood there and watched it like the rest of the audience, a passive onlooker, like someone watching a nature documentary. When it finished he tipped his head, turned toward us, and smiled.

Then the host asked the audience and those at home or on their PEDs to vote, reminding them they could only vote for their top three picks. The live tallies showed up on the screens all around the stage. The data changed in real-time. As people voted the announcer reminded them that only seven of us were going to appear on Fugitive Theatre.

I looked at the screens as the host excitedly explained for the viewers and the audience in the studio what was happening.

"Would you look at that! Jose Mann has 100 percent of the possible votes. 100%! And second in the tally is our terrorist bomber."

I had no doubts Burgess had fixed the results. It was never possible I wouldn't make the cut. I hadn't killed anyone but somehow I was second choice on The Lottery. I didn't buy it.

It also didn't matter.

"Come on folks, get one last look," the host said as they paraded us out to the front of the stage at the end. "They are moonbound and they won't be coming back."

One guy singled out as the star and six patsies along for the ride. It was the Jose Mann show. A few of the guys were clearly pissed off. The rest of us were simply window dressing.

I was marched back to the same room I had spent time in the previous two days and nights. I'd had a good look at some of the men I would have to face on Fugitive Theatre. They were hard men, like the gang members from The Edge, or the types who roamed Skin after dark, badasses with chips on their shoulders and I-don't-give-a-fuck attitudes. People who didn't value life. I spent the evening pondering the problem and asking myself the same question again and again. Could I abandon my humanity and become the thing necessary to survive?

I had to think it through. It was a big ask. But I saw no other way. I had a fitful night. I couldn't sleep, tossed and turned while my mind wrestled with foreign thoughts and ideas. Somewhere around three a.m. I sat up in bed. I rubbed my eyes, wrapped the thin, coarse blanket around my shoulders and realized I had no other choice. I either became that thing, the one that put survival above all else, or I was a dead man. Dying wasn't an option. I'd made up my mind. It felt good at least to arrive at that point. Even though I had a lot to figure out, the big ticket item was behind me, settled. I knew what I had to become.

I had to become Jose Mann—times ten.

I fell asleep quickly after that. But not before visions of Sarah warmed the night and smoothed out my thoughts, until they didn't, and I felt like crying, sorry for everything I had brought down on her and myself.

Early the next day I was pulled from bed and thrown into the showers again. When I was finished they marched me outside to an old bus. I was seated on the bus, hands zip-tied to the seat. Some of the Lottery winners were already there. The remainder joined us shortly. The driver closed the doors and we were off.

It was a two hour drive before we reached our destination, a private airfield with one of the new small and reusable rockets on the far side of the tarmac. They marched us into a small hangar. A nurse was there and they lined us up to meet her and then move on to the area where we donned suits and got a few instructions.

"What's this?" I asked the nurse.

"Should keep you from getting sick in space. Happens to most people their first time."

She stuck the needle in my arm and motioned with her head for me to move on.

Space. I hadn't even thought about that. I had too many other things to worry over. But there it was. Big and bold, the adventure of a lifetime, just waiting out there on the tarmac. It was supposed to be a one-way ticket, but I had other plans. I was going to find a ticket home.

They removed my bindings and I climbed into he suit. They snapped the helmet on, checked something, patted my shoulder and pointed for me to follow the others ahead of me. Several guys with stun guns were watching over us. But once we were in the suits there was no way to move fast enough to cause any trouble. It was difficult to walk, no way to run. These weren't modern suits that fit snuggly. They were more bulky, too much room in the legs and arms.

Out on the tarmac I stopped walking and looked to the sky. A daytime moon, white and crisp, floated not far off the horizon. My new home in a few days. The far side of the moon was a graveyard for some of the old space agencies. Satellites and lunar landers crashed there. Dead machinery. I didn't want to end up there, another dead machine stuck forever in the cold and dark. And no bot was going to push me out an airlock, despite the promise Burgess had made. My heart was pounding in my chest, my mouth dry. Remember the mission, spaceman. Remember the mission.

An elevator took us up a short distance and we were strapped into seats in what looked like a cargo hold and then rotated into place and locked in. It was agony waiting to take off.

"This is mission control," came over speakers in my helmet. "This is a one way trip into space. If you are on the wrong flight please disembark immediately." The man laughed. "Sorry, folks, just a little humor. Liftoff in one minute. Enjoy the ride."

There was a roar, some shaking, and a brief feeling of vertigo. Then we were pinned back in our seats and gone. I found it strange traveling without seeing where we were going. I think it was less than an hour before we docked at the near earth orbital. The automated systems snapped into place. After a few minutes the doors opened and two security floated in.

"Look who won the lottery," one of them said over comms. The other laughed.

The first floated up to me. "Well, dead man, how ya feelin'? Sick yet?"

While I was still locked in place I caught him off guard and put my hand into his chest as hard as I could. He tried to grab onto my arm but slipped and flipped back, hit someone in front of me and spun into the far wall, feet over head.

He came right back at me.

"I ought to slit your suit and leave you here to die!"

"Kind of redundant, no? You just said it. I'm already dead."

9

THE LONG DESCENT

"You won't last long, homey." He stuffed some mashed potatoes into his mouth and smiled while chewing, then pointed his plastic spoon at me. "You ain't made for it. Look at me, gang born and raised. Streets in my blood. I killed a man on my twelfth birthday and never looked back."

Like everyone else at the table, except Mann and myself, he was all tatted up. Fingers, arms and the side of his neck had some nice artwork—a skull, a tribal sign and some wings. On the left side of his face were three bars, just a couple millimeters thin, maybe a centimeter long, evenly spaced in parallel. Somewhere in there was his tribe, his identification. I guessed each one meant something to him, but I wasn't versant enough in tattoo or gang symbolism to know what. But as I watched him I realized he was working hard to convince me I was out of place because of his own insecurities. He was trying to act nonchalant about our situation but he was struggling, pawning his fear off onto me. I kept my mouth shut.

"Now look at you," he continued. "You're more like some pansy office-worker. I mean, you're big enough, but what you ever done. Hell, homey, you blew up a factory and didn't even kill anyone. You ain't got no chance against the pros, and that's what this place is."

A couple acolytes grinned and waved a spoon while they ate. A huge Polynesian guy sat at the end of the table across from me. He had a permanent grin on his face and such a relaxed vibe I found it reassuring to watch him. He wasn't paying any overt attention to the gang-bangers. He was enjoying his meal, printed from an algae base or not. He was in his own little world. At one point he looked up at me, the glint in his eyes made me think he was having fun, then he smiled, shifted in his chair and slipped his spoon inside his shirt. The whole time the lecture from the gang banger kept going, but I was oblivious. I was thinking about some of the things I had learned. The lecture wasn't for me, anyway.

The near earth orbital was like a giant hotel in space, at least the portion where they housed us was. We were sealed off from the rest of the structure. What we saw was a big conference room, a small dining area and some small and basic quarters with a communal bathroom. We spent the late morning "acclimating," which meant throwing up for most of us. It took some to time to get used to space. Even with the shots most of us chucked at least one meal the previous day. A light amount of gravity tugged at me, but I couldn't say how or why. There were no windows in our area.

The gang banger scowled at me. "You should be more respectful, all things considered."

I just stared. This was heading in a bad direction.

"Any one of us could end you right now. Ain't nothin' gonna

happen if we do. We're all dead men anyway. You might need some help, you know, when we get there, some protection, I'm thinking. I'm trying to talk to you, help you out, and you just got that smirk on your face."

"Guy like that," said a plastic spoon waving minion, "might not even make it to the moon."

I smiled and got up to leave. "I'm no sycophant and I don't need help, especially yours."

Jose Mann was grinning. The big Polynesian guy nodded his head a slight bit and stood up. This guy, the gang banger, was trouble. Maybe, I thought, I needed to deal with that sooner than later.

After the meal two security showed up and escorted me to the doctor. Her office was about three times larger than our quarters, but it wasn't large.

"Take a seat, Mr. Alexander." She motioned to the treatment table. The two guards stood near the door.

"Just Clay, please."

"On a first name basis with a terrorist? Me?"

"Whatever. Did you see my trial?"

"I did not."

"Me, either, there wasn't one."

"Well, you confessed, according to the news networks and the authorities. They probably didn't feel you needed one."

"Uh-huh. Did you hear me confess? Was I on the news pouring my heart out, releasing that pent up anger they claimed possessed me?"

"No, you weren't," she said solemnly. "Come now, *are* you claiming to be innocent?"

"By now that's irrelevant, doc."

"Open up."

She looked down my throat, into my eyes and ears, and then listened to my heart. Then she grabbed a mobile scanner and ran it around my body and head.

"Lift your shirt up, please."

I did as she asked and she examined my bruises, including the one that had emerged on my arm. "Those appear to be fairly deep and it looks as though you were hit with a taser in your arm and in the chest."

"Charge round, at close range."

"That must have hurt. But those knock you out, I believe. So, maybe it wasn't so bad. Would you like a painkiller?"

"Didn't knock me out. I did get to a couple of the security team before they took me out though. And I can manage without the painkiller."

"Suit yourself. There aren't any niceties where you're going, I'm afraid. Let me know if you change your mind."

She nodded to security and they escorted me back to my quarters.

Niceties, she had said. But I didn't want to ease the pain. I wanted hardness. I wanted the universe cold and exacting, to know precisely where I stood and what was required of me. My perception was shifting, my view of people took on a new level of clarity that I hadn't seen or felt before. The doc had been nice enough and my security escorts hadn't said a word to me on the march to and from the office. But they were both hiding, wearing a uniform that shaped and controlled their worldview. Everything they knew about the world was wrapped up those two identities—doctor and guard. But strip that back, peel away the facade of their uniforms, the doctor's smock and tools, the guards' weapons and demeanor, and break down their position within society and they were simple things. Without the uniform they were hairless apes, evolved to survive on a blue-green ball spinning through space. They were chemical concoctions ruled by electrical impulses. What did the universe care? Could either of them forego their perspective and position, abandon who they were, to survive like the animals they were? Or, were they so insulated and cocooned by society and its imagined metaphors of importance that they couldn't break the illusion?

More importantly, was I?

I hadn't had any real time to myself since I had made the decision to survive regardless of the cost, to become whatever was necessary. Understanding the vengeance that fueled that desire wasn't difficult: I was going to get revenge against Edward Burgess. I also understood that vengeance was an all too human trait. Despite my desire to slough off everything I knew to be human—civility, mercy, care, order, all of it—I knew I was motivated and fueled by the most human of desires and emotions. But I could operate within that bubble, cold, calculating and ruthless, until I found a way back.

Fights aren't always won by the strongest or fastest. Sometimes it would require smarts, sometimes guile, often just mere brutality and the willingness to do what was needed. Acting quickly and decisively would be just as important as strength. Most people get caught up in the things going on in their own heads, like the gang banger at mess. I needed to avoid that. But most important of all, I reasoned, was the desire to live, to never give up or lose sight of the goal. Broken people—minds and psyches—don't survive.

The gang banger had me marked as a weak link. He probably thought killing me would give him some breathing room, some cred with the others. That wouldn't happen. I wasn't going to let him have that.

Personal demons take on many disguises. They call at odd hours, just when their presence will have the greatest impact. But they are mostly figments of the imagination, some dark corner of the mind designed to prevent us from wandering too far afield, maybe, to remind us of past transgressions. Mine, it seemed, had become a blonde headed thing full of grace and understanding, those ice blue eyes like daggers. I swallowed hard at the vision and buried it. I had no control over its impact, yet. I still hadn't come to terms enough with my new outlook and surroundings, and the uncertain future before me, to entertain it—*her*. I tried to shunt it from my mind. Later I would welcome her and turn her from a demon to a vision of hope, or something like that. Then she would be a reminder of what I was fighting for. But for now the thought of her, what was left behind, what I had done, was too raw, too much of a reminder of all I had to push aside to keep moving and stay alive.

Someone wrapped on my door. Security was there to escort me to the conference room. We were all gathered again for another session on what to expect. It seemed a useless exercise, but then I realized they needed people to survive a while for ratings, if nothing else. When I tried to enter the door the gang banger forced himself past me and knocked me into the doorframe.

"Stay out the way, homey."

As he walked away I tripped his left foot into his right. He stumbled for a couple steps. I walked past him and found a seat.

"Wait 'til we get to the moon, homey."

His spoon waving minions eyed me as I walked by.

The man speaking was an engineer and one of the designers

of the base. After he welcomed us he began explaining a few of the technical features.

"I can't go into the specifics of it all, not that any of you would understand it, anyway. But the local area around the base has additional gravity. Basically, about a kilometer or so below the base is a blackhole generator. The blackholes are small and die out almost immediately, but by constantly creating new ones we generate about seven-tenths earth gravity in the local area."

"Artificial gravity?" I asked.

"No, not artificial, the gravity is real. The base is more advanced, in some ways, than anything on earth. The important thing for you is to know how to find food and water. Both, you will be happy to know, are abundant. An algae farm is under the base. It is controlled by robots. In fact, you will get very used to seeing the robots about. It wasn't originally designed like this, but for the show, Fugitive Theatre, we thought it necessary. Printers have been installed throughout great cavern. You can actually request five nutrient bars a day, though that is far more food than you will need. The printers are the same as here on the near earth orbital, Olympus. One difference is on the moon the food simply comes out in chunks, much like the size you get in the stores. In the stores, of course, they get wrapped and packaged. Yours will be the raw thing that gets printed."

In other words, we'd be getting the same food we had been eating on earth, just without the wrapper, the same food produced at the factory I supposedly bombed. The guy giving the presentation liked to talk. He rambled on for quite a while. Most of the guys, it was easy to see, were bored. But I found it interesting.

I also found something I thought I could use. The seat before me was broken in the back, a six inch piece of the thick plastic was torn along a seat edge. I put my foot on it during the entire presentation, trying to weaken it or break it off.

"It was decided early on to acquire water for the base," he continued. "There's a lot of water on the moon at the lunar south pole. But the designers decided a nearby comet was a better solution. They didn't want the base in the South pole. Remember, this was a generation-long project. An unmanned spaceship was sent to collect a comet relatively near to earth while a team of robots on the moon drilled down under where the base is now. Once the fusion engine was installed and working properly the comet was ready to be delivered. Under the Great Cavern, as it is commonly known, that makes up Fugitive Base, off to the side of it, actually, basically is another cavern now filled with water, like an aquifer. The comet was broken into pieces and put in place, the hole was then closed up and sealed with plasticrete. Then the comet was melted down using the heat generated by the fusion engine. There is enough fresh water in that closed system to last several generations. And that fusion generator can last that long, as well. It may need more fuel but that's relatively easy to deliver. Of course, the solar field on the surface, that runs all secondary systems, could be used to run the entire city if it were necessary. It's a beautiful system and a remarkable feat of engineering."

"And now it's a prison," I muttered.

"Yes, well," the guy looked at me, "times change. Opinion and desire will come around again. People will get interested and some will want to live on the moon eventually."

"Anything else we should know?"

"There is more, but it isn't necessary I go into it. You will see different things there. Not a lot different from here on earth, just a bit. You may not notice much."

"Such as?"

"Let's let that be a surprise, shall we."

After more than an hour we adjourned. Everyone got up and filed out as if they had been forced to go to church and listen to a long sermon—in Latin, by a crusty old priest bored with his own reading. I stayed a little longer in my seat and saw security lingering outside the door. I gave the plastic one final hard kick. The noise from it breaking and falling to the floor was covered up by the commotion of everyone shuffling along and talking about the base. I picked up the plastic as calmly as possible and slid it under my shirt into the waist of my pants.

I had thought of something that might be useful to me so I waited as everyone shuffled out the door.

"Tell me something, doc," I asked when we were alone and he was gathering his things, "how are things controlled on the base. Everything can't be automated. It would seem too difficult to manage the entire base—the city—from earth. Besides, I can't imagine those who built the place wouldn't want complete autonomy."

He smiled but clearly was taken off guard by the question. But, as I said, he also liked to talk. "You aren't wrong. Mr. Alexander, is it?"

"It is."

"Yes, well, the entire city was designed to run itself. We have dumbed down the place for its current use, but it was designed to exist without earth assistance."

"So, what are you saying, there are engineers on the moon managing things behind the scenes?"

"Oh, no, we covered up the control room. It is all automated, for the time being. If anything serious happened we would have to send up a team. We can monitor it from here, of course, and the robots can effect many changes and repairs per their programming.

But that only goes so far. We haven't had any reason to send a team in yet, nor would I expect to. You needn't worry, really. The environment is remarkably stable."

"That's reassuring," I said. "Environment: you make it sound like the place was terraformed."

"That's not so far off, you know. There is an entire bio system up there, under the surface. We even imported bacteria."

He smiled and walked me to the door. "Good luck, Mr. Alexander."

The guards escorted me to my quarters. Inside, a box was on the bed. I opened it and found a new set of clothes and a breakfast bar and some water for the morning. We wouldn't be meeting in the mess area. Orientation was over.

I pulled the piece of plastic out from under my shirt and examined it. Given the proper opportunity it was sharpe enough, long enough and stiff enough to use as a knife. Jose Mann could probably kill us all with it. But I only wanted to kill one person and then leave it behind. That was the plan forming in my head.

At night security locked the place down and only left one guard at the doors outside our area. Water was cut off to the communal showers but the toilets and sinks still worked. It was a small space, which was why they had never let more than three of us in it simultaneously. Once things quieted down for the night I slipped out the door and headed to the bathroom. With things so quiet at night every creak and ping could be heard traveling along bulkhead floors. There was a white noise hum to the orbital. I paused outside the bathroom and listened. Nothing.

I would have gone straight for the guy, but there seemed to be more risk in that. First, I didn't know which quarters were his, or if they were the same size and layout as mine. Second, that would be too noisy. I liked the odds of waiting him out better.

I camped out in the last stall and waited. I didn't care how long it took. Time was irrelevant and something I realized no longer had a say in my life, no expectations, no where and no when to be. Aside from the trip to the moon in a few hours, I was no longer slaved to a schedule. I closed my eyes and rested, and listened.

Sometime later the door opened and someone walked to the urinal. I peeked over the door. It was Jose Mann. The little guy took his time, slowly messing with the tie to his pants and then loosening them. Just as Mann got down to business the gang banger walked in, noisy and tired. He banged into the door on the way in.

"You, too?" He mumbled to Mann. Mann just looked at him like he was an annoyance. The gang banger dropped his pants and leaned his head forward against the wall. "Still sick," he said. "Can't wait to get on solid ground, even if it is the damn moon."

I slipped out of the stall and snuck up behind him as quietly as possible, which probably wasn't necessary. He was practically asleep standing up. Mann saw me at the last minute, saw the pointed plastic in my hand and grinned. My heart pounded in my chest, but I focused on my one objective, raised up stabbed as hard as I could into the gang banger's neck. I had placed my thumb over the end of the plastic and stabbing him caused it to dig into my hand, but that prevented it from slipping out on impact. The gang banger couldn't scream or lash out or fight back in any way. He was caught so unaware he was clueless what was happening. I dug in deeper, cut a major artery and the plastic sank in several inches as he slumped to the floor, blood arching out a foot or so. I made certain to avoid getting any blood on me. The gang banger reached feebly for his neck. I rode him down to the floor when he collapsed, took a quick glance at Mann who seemed to be enjoying himself, and then stood up and put my heel into the gang banger's face, crunching and shattering bones. He was still. Dead.

I looked at Mann. I was fighting off throwing up and desperately wanted to leave. Mann was as unemotional as possible, calm and quiet. He had an eerie quality about him, like some alien observer always on the fringe of things but not participating. I thought he was enjoying it all, but he didn't give an impression one way or the other. He walked to the small sink and washed his hands, looking back at me as he toweled them dry. I forced a shrug through the massive adrenaline dump in my system and turned and left.

I was shaking and breathing hard as I walked and nearly stumbled back to my quarters but I made it. I sat on the end of the bed and tried to fight off the shakes and the crazy amount of energy that coursed like lightening bolts through my system. My mouth was dry and I couldn't focus well. Eventually, I quit fighting it. I gave in and just let my body release the energy. I got so tired and knew I was going to pass out so I got on the floor and put my back to the door. If anyone tried to enter I figured they would have to wake me up to do it.

A commotion in the hallway outside my room woke me in the morning. I could hear security running to the bathroom. I tried to get up but I was exhausted and weak and every muscle and joint ached. I pulled myself up to the bed and forced a drink from the bottled water. It was difficult to swallow at first, but once my throat was wetted I was dying for more and downed the entire bottle. Then I ravenously tore at the breakfast bar, and contemplated what I had done.

Just as I was finished eating security burst through the door.

"Time to go?"

"What do you know about Perez?"

I shrugged. "Who?"

He was angry, the guard, and took a menacing step into the room. I wasn't sure if he wanted to hit just me, or each of us. It didn't matter. He had orders not to hurt anyone else, I'm sure. "Get dressed, now."

I discovered everyone was certain Mann had killed the guy as I walked into the hall where they lingered, nervous chatter everywhere. They were even talking about it around him, as if Mann weren't there. But Mann just stood there, hands behind his back, leaning against the wall, calm and detached. The guards came and took him away to one of the rooms, for questioning, no doubt. But they brought him back a few minutes later. His expression had never changed. He gave me a quick conspiratorial glance as if to say all was good. Then he resumed the same position he had taken against the wall earlier.

The big Polynesian guy stood in the doorway to his quarters across from Mann and beamed a smile at me. He knew. He listened to the others burning their nervous energy off by talking smack about revenge while he finished his breakfast bar. But he knew. I was certain he knew. I was calm standing there with everyone else, chill and relaxed. The previous evening felt like a long while ago. Him or me, I reasoned, and then dismissed it from my thoughts. I had other things to focus on.

The guards came a few minutes later and it was time to go. No one cared about a bunch of criminals killing one of their own. We were all expendable, anyway.

Suits were waiting for us, similar to the ones we wore on the trip to the orbital. They looked and felt ancient, nothing like the stuff shown in any movie or show, nothing like the astronauts were pictured wearing.

One of the guards spoke. "The suits hold half an hour of oxygen and aren't reusable. Once you get to the moon you enter the airlock and remove the helmet and suit as quickly as possible and make your way into Great Cavern."

He showed us how to snap the helmet in place.

"Even though it's a long trip, keep your helmets with you always during the trip, never know what can happen. Use the built in heads up display for entertainment. You can watch a thousand things on your HUD. As you were told during training, make certain you are properly prepared for deceleration. We would hate for you to come this far just to be killed at landing, wouldn't we?" He smiled sarcastically.

It was an eight hour trip. The shuttle had a fusion engine similar to the one running the base. We were locked in place and told to stay in our seats unless we absolutely felt the need to get up. The shuttle was fitted with two rows of seats facing each other. It was a crude set up, just an old cargo hold, but they weren't trying to impress us. Creature comforts weren't a consideration.

The ride was boring, too much chatter along the way for me. The gang bangers liked to talk, which seemed at odds with their reputations. Mann sat across from me. I could tell he was watching a show on his heads up. The big Polynesian guy sat next to him, head lolled back a bit and he was slid forward to the edge of his seat, almost reclining. He was sleeping. I liked that guy. He was calm and quiet, relaxed enough to sleep in our ridiculous situation.

I watched a few minutes of a movie but couldn't get into it. It seemed so small and insignificant. I considered my position for a while, tried to think of a plan for when I got to the base, and then shifted through thoughts of Miyamoto and Tabitha. I was going to miss my home. But eventually I settled on Sarah, concentrating as long as I could on her beauty, smarts and the incredible time we had before everything went to hell. It was a painful time, to be honest. Sweet memories are like that, though. Every ounce of sweetness is accompanied by two ounces of heartache.

The signs flashed for deceleration, a red tint throughout the cabin. I kicked out at the Polynesian guy, jarring him from sleep. He straightened up like the rest of us. I locked myself in tighter. Three flashes of light came a minute later. Our chairs wrapped around us, the belts pulled tight. Then the chairs rotated toward what I thought was the back of the shuttle and my back slammed against the chair. It was like an old amusement park ride, only ten times worse. But it didn't last long.

A few minutes later the cargo doors opened and we were instructed over comms to jump down and go. I stopped at the lip of the shuttle as everyone else jumped and looked out on the moon and farther into the darkness beyond. The airlock door to the moon base opened and everyone filed in. I jumped down then. It was just a few feet. The difference in gravity was noticeable, both the physical gravity and the immensity of my situation. I turned and looked beyond the moon landscape again, searching for home, for earth. But the shuttle blocked the view.

How ironic, I thought, pushed so far from home only to become intimately involved with millions of people. But then, it was a one-way transaction. I was the caged animal. They were simple voyeurs.

Trailing the others, I entered the airlock and began the long descent.

10

EXTREME CLOSE-UP

Conspiracists describe convoluted associations threaded throughout history based upon the flimsiest of tentacles, whose logic defies facts and exists sans support of empirical data, proof as much in a nod and a wink, or a leap of faith, as in the real world. The story of the Oligoi was no different from many others, the latest iteration of the secret society pulling humanity by the marionette's strings. The Lords, Kings, Oligarchs and others who wielded power in the past, the story went, organized and plotted the course of human doldrum in a manner that left most with just enough, most of the time, but never plenty, at least not for long. It was easier, said the conspiracist, to control the masses when their next meal or rent payment was their immediate concern. Keep the masses from looking up, noses to the grindstone and all, and they won't look about.

Secret societies have always existed, of course. The Illuminati were real, but they never possessed the breadth of power required to rule humanity. They also suffered from living in a world separated by vast distances. It took weeks to travel small distances. Mass communication only existed when one human spoke to another, both physically present at the time. In time, this changed. Ships were invented and the world shrank a small degree. Gutenberg's printing press spread books and knowledge like wildfire and through its dissemination the world shrank a massive amount.

But the conspiracy of oligarchs pulling strings from behind the veil suffers from another simple fact: The Lords, Kings and Corporatists of the past weren't team players. They were egomaniacs, some hell bent on running the world their way, most, like the dragons of myth, were only interested in sitting atop the largest pile of gold they could acquire. They were brutal, self-centered and only concerned, for the most part, with their immediate locale. They didn't have the time, desire or means to expand.

All of that changed with the development of the network. Instantaneous communication to anywhere on the planet changed the game. Instantaneous coordination across the planet among those in power was simple. All that was needed was a push, a nudge in the correct direction, and the impetus and gall of the few to look down upon the rest. Climate change provided the needed boost. When the world was rearranged through catastrophic rising seas, as the coastlines disappeared when billions of gallons of water trapped under the earth's crust were released and the maps were rewritten, the Oligoi used their power to shape the new world. After the Wars, when the dust had finally settled, the conspiracy became fact. The remaining players from the Oligoi Wars banded together and for the first time in human history a group of individuals and organizations stepped beyond influence and began curating humanity's future.

"When The Conspiracists Got It Right: The Oligoi Emergence", The Oligoi Wars, 73.

She sprang from bed—empty and unruffled beside her, she noticed in her haste—and clamored into the bathroom, knocking a small tin of makeup to the marble floor where it danced and flipped on any number of sharp edges before coming to rest without breaking or spilling open. For the briefest of moments she thought the nausea would abate. In the mirror, looking back with something bordering on contempt, or maybe pity, she couldn't be certain any longer, was someone she didn't recognize—blond hair a ratted mess, vacant eyes, the energy only a whisper of its former self and something even the most expensive of makeup couldn't fill in, gloss over or fabricate. What had become of her life?

Then she dove for the toilet and threw up, pulling at the handle to flush it as she unloaded the meager contents of her stomach down the bowl. I need to see a doctor, Sarah thought. Since Clay had been arrested, detained, taken, *what?* Since the day he had allegedly bombed one of Edward's factories—the veracity of which seemed implausible—she had sunk into one episode after another of illness, caused, she decided, by nerves. She was a wreck and she needed help, but the last thing she wanted was something to deaden the pain, to gloss it over and leave her in a clouded, medicated fugue state.

All of the hours and hours of reporting in the news feeds, she couldn't take her eyes off it, but couldn't stand watching it, either. The pain was overwhelming. She wanted to scream. She knew the man, the accused. It couldn't be true. None of it was true. The coverage waned over the days, less sensational with each passing news cycle, replaced with events more immediate and equally sensational. But each tidbit, each reference, no matter how small, siphoned her energy and hope. Plus, today was the day Clay was to make an appearance on Fugitive Theatre. My god, she thought, sitting on the cool floor of the bathroom with her back to a wall, he could already be dead. As her mood turned sour again, tears flowed down her cheeks, and she felt more tired than she ought to have been. She had barely slept during the night, dream interrupted sleep that raced along helical lines of despair for both Clay and herself. Still, her level of fatigue was monumental.

Her mouth was dry and she wanted water, the sink so close. But she wanted to stay where she was more. She didn't want to move so she sat, and dwelled. But nothing was in her thoughts at the moment nor in her heart, no sense of fight, no rebellion or determination, just a blankness. "This," she muttered to the high-end cosmetics and gold leaf trim, "is what hopeless looks like."

Her stomach settled while she sat there. Then a few stray thoughts popped into her head. She felt shame when she thought over the past few days. But at what? And why? The shame wasn't attached to Clay and what they had done. She felt it every time she had seen the coverage on the news feeds of the bombing, as if she had been a part of it. It wasn't guilt she felt. She played no part in the attack. It wasn't humiliation, either. No one knew of her relationship with Clay, except Edward. Edward, that's where the shame came from. What he had done was disgraceful, a level so far removed from anything in her experience that she had difficulty processing it. That much spite—to bomb a factory and put others at risk because of his anger, and she was certain he had been the bomber—was beyond recognition for her. Then she realized, with Edward's resources, Clay never had a chance.

She could have gotten angry then. Under other circumstances it would have risen and turned her into a seething ball of fire. But she lacked the energy.

As she pondered Clay's position the doom thickened over her head, weighed her down and suffocated her. She became aware she was trapped, but Clay was in a truly hopeless situation. He was 250,000 miles from home with no chance of getting back, in an arena and situation built for death, his death.

Her sense of shame shifted then. Clay was off world fighting for his life. The least she could do was keep up her part on earth. It wouldn't do any good to cry over her lot when he had it far worse. How could she count herself among the hopeless when sitting on her marble bathroom floor and staring at her nicely pedicured toes? She got to her knees, picked up the makeup that had fallen to the floor, and then stood and turned on the shower. This wasn't just soldiering on, she told herself, it was about more than that. It was about control and refusing to yield or give up.

Edward's ebullient mood carried him through the gray morning: droll reports from middle managers that never should have found their way to his desk, calls that only offered a few minutes diversion and messages that were deflected to another day. Despite the middling nature of the work he wasn't put off or bored, simply unfocused. After his private chef had left in the early afternoon, stomach filled with farm-raised chicken and creamy mashed potatoes, a private indulgence he favored several times a week, he instructed his assistant, Thomas, that he wasn't to be disturbed until otherwise informed.

"Talk to me, Sammy," said Edward, sitting at his desk. He was speaking on video to Samuel Verita, producer of Fugitive Theatre. Edward had learned long ago to hire good people he trusted and then to stay out of their way. Verita shared Edward's passion for the project and his team had performed well in the past. He was trusted to deliver, both in the industry and by Edward.

"It's a good week, Edward. Some interesting new characters you sent us." Verita was nodding his head up and down as he spoke.

"That's great to hear. How is Mann?"

"Mann, well . . . it's hard to say just yet." Verita craned his neck and stretched out his thought and diction. "Strange little dude. Wasn't what we expected. But that's true of many of these guys when they first arrive. He'll come on."

"Any issues or glitches?"

"Nah, none," said Verita. "Those immersed will get a nice show this week. There were a couple fine episodes caught on video from multiple angles and we extrapolated some fantastic VR experiences."

"Very good. We have to get it right over the next few weeks, Sam. The Lottery has generated some good buzz and the Fugitive Fantasy League is performing above expectations. A couple good shows and she'll jump the charts."

Verita grinned and nodded.

"Any other developments?"

Verita blinked then looked at Edward, eyebrows raised in an "Oh, yeah" expression. "I almost forgot. We've had a . . . development. There appears to be a faction developing."

"A faction?"

"Two guys who are from the same gang, can't remember which, have teamed up and recruited a few other guys. I believe they were from gangs that didn't have a violent history between them. They've taken over one of the housing units. They are offering protection and a little organization. So far they've got about a dozen members. They go out in packs, when they go."

"Do you know who it is?"

"Um, yeah, Escobar, he's the leader."

"Okay, stay on it and get me a report with as much detail as you can. We'll see if it impacts the ratings and how much chatter it generates on the networks." Edward shrugged, "Not much else to do right now. How much CGI was required this week?"

"Much less than we needed previously. As I said before," Verita looked off screen then back, "we got some fantastic footage and didn't have to embellish as much as previous shows. Hey Edward, I've got an issue to deal with before we wrap this up and get ready to air."

"No problem, thanks for the update, Sam."

Edward cut the connection and leaned back in his chair, both hands behind his head, looked to the ceiling and exhaled. This was it, countdown to liftoff. He could feel it. He felt invigorated, energized. Maybe he could use this to turn things around with Sarah. With Alexander out of the way completely, meaning dead, she would start to come around again. Just a mistake, that's all it had been. Put this behind them and move on. Give it a month and the past few weeks would fade away, she would understand her place and all he had done for her. Maybe then they could get started on that heir he desperately wanted.

"We should do this more often."

Sarah, hair pulled back into a ponytail, wearing a long-sleeved, oversized shirt, pulled her feet up under her body and hugged the edge of the couch in an effort to get more comfortable and farther away from Edward, a distance she found impossible these days whenever Edward was in the room. Edward hadn't been kidding about the popcorn, though his choice of wine to go along with it seemed at best odd, if not insulting to the wine, or maybe the popcorn. But that's how things had been since Clay had been arrested and railroaded onto the Lottery and then Fugitive Theatre, anything Edward did was going to seem obnoxious or insulting with a layer of underlying disgust that she would never be able to circumnavigate. She wanted nothing to do with him, but he acted as if there was nothing going on between them, as if he had never hit her, or as if he hadn't set Clay up as a terrorist. So, instead of getting caught up in his make-believe she screwed her face up into a you've-got-to-be-kidding-me look and tried to fend off her growing anxiety over Clay's plight.

The truth was Edward seemed too happy, as if he already knew the outcome, which would have been odd. He never intervened with the talent, only overall goals, vision and direction, never micromanaging or getting involved in the day to day operations. It was one of his rules and he knew his creative limits. His confidence, stemmed either from being informed earlier in the day of the previous few days of gore and violence, or an over saturated sense that Clay couldn't possibly survive in that godforsaken place. She would learn which it was soon enough.

"Popcorn?"

"No, not feeling well."

"Still sick to your stomach? You should go to your doctor." He considered something for a moment, "We could VR this, you know. Sam tells me the some of the footage is fantastic for it."

"No, thanks. I hate that stuff and you know it."

The wall went blank as Edward grabbed a handful of popcorn.

A blood-curdling scream came from the surround-sound system and slowly the wall faded in. From a low angle shot, as if the camera were perched upon an outcropping of rock, a body lay face down on the surface below, left arm and leg in an impossible position.

Not Clay, Sarah pleaded silently, her heart skipping beats and then violently pounding in her chest and head. No, she could see, it wasn't Clay. So, she thought, that's my night, tragedy around every corner.

Two men, off camera, were chuckling as the image faded in. Jose Mann walked into the shot and stood over the dead body. He looked up impassively at the two men then down at the body, nudged it with his right foot, reached down and took something from around the waist of the corpse.

"Hey, get away!" One of the men yelled. The camera panned up to him, standing on the edge of a rock wall, the other sitting next to him, feet dangling over the edge like some innocent school kid.

"Let's get him," said the second, leaping to his feet and scurrying behind his friend who had already turned to run.

But by the time the camera panned back to the dead man Jose Mann was gone, disappeared. Only the awkwardly arranged body and a small splatter of blood remained. The credits were cued and came onscreen with the Fugitive Theatre theme song.

Sarah's level of disgust found new heights—or lows, depending on perspective—her stomach turned and she gripped the arm of the couch to keep from shaking. The show passed from gore and conniving to more gore, statistics now populated the right side of the screen, something she hadn't seen before. At one point a brief sixty-second profile of the Fugitive Fantasy League leader was played, some low life from somewhere like The Edge, who hemmed and hawed over his insights and strategies for picking winners. At the end of the profile the man was presented with credits and a large box of gourmet food, not the real stuff, of course, but a higher quality algae concoction than he was used to eating. "The good stuff!" He blurted, all smiles, pride beaming through his crooked teeth and dazed eyes, as if he had accomplished something of note.

Edward laughed, "Fucking losers, unbelievable. This is a good show, isn't it?"

Sarah had no answer for that, wondering about the minds that could enjoy it, or worse, dream it up, glancing sideways at Edward as she thought about it. Her thoughts traveled the long road of history and the things that would have qualified as the Fugitive Theatre of their day, gladiators in giant stadiums, jousting, two men beating each other senseless and calling it sport. Humanity could justify anything, any action. And entertainment, she decided, was probably the true measure of human development. When we can cheer for one man while he beats another to death then how far removed, collectively, can we pretend to be from anything else in the natural world, how much more enlightened can we claim to be? Or perhaps, she mused, that is what separates us from the rest of nature—that we use violence as an outlet, as entertainment, or, worse, that we need to.

Just as she was finishing that thought Clay came onto the screen. He was right there before her. She wanted to reach out, to grab hold and tell him how sorry she was. She wanted to connect with him. He was shirtless and had turned his pants into shorts. The camera panned back and he was walking along the roof of one of the buildings, stealthy, measured. He paused at the edge, something in his hand. He was waiting for something, or maybe just watching. But then, no, cat-like he crouched and leaped from the roof. Frozen mid-air in the act, rock lifted above his head, poised and ready to be used, right knee bent, eyes focused below as he descended. The camera switched to super slow motion and he was nearly suspended in mid-air and then quickly the camera pulled away and into real-time and Clay crashed violently into two men below him. One of the men was killed instantly, the rock bashing in his head. The other took the full impact of Clay's knee on his shoulder. It happened so quickly he didn't have the chance to scream or yell. He went down in a heap. Clay hit and rolled and quickly got into a crouching position, looked right then left. The second man was on the ground, groaning lowly but not moving. Clay stood up and slowly walked to the dead man, the one who had been hit with the rock, and searched him, taking a couple items and placing them in a makeshift bag Sarah hadn't even noticed before. Then he moved to the second, paused over him, contemplating. Sarah sensed what came next and averted her eyes, still the crunch left her shaken.

Clay looked around again, walked to the first man and dipped his finger into the pool of blood next to his head, then wrote something on his face. He stood, crossed to the other side of the path and climbed a small wall then disappeared into a small wooded area next to a lake. The camera came back to a close up of the dead man's face—LIES was written in blood.

The scene transitioned but stayed with Clay. "Come on, tell me, don't be bashful, you strange bastard." From the side the choker shot showed the sweat on his brow, a scratch on his left cheek that was mostly healed, and the intensity of his focused eyes on the task he was performing. It was riveting to watch him. "At what point," he said, "do we admit you are more human than I am? What form of insanity is this, where people are happy to watch other's lives instead of living their own, other's deaths, and call it entertainment? At what point, my friend, do we admit what we are?—a species of voyeurs and easily distracted foils for those in charge."

The cameras pulled back from the extreme close up to a medium shot, bag and shoes tied together and slung over his shoulder, muscles rippling along his back with each movement, and continued to move out into a low angle long view and eventually to an extreme long shot. Clay Alexander was climbing more than two hundred feet up, alone, toward one of the massive skylights of Great Cavern, his body growing smaller and smaller each second the camera pulled back from the wall, by the end he was just a speck on the landscape, a dark silhouette against the steep and rocky background.

The scene faded, the theme song came over the speakers and the credits rolled. And Sarah, remembering where she was, released the white knuckle grip she had on the arm of the couch, and heard Edward sigh aloud in frustration.

11

LUNACY

The moon holds a nearly impossible station in the human experience, an odd history of folklore, myth, and Godliness all shrouded in mystery and imaginative suppositions. Lovers and poets have called to it in their ecstasy and angst. It has been celebrated in song and art. Ancient Mariners gave thanks for its luminescence and companionship. It is the progenitor of transformations and evil, and an omen for seed-sowers. It pulls invisibly at us, and it is the regulator of earth's tides, a rhythmic pulse that prefers its influences subtle in nature and loud and vociferous in our lore.

It may also be the home of humanity's greatest achievements as a species, or, at the very least, one of them. Several generations ago humans kissed its surface but barely returned for decades, preferring to keep it at a distance rather than reel it in. That changed when the planet expressed itself rather angrily after centuries of human abuse.

A group of powerful and wealthy individuals—the Oligoi—then transformed a piece of the distant rock into a home, a distant sanctuary for the uber-wealthy as a way to escape troubled times on the planet they had angered. The way I saw it, with their lack of care for the home world, with their abuse of power, their avarice and negligence, they were the principle architects of the earth I knew. But perhaps I was too kind to the rest of the population. Maybe blame should have been spread as wide as the oceans currently reached. Maybe we were all to blame.

Regardless, for all its human entanglements the moon was still a distant and lonely place. Lying on my back, one of the two massive sun windows above me, light deflected and angled into Great Cavern, diffused by a form of nanotech not found on earth that was designed to filter out harmful radiation while giving the cavern a daytime glow, I contemplated my situation. I needed a way off that rock, a way back to earth. First, that meant survival, something I was, thankfully, excelling at. Then I had to find a way to navigate through a quarter million miles of vacuum.

I tossed a ball of torn fabric fashioned from t-shirts and pants of men I had killed, collected when I had the time to strip them for anything useful. I was thinking back to several days before, when I had slipped into the water's edge near the wall to my home, swam slowly along the shore, only the top of my head out of the water. At the other end of the lake, several hundred yards away, a plasticrete road ran along one of the housing and entertainment sections. Beneath the road, up against the wall, the water cold but not so much I couldn't handle it for long periods, I listened. Nothing more. It's amazing what you can hear if you just listen, with no intent to speak, or even be seen, just a ghost of the moon. From my location, near the shore and the road, hidden by some bushes that hung over the lake, I heard the two remaining gang bangers from the orientation on Olympus. They had already become creatures of habit, developed carelessness because they were two men working together, a false sense of security in their numbers and trust in the other. This was the third day in a row they had made the same walk at roughly the same time.

"Cain't have been no one else, what I'm sayin'—no one else."

"Hear ya, man. Motherfucker needs ta die, see what I'm sayin', needs ta die ugly. Fo Perez, man. We owe him dat."

They stopped walking. "What you hear?" one of them asked, voice quiet but stressed.

"Cain't say, but we gotta go."

Then they were gone.

I had overheard chatter the day before that they were hunting me. I had been hidden about thirty feet up behind some rocks then. Either they had guessed correctly that I was the one or Mann had told them I had murdered their leader. I doubted Mann had said anything. He never talked from what I could tell. I turned the tables then, out of necessity, and the hunters became prey. My time on the moon was different from most from what I gathered. I chose to go it alone, not forge any alliances or temporary arrangements. I learned quickly through observing others to take advantage of the unique things found in Great Cavern. Gravity was less than on earth, yet no one used that to their advantage. They continued to view things from the perspective they had back home, down the gravity well. On the moon it was possible to leap from greater heights compared to earth and not get injured. Nothing outrageous, but jumping from a second story building was less suspect than most imagined. I was fully aware that injury would lead to my death, but some risks were warranted. One key, I reasoned, was to maintain physical strength in the slightly lower gravity. Each morning, and often in the evening, I worked out with weights. I used rocks of different sizes and pushed myself hard, dead lifts and squats, bicep curls and even pull-ups with rocks in the bag I had fashioned from the clothes of the dead, anything I could think of that I could do alone without risk of serious injury. That was another advantage to living where I did. I didn't have to worry about being ambushed.

Next day I didn't have any trouble disposing of the two gang bangers. They made it easy, really.

Climbing became easier in the reduced gravity, not necessarily any less dangerous, but danger, as I said, was a relative thing. I decided to climb to safety and made my home far up one of the walls of Great Cavern, beneath one of the enormous skylights. From my base I could see anyone coming my way and easily defend myself. My birds-eye view revealed patterns below, patterns in the layout and in the movements of people. To get to the wall required swimming a hundred yards or so in the lake that stretched through a large portion of the cavern. All around one side of Great Cavern was a forest, not typical of anything on earth. The trees were different, smaller, leaves harder and sharp. The underbrush wasn't thick but it was gnarly and spread out everywhere under the trees, rabbits and squirrels scampered around. A few smaller birds, swallows, I believe, flitted and flew through unrestricted airspace, groups of birds moving as one, spiraling and diving, zigging and zagging, high above the lake and floor of the cavern. I couldn't be certain, but I would estimate the cavern was nearly a kilometer tall, tapering at the top to the massive skylights.

Most of the prisoners preferred to stay in the housing units that had been built for the Oligoi when they wanted to retreat to a safe haven from the chaotic times on earth. The Oligoi died from the spillover pandemics just as easily as the rest of us, despite the claims they were different. The apartments weren't large places but there was plenty of room with the small population that currently resided in Great Cavern. Seemed a dicey strategy to me, too many opportunities for someone with an axe to grind to easily locate you, too easy to break through locked doors. Given that food and water weren't an issue, it didn't make sense to remain in harm's way for a soft bed and comfortable living quarters. Those guys died the quickest, choosing to prove they were the real badasses of the place, to themselves and the viewers, and not hide, somehow deluding themselves that their brief encounter with fame would cause them to be remembered. For many, I suspected, that was all they wanted: to go out in a blaze of glory.

I sat on the edge of a rock carapace, a forty foot drop below to the next outcrop of moon rock. The wall wasn't steep immediately from its base to the roof. It had sections that climbed nearly straight up. From here I could see how there were large vertical sections before it eased and tapered off to a flat ridge five yards or so wide, probably for the robots as they created this place, boulders now gathered about the base of the next vertical section, until the wall reached high above and rounded into the ceiling.

I needed to learn the place, all of it, if I were to be successful, if I had a chance to get off that rock. The robots were the best place to start. I didn't care about the comfort of housing or the areas that should have been dedicated to entertainments and dining. I wanted to know how the place worked, how it operated. I had to look behind the screen and the facade at the inner workings. One way to do that was to follow the robots.

I had seen four different types of bots at that point, maintenance bots that were small and agile, landscaping bots that moved slowly with a flat bed and multiple tools it could manipulate for digging and working in the soil. A food bot delivered raw resources to the printers that had been installed for Fugitive Theatre. Then there were the drones. Some were cameras for the show, easily identified and avoided when needed. Others were closer to science drones, testing soil and air and water. It was difficult to tell what their purpose was precisely, but it most likely revolved around maintaining the environment.

"Caw-Caw-Caw," came from the sky to my right. The strange raven landed several feet away, cocked its head in an odd manner, its iridescent feathers shifted colors through the spectrum of visible light. "Caht-Cow."

The bird was speaking to me. I swore it was. I had been observing them since my arrival. It wasn't a normal corvine. Crows were smart, always among the smartest things on earth. But this one was different. The whole group was different. They congregated in a group. They continually talked among themselves. Not talked, really, they argued back and forth, sometimes they laughed, a higher pitched sound with their heads lifted toward the sky. They hunted in packs with amazing precision, but not for food. It appeared they hunted for sport, population control for the rabbits, at any rate, their feathers changing colors and blending in with their surroundings as they landed and surrounded their prey. I watched them for an hour one morning I heard a ruckus down below. I climbed down the side of the wall and stopped and watched a short distance away from the top of a boulder.

The rabbit ran frantically. Each time it approached the circle of ravens they raised their wings and let out a loud screech. When the rabbit got to close they attacked with their beaks. Eventually, the rabbit ran out of energy, gave in, and the vari-hued crows marched toward it like bullies on a playground. When they finished there was a great deal of chatter among the birds before they flew off. They left their prey and only later, I noticed, did a few individuals come by to make a meal of it.

Epigenetics and gene modification was supposed to be illegal on earth, but that was for appearances, I'm certain. Most people were fearful of messing with the human genome. It went against too many religious beliefs—the sanctity of God's design—for the Oligoi to ignore them. Odd as that seemed to me, I understood the fear, science run amok while the earth was in such upheaval was too much. But those same people had no issues with generations of gene modification in animals, breeding dogs to be one flavor or another, corn to output greater yields. But this was the moon, not earth. I'm sure the scientists had found a way to express several dormant genes in the crows to run the Oligoi experiments.

"What gives, bird? Come to hunt me, now?

"Ka-Ka-Ka."

"Uh-huh. Well, I'm heading out when nightfall hits. You are welcome to join me. We're going hunting, if you're interested."

Great Cavern kept the day and night cycle similar to earth. The sky light filters would slowly dim, as would the other lights in the ceiling that ran off the solar grid on the surface, until darkness settled in. I traveled at night because most of those on the moon kept active in the daylight hours. The nights were spooky. That's when my senses reminded me, amped up and adrenaline fueled, I was some place other than home. Nature was more quiet in the evenings and I was more aware of the smell, so different from earth. It lacked earth's richness and underneath there always seemed to be a looming cold, something metallic. During the daylight hours a slight breeze that circled around, not so during the evening.

I swam the distance from the wall to the road, pulled myself out of the water and waited, listening, wary. Once I was certain I was alone I made my way to a passageway where I had seen a couple of the bots disappear. This was risky. Running into someone else here meant things would get physical. But the risk was necessary. Signs warned everyone away, off limits to humans it said. Most of the roads weren't very wide and they were nothing more than rock. In the primary areas around the living quarters and entertainment sections they were plasticrete. This was a narrow road, bike path wide, made of dusty rock. Up ahead, trundling along, was a landscape bot. I hopped on its flat back for a ride. It paused for a moment to recalibrate, then began moving again. I had seen something like these bots on earth, though never worked on one. I wondered if it could be put to another use. I didn't expect them to lock down the code. It might be possible, something to keep in mind, anyway.

After ten minutes the path spiraled downward. It was still warm. It didn't feel as though the temperature had dropped and I guessed it would stay that way. The path straightened out again and a fork was up ahead with a sign: Farm, to the right, and Maintenance to the left. The bot was going to maintenance so I hopped off. I wanted to see the farm first. Before too long I could smell it.

The farm cavern was large, lines of microalgae ran side by side. I didn't know enough about it to say, but they were probably different types of algae for different purposes. It was warmer and much brighter in the farm than in Great Cavern. Sensor bots moved along the ground, constantly testing and probing. At the far end were giant vats that separated the algae from the water. From there it went through a series of processes before finally being sealed in smaller containers and stored. I recognized one of the large printers at the far end. I had worked on one similar to it before. That machine would inject proteins, color and flavors into the raw algae form.

As fascinating as the place was, I reminded myself of the purpose I had to be there; I needed to figure out where the Control Room was. When I was on Olympus I had asked the engineer who spoke at orientation about how the place now ran. He had said it was automated for Fugitive Theatre and that they had covered up the control room. He hadn't said they had disassembled it, only covered it up. That was key. If the control room were still functional I could figure out a way home. It was a hope, anyway, but one I had a great deal of confidence in. I spent hours looking through the farm for false walls and covered sections in the few rooms I found, but to no avail. Then I made my way back to the fork on the path and traveled down to maintenance.

Maintenance was even more fascinating for me. I thought of multiple possibilities, including weapons I could manufacture from tools and parts. But that turned out to be false. Everything had been stripped away, nothing lying around, just a bunch of bots aligned and quiet, possibly charging their batteries in the light. After a couple hours I found a long flathead screw driver, some duct tape and several feet of rolled up netting that was heavyweight enough to support me, all stashed in a corner behind a damaged bot. I took it all. I wanted to stay but the time was stretching long and I didn't want to press my luck.

Then I noticed a key pad on the wall. A small sign over it: Suits REQUIRED Beyond This Point. No Atmosphere. It was an airlock, the rock smooth over its surface, but I didn't know where it led. It could have gone to the underground aquifer they had created, or maybe the fusion engine that powered Fugitive Base. It didn't make sense to me that it housed the control room, and that was my primary target.

It tore at me not to pursue the lead. I was antsy and time was running short, the night slipping toward daybreak in Great Cavern, which meant people moving about. It would have to wait for another night. I grabbed the netting and other supplies, strapped them to my back, the screwdriver in the waist of my pants, and started the long climb up.

Going back was quick and uneventful until I got to the turn-off to the farm. Shuffling toward me was the big Polynesian guy. I stopped walking when I saw him and stood up straight, adrenaline boosting through my system. I liked the guy—but that didn't mean he felt the same for me.

When he saw me he slowed, then I saw the grin in his eyes. I smiled big. "Out exploring, eh?"

He raised a hand slightly. My pulse quickened and my mouth went dry. I didn't want to scrap with this guy and the passageway was too narrow, I thought, given his girth and the athleticism I had seen in him, for me to slide past safely.

I looked behind me. "Pretty interesting stuff down there, especially if you enjoy science. You might find something of use in the maintenance bay."

He nodded his head, that permanent grin still unnerved me.

He turned and I heard a flutter from behind him. The crow landed several yards away.

"Ka-Kah-Tah."

"Crow, what gives? You shouldn't be here."

"Kahack."

The bird ambled forward, almost a swagger in his walk. It made sure to keep its distance from the big guy. "Come here."

My Polynesian friend turned, looked at me and grinned. He stepped back to the far wall, watching the crow as it walked opposite him, looking back and forth between the bird and myself. I took it as a sign that the guy wasn't interested in fighting me and stepped toward the crow and then knelt down, keeping a wary eye on my big friend. I looked down at the bird, only a few feet away, put an elbow on top of my knee. "You shouldn't be here, dude."

Then I stood up, sensing it was my chance to get away without conflict. I looked at the big guy, "Glad you're doing well. Stay safe, and be careful. It will be light soon."

He nodded, the crow squawked, and I walked up the path, my heart racing and jumping out of my throat. I looked back once but the guy was gone.

"I don't know what that was all about," I said to the crow, "but thanks."

The bird fluttered its wings and then took flight up and away.

For some curiosity is a way of life, a chance to open our eyes a little wider, broaden our minds a tad more, and submerse ourselves a bit in the puzzle of the great unknown. It is the breath of life.

To others curiosity is the death knell of humanity, and where the cat gets its comeuppance. Fear, however shallow or unwarranted, guards curiosity's doors and shuffles us along our way. Nothing to see here. Perhaps their lack of curiosity affords them a degree of ignorance or innocence that filters out some of life's harsh realities. My walk back to Great Cavern made me think about what I had just learned. My Polynesian friend may be just that: a friend. One thing was certain, the man was curious and he wasn't afraid to explore his curiosities. If only he would speak, I would learn a lot more then. And the crow, clearly, was more than its natural genetic make up. The Oligoi had messed with this place, from the plants to the animals. Some of that may have been out of necessity to get plants to thrive here. I couldn't say. But I saw no reason for what the crow was.

As I climbed home I thought I heard the crow nearby so we had a conversation, one way because I never heard him respond, but it felt good to talk to someone, something. Curiosity was still on my mind and I thought back to the Merit Analysis and how they used my rant at the priest against me in the media when Burgess had framed me for the bombing of the factory.

"Why do you suppose there is this great divide? Why are some of us curious, understanding that the newfound thing uncovered by our curiosity might change our perception of the world, while others are so frightened by it that they will actively avoid asking the question? Is it better to go through life not knowing something—how things work, how the universe is organized or how the past unfolded—so that we can continue to exist with our current beliefs? Curiosity, and its brother experience, are the assassins of innocence and naïveté. They strip the world of a certain type of magic and wonder. They peel back its layers and expose something closer to the core. The answer seems obvious to me, but that isn't necessarily so. I would estimate there are as many people happy to live in darkness as those who want to see the light. I suppose, my friend, the answer to that question, it could be argued, is more philosophical than right or wrong."

"Does it change anything when one group imposes its view on the other? Can the two perspectives really coexist? Take the Merit Analysis as an example. The propaganda sells the notion the test identifies the best among us. That isn't really true. The Merit Analysis measures conformity, docility. It identifies loyalists, those who go along with the status quo. They don't want seekers. They want followers. But let me ask this: Is it wrong to be curious, to ask questions, or to have differing ideas based upon the facts and evidence? Should that be a crime, or disqualify the individual from a better life? Should it?"

I reached the level where my bed was. I was hungry and grabbed a food bar and sat on a boulder. I still had several days of food stashed. I could sleep in if I felt like it. The sun was coming up, light slowly painting Great Cavern, drawing out the colors and defining the shapes through shadow and light.

I hadn't found what I was looking for, but I had learned a lot. And now I was certain the control room was here, in Great Cavern. It made sense, really. I just had to find where it was hidden.

Lunatic. I grinned as I looked down upon Great Cavern, thinking again of the myths and lore we've framed the moon with. I just had a conversation with a crow that I believed to be smarter than the average bird, capable of understanding me, and that I thought may have purposely intervened in a delicate situation. And I believed now I could survive this place and find my way off. "I wonder," I asked aloud, good humored, "given that I live here on the moon, is it an insult to call me a lunatic, or just a way of describing my situation?"

From up behind me came a response. "Squawk!"

12

NIGHTMARES

No matter where I went, how deep into the water I dove, how high I climbed along the steep walls, or how far I buried myself in denial, he was there, shadow-like, scraping at my heels, lunging desperately at my burning, lactic acid laden legs. I ran across Great Cavern floor, shoulder glancing, sweat dripping and flinging about with my movements, breathless, only to blink or turn my head and find him below me, scaling up the wall, effortless and faceless, under my tired legs. My fingers bled, my lungs exploded and I felt heavy with effort and panic despite the slightly lowered gravity, the singled-out antelope on the Savannah. From above the crows appeared, dropping from the top of the wall, attack formation, a vertical blur of speed and momentum, beak first and inescapable. Or, if that scenario hadn't inspired enough dread, he was a ripple of wave on the water moving with speed in my direction, panic causing me to breathe in water and choke, sinking under the weight of his menace.

The bird squawked loudly.

I turned over, the sound of the bird misplaced, and felt the netting against my skin and bolted upright. Another nightmare. For a place so new, so cold and lacking in history, the moon had its share of ghosts, specters and wraiths that haunted and shattered my sleep, that rattled the cage that was Great Cavern. I was sweating and my heart beat fast, eyes blurry. At least this dream wasn't about Sarah. I found some consolation in that.

I rolled out of the hammock I had fashioned out of the netting I found in the maintenance facility and checked the surroundings. All clear. It was daylight, a day since my visit into the tunnels below to the maintenance area and farm, a brief sojourn to rest and consider my options, though the dream-shattered sleep left me feeling exhausted. Perhaps it was best to keep moving, if nothing else then to hold off the haunted things this place produced in abundance.

Funny that, I snickered, the place was a bloody hell but I preferred the reality to the things that manifested in my dreams. Reality was easier to navigate.

I still had to locate the control room, my second priority after staying alive. I grabbed a food pack and walked to the edge of my home area and sat on the dusty ledge, legs folded under me, and studied Great Cavern below.

I didn't believe the control room was located where the town center was. That left a couple possibilities and both had their merits. The first was to my left. From the end of the lake, where the wall jutted out in a vertical slice of imposing rock, was a thin area of wood and open space. Beyond the wood and open space were more housing units. The only one way to get there was tricky and possibly dangerous. Swim to the shore along that side, past the vertical wall, and walk through the wooded area and then the open space to the small housing section. I could keep to the wall, along the edge of the cavern, but that might be risky, only one way to run from there. The wall in that section was too difficult for me to climb.

I had studied the housing section—printed and similar to the places in The Edge, just nicer and more finished and polished—and made one foray into it before, on my second lunar day when it was still empty. The control room wasn't there. Beyond the housing section was more of the Great Cavern wood. It wasn't large or thick, or even tall, but would provide enough cover if I could get there. It was also a small hill. It wouldn't take long to get to the other side.

If I didn't have any success in that area I would have to travel across the lower part of the cavern to the area where new arrivals entered. Several maintenance buildings were up against the wall and, being so close to the entrance, it might make sense that the control room was there. After those options were exhausted, I would have no choice but to go into the town proper, amongst all the housing and other buildings—and the bulk of the residents on this rock. That was the riskiest area and I wanted to avoid it.

For a long time I watched the housing area closest to my home. I saw little activity until I heard a loud whooping and a few guys moving around quickly. It was too far away to see much detail or hear what they were saying. It looked like trouble, though. But this might be the best time to go. Once the excitement died down their guard was lowered, relaxed in the afterglow of their violence, for those who survived.

But I was worried. "I don't know, bird. What do you think?"

A flutter of wings behind me. I figured he was hanging around. The squawk I had heard during my dream, the one out of place that pulled me from the nightmare, had to be him. Waiting wouldn't get me off that rock and back to earth. I got up and grabbed some of the things I had been gathering and wrapped it all around my shoulders, except the screwdriver. That I slid into the waist of my pants in the small of my back.

Aside from finding the control room, I had to create a few more traps. I wasn't willing to bet that no one would ever see me climbing up here, or try to follow. There were only a few ways to get up this high, and I could probably defend myself with rocks if I needed. But I had other ideas, not just for here, but around the cavern, that I wanted to put into play. Several levels down I built up a series of boulders, precariously placed and easily dislodged, that I could activate and have them tumble on anyone approaching from below. I created a trigger I could activate from above by pulling out some of the material I had gathered. It wouldn't take much to break the hold of the boulder and make them fall downward. The piece of rock they rested on was broken and ready to collapse under the weight. My trigger involved dislodging a rock that was out on a ledge twenty feet directly above. The force of it hitting the others would cause the avalanche. It was possible the trap might come down on me mistakenly when I was climbing up here, but this place was about risk and reward as much as anything else. Some risks had to be acceptable.

Once I had that set up and run the trigger material back up to my home, I climbed down to the lake, slipped into the water and swam to the shore off to my left, where I waited and watched. Since time was no longer something I needed to keep or worry over, other than to use it as a tool, I had become surprisingly patient. The only problem with time was killing it—without the ghosts returning.

I kept thinking of Sarah. What was my being here like for

her? She probably worried and stressed over my situation, but I couldn't imagine her watching the show. That would be too much, I thought. I couldn't put myself in her position or begin to understand the impact it would have watching me. And, too, she was smart; she would figure out what Burgess had done. I had to believe that. I couldn't face things if I thought for a moment she viewed me as a terrorist. One question was always ever present when thinking of her; would she be able to forgive what I had become if I ever made it back? I wasn't able to convince myself she could look a mass murderer in the eye with anything but fear. Nor could I imagine her trusting me enough to turn her back to me. I was at peace with my actions. I was going to survive and that required ruthless commitment. But that also meant others would see me for what I had done and become, which brought another question to mind; if I returned from this hell, would anyone view me as human, ever? I had to lock it all away. It was toxic to my primary goal, intrusive and debilitating.

Nothing was out of place so after a while I decided to move on. But as I climbed from the water I heard an odd noise and froze in my tracks. Eventually, I heard another sound and identified the direction. As quietly as possible I made a long arc around it and then stopped and knelt down. Jose Mann was sitting on a rock, his back to me, lightly tapping a stick on the ground. He was well hidden but too noisy. Of course, I didn't know if anyone else was as stealthy as I was. I imagined others were taking a similar approach, but that was supposition and conjecture. Just because I did it wasn't proof anyone else did. Most, it seemed to me, hung onto their need for social involvement, which was why they grouped together in twos or threes. That had the appearances of a good strategy, but I wasn't convinced. I chalked up my lack of trust to being an orphan. But that lack of trust may have kept me alive. It isn't paranoia if your life is always in danger and your fears are grounded in reality. Then it becomes strategic thinking.

I left Mann—strange lunar dude that he was—to himself and made my way toward the housing complex. Jose Mann was not who they said he was. He couldn't be. It was possible he had changed after his killing spree, sure. But that much? I wondered, was it possible he was here under false pretenses as well?

Things were rambunctious around the housing. Someone had placed a dead body on a landscaping bot. It moved slowly toward the main area of Great Cavern. There was no other way past the housing. I had to decide the way forward. I saw a flat section along the wall that was about fifty feet up. I couldn't see a way to climb any more of the wall beyond that, but I could hide along the ledge and wait until I deemed it safe. I climbed up as quickly as I could and then scampered over some rocks and sat quietly and listened.

My crow friend fluttered and came to a stop on top of one of the nearby rocks, a strange iridescence to his wings. He cocked his head at me, his wings changed to the gray of his surroundings. "Let me ask you something, crow. What makes our lives any different from yours? You are smart and adaptive. You are a social and cooperative group. Some of you are pretty damn chatty. From what I can tell, you like to laugh. Of course, I could have that all wrong. We're just a different form of life. Are our abilities in math and art the only things that separate us?"

The bird fluttered its wings and rocked back and forth, working its claws on the rock as if kneading bread. I checked over the edge to see if anything had changed. It was more quiet now, but I could still hear the men talking.

"I suppose the real question is this; when I get off this rock, will I ever be accepted into society again? Am I the same as a man gone off to war, a license to kill and maim without stigma upon his return? Perhaps. But look at ancient history and how Vietnam impacted many of the guys who served in that war, how people treated many of them, always at arms length, never a part of. Look what that isolation did to many of them. How far is too far here with what we do, and what is life without our social constructs and connections?"

"Caw."

I looked at the bird. Its eyes shifted between gold and green, perhaps the light or possibly some other modification. "Hm, exactly right. It's all bullshit unless I find a way out of this place."

The crow took flight, light and easy, swooping down the side of the wall and then arcing up and over the housing complex. It circled around once then let out another cry before disappearing. I took that as an all clear signal and climbed down and quickly snuck past.

I spent hours searching the area between the housing complex and the far section by the entrance to Great Cavern, but didn't discover anything. I looked for obvious clues; roads or paths that had been covered over, rock sections by the cavern wall that seemed out of place, even footprints that led to nowhere. But the control room wasn't there.

I grabbed a food bar from my makeshift bag and sat on a loose boulder not far from the wall. I wondered then what was being said about my mother. Burgess had said to me, and the newsfeeds echoed it, that she was considered a dissident. He probably played that up as much as possible. I looked across Great Cavern, almost misty in the sunlight, and wondered what she would have thought of my predicament. It wasn't a good thought, her seeing me like this. What my twelve year old self remembered of my mother was that she would kick me in the ass and tell me to get going.

The day was running long and I was worried it would get dark before I could recon the other area. I heard a noise behind me and climbed from the boulder and ducked behind some of the rock and brush. I was several yards from a rock path and a maintenance bot slowly moved down the path. Just as I was about to relax and get up I saw two men running down the path. Something was happening. After they passed by me I heard more loud screaming from the housing area I had passed earlier. I debated between making a beeline to the lake and on to home, or following the noise to learn what was happening. I stood on one of the rocks next to the boulder to get a better view. There wasn't anything happening far off in the city center. I saw the two men more clearly, their backs to me, all elbows and heels as they ran toward their home. I decided to chase after them.

As I ghosted up behind them, I maintained a safe distance and always kept options in mind for a quick escape, if needed. I pulled the screwdriver from my pants in case someone waited along the path. A feint whisper of the paranoia slipped into my thoughts and I slowed and eventually stopped following them. Those two had been following me. They were returning home which meant they had been on my trail. Were they stalking me? Had I been unaware, completely unguarded? Or was it coincidence? Coincidence wasn't something I could afford to believe in. There was too much risk in it.

I jumped off the path into some of the Great Cavern scrub before the wooded area began. Something was warning me to be on the lookout, the hair on my arms raised, my heart-rate quickened. I ducked down and did a quick look around, but didn't see anything improper or unexpected. The place smelled as it always did—less of the tanginess of earth, suppressed with moist rock mixed in—and the background noises that had become white noise over the past few days were no different from before. Staying crouched I moved through the brush, senses alert. The commotion was coming from the housing area I had stopped behind earlier.

A few guarded steps later I came to a stop and stood. That thing from my nightmare had raised its head, crossed the threshold from synaptic fantasy and journeyed into the real. Fear immediately gripped me, though I wasn't certain why. Four men, the two I had followed and two others, laughed and joked about, boisterous and celebratory. Though I wasn't too close to them, I could see clearly what was going on. Hung from the top of one of the housing units, facing the front for all to see, was Jose Mann, naked, split open chest to guts in full technicolor display, his thin and frail body slowly spinning back and forth.

Fear transformed to anger then, a rush of energy too feral and primitive to contain. It swelled and fed upon itself and without my assistance quickly became a consuming rage. I wasn't certain why, but it didn't matter. It was all-consuming. Jose Mann, The Edge Knife, was dead. On earth he might have deserved it. But here it was wrong. He was like a quiet little boy, out of his element, unaware.

The bastards below Mann's swinging body continued to celebrate. My fists were clenched tight and before I took another step I knew what I was going to do. I was going to put an end to their party.

13

BITTERSWEET

Sunsets were brilliant from his office on top of the world. The world painted magnificent masterpieces no artist's brush could ever replicate. Paint on canvas couldn't capture the magic or expose the majesty. The sky was lit up, reds and oranges, yellows and purples, and the last of the day's blues before they faded to black. Up here, towering high above humanity and its mundane slogging against the clock, was the rightful place for the dreamers, the men who raised up the rest and carried them forward. Up here was vibrancy, life fully saturated. Even the angels, he had always thought, would weep at the views.

And he owned it all, not literally, of course. But he was one of the few.

Edward Burgess looked from the horizon, darkened to near black with the clouds above on fire, toward the lights below, yellow, red and white in the sparsely populated areas, neons the closer his eyes wandered toward town. Someone like him, *family*, had dreamed it all up, packaged it and made it real for everyone. That's all the world was, the imaginings of the brilliant and the mad become culture.

Dark roads like black veins spiderwebbed away at the fringes of his sight. Some led to dark places, just as the dreams of a few of his forefathers had, but sometimes the darkness was a good thing because it led to better dreams, born from the ashes and fires that came before them.

The setting sun reminded him he was proud of his place in the scheme of things.

"Sir," Thomas interrupted over the speaker on his PED, "Mr. Verita is here."

Sam Verita, producer of Fugitive Theatre, was all smiles when he entered the office. "Ah," he said, "I never get tired of that view."

"It's almost faded for the day, Sammy. The light's about gone, I'm afraid."

"Still . . ."

The two sat and casually viewed the sights for a few moments.

"The news is good, sir. We're turning the corner I think. Midweek ratings were at an all-time high. Followers are up and advertisers are beginning to call us, instead of us reaching out to them."

"What can you tell me specifically about the growth and changes? I have to meet with the board tomorrow. They want details."

"I understand. A huge percentage of viewers are also participating in the Fugitive Fantasy League, far more than anticipated. It seems they like having someone to root for. The recruits over the last couple weeks are great and making an impact. We've also seen a spike in ratings for The Lottery."

"Very good, Sam. So, Jose Mann has everyone's attention?"

"Oh, no, not Mann. In fact, he's dead."

Edward was shocked. "Mann is *dead!* How did that happen? Jesus, I thought he was going to be the star we needed."

"Not so much, I'm afraid. He was a strange little dude. Kept to himself, or at least tried to. One of Escobar's groups, living in the far housing section, got ahold of him. Gutted him good."

Escobar's group? He might have to do something about him after all. It wasn't good for the show if too many of them teamed up and ruled the place. They'd just be recording a prison day then, no rules, but still just a prison. There was something enticing about an individual fighting for his life, something of the old gladiators in it.

Edward looked out upon the now dark landscape, ran his hands through his hair and sighed. "Is Escobar a problem now? Are we going to have to do something about his group?"

"Oh, I don't think so. Factions are forming, groups other than his are becoming a resistance to their rule. Besides, he lost face in the aftermath."

"Aftermath?"

Sam was perplexed. "You didn't watch the mid-week showing last night?"

"Didn't have time. It's all in the weekend show tomorrow, anyway."

"I see. The men in the far housing section, Escobar's men, they were murdered. Someone was angry that Mann had been killed. Maybe they were angry at the way he was killed. It just happened yesterday, only just made the show for tomorrow. We're still sifting through the details for the weekend airing."

"One of these rival groups took revenge. That's actually good, isn't it. Now we have a war going on. This could get really interesting."

"We have a war, all right. But it wasn't another group. It was one man."

"I don't understand—how many did this one man kill?"

"There were four and now Escobar is pissed and he's put a bounty out on the guy."

"This gets better and better. No wonder the ratings are going up." Edward thought for a moment. "Who was the guy?"

"The guy that took out Escobar's men? He's your star, Edward. The real star. He's smart, different from the rest of them. He's a loner. One of the few guys who hasn't teamed up with someone else. He's made a home way up high in the cavern, climbs up and down the wall all the time, built booby traps everywhere. He's stealthy and, when he needs to be, he's ruthless. Oh, and get this, he talks to the birds. One of them damn crows follows him around everywhere. They're like a team. Viewers love it. He's like a philosopher up there, always asking the bird odd questions. It's one of the experimental birds. The online chatter is that the bird talks back to him. People think it's uncanny the way the bird understands him and always hangs around."

"Wait a minute, you're telling me our hero is a fucking bird-whisperer? Come on, Sammy. I don't care if it is one of the altered birds, what the hell?"

"Watch this weekend. You'll see."

"You think this is driving the ratings, Sam?"

Sam logged onto his PED and pulled up the social networking statistics and showed them to Edward.

"Okay. I need you to send everything to me for the board meeting. What next? Can we use this, play it up?"

"We are, in a big way. The guys are working on new promo ads right now for next week. What we really need is to hope he doesn't die any time soon. This guy can deliver the ratings we need and launch the show."

Edward smiled and nodded his head.

Sam put his PED under his arm and stood up. "I need to get going. I should have been home for dinner. You know how it is. But I wanted to update you."

Edward got up and walked with him to the office door. "I understand, Sam. Say hello to everyone for me. Oh, by the way, who is this guy, our new hero? What's his name?"

"It's that damned terrorist, Clay Alexander." Sam smiled and shrugged his shoulders as he exited. "Have a nice night."

The door to the office clicked shut. Edward leaned his forehead against it. His mind darted from one thought to the next, none of them really registering, scattered visions that taunted and haunted. His breathing escalated and he lost focus. Finally, he pulled away from the door and walked back to the floor to ceiling windows, tried to understand what he had learned and what it meant.

The reports were good for Fugitive Theatre. Ratings were up. The Board would be happy. The Fugitive Fantasy League was taking off and the social networks were buzzing. All good. Except none of it was good. Fucking Clay Alexander was driving ratings, turning himself into a hero. What did that mean for Edward? It couldn't go on, that was certain. Edward couldn't imagine how Alexander had survived as long as he had. It was ten days now. How was that possible? What would the bettor odds have been on this scenario? Fucking Alexander! After long moments of panic, he reasoned he could at least use Alexander, ride him all the way to the top. In the end, Alexander would be dead anyway. No one survived Fugitive Theatre.

The last time he had seen Alexander was after he had been detained and was waiting to go on The Lottery. "Says the dead terrorist." Those had been the last words he had said to him before walking out the door of the interrogation room. Nothing had changed. Alexander was still surely dead. It was a matter of when, not if. Edward could live with that. If it meant the show was going to be successful he could live with his wife's ex-lover stealing some of the limelight before he was gutted and left to die on the moon.

Edward looked down on shimmering lights, the glittering jewels of humanity. Darkness had settled over the land. Those black veins leading to dark places faded into the black. Only the glitter showed now. Each point of light was like a human connection, strung out across the landscape but still touching, interacting, one light bleeding into the next. He could overcome a few minutes of Alexander's fame if it meant his dream took flight. He'd have to.

He closed his eyes. Restless visions played like an old celluloid newsreel across his eyelids. Sarah and Alexander burned his retinas. He tried to exorcise them, dismiss them. But they persisted and left a bad taste in his mouth and a knot in his stomach.

He opened his eyes and looked below. Everything was so tiny down at ground level. Despite his lofty position, despite being so far removed from humanity and looking down on it all, he couldn't escape the nagging feeling the color had been stripped from his dreams, just a grainy black and white shot left over. He looked up and saw his own face in the reflection in the windows. He was anxious, nervous, and swallowed hard. You're an animal, he thought, pacing the cage. Fugitive Theatre, this budding success, was beginning to taste bittersweet, but he wasn't really sure what he could do about it.

He knew the voice before the words registered, before he turned around and made eye contact with Tilda Hogue, whose smile was beaming across the space between them. She rushed toward him, her slim figure gliding effortlessly.

"Okay, I give, you did it." She reached out with her right hand and placed it on the crook of his elbow. "Those changes made a difference. I may not understand it, but I do understand the numbers and the chatter. I just hope they are all as good as I'm hearing."

"Hi Tilda. And they are."

The two entered the conference room. "Thanks for meeting on a weekend. I know it's unusual for us, but it seemed like good timing."

Edward sensed immediately the upbeat mood in the room.

"Brilliant changes, Edward," said Jonathan Sterling.

"This Alexander guy is quite athletic and smart," Tilda put in.

"I think," said Thomas Ulbright, "the fantasy league has everyone's attention."

Edward figured he had been correct in his previous assessment; Ulbright was playing the fantasy league. "Well, I'm glad you are all happy."

"So, now what, Edward," someone asked, "let the show run for a while? It seems the formula is good."

"That it does. Yes, I think we see where it leads from here. Shall we go over some of the numbers?"

It didn't take long to run down the trends and direction things were headed. Breezing through the numbers and building them one on top of the other, and the accompanied expectations, was easy for an old media hound like Edward. The board ate it up and Fugitive Theatre was the only part of the business they were interested in. Unlike the previous meetings, Edward wasn't having to fend off questions regarding the show's viability, nor the doubts regarding his approach. Each member of the board seemed genuinely pleased, almost as if they had some responsibility for the show's gathering momentum. They were more interested in their imagined plot twists for the evening's airing than the numbers. Much to his own distaste, the conversation twisted, vectored and finally settled on Alexander and his bird friends. Edward was squirming, uncomfortable with his fate hingeing on the success of Alexander. Several of the board genuinely seemed to be rooting for the man.

"There is one issue I have to consider," said Edward, needing to change the subject. Everyone quieted down and looked in his direction, alert. "There is a faction developing with Escobar. We can't have him gain too much control. If he seizes power then we'll have nothing more than another prison reality show, just with no rules. We don't want that. As of now, other factions are organizing against him, but it is something to watch."

"What if," asked Sterling, "he does gain power and persuades most of them to work under him?"

Edward shrugged. "We'll deal with it. We do need to monitor it though."

"I don't think it's an issue," bleated Ulbright, "this Alexander guy will take care of that!"

Several of the members laughed. "Right! Just like when they got to Mann."

Nods all around, eyes sparkling and eager. It was too much for Edward. He just wanted to get out of the room, go somewhere, have a drink and consider things. And that's precisely what he decided to do. The meeting ended and the board members left the room together.

"Wonderful job, Edward," "Great stuff, really," more smiles and hand shaking as each passed by. When he was finally alone in the room he collapsed into a chair. The bar down the street felt like a better option than drinking alone in his office. Lunch at the bar might be just what he needed. Take the edge off, dull the senses and wait for a glimmer of hope to appear inside a chemically altered fog. And maybe, just maybe, get rid of the feeling that he was still pacing the cage.

Sarah sat herself before the wall screen. It wasn't like Edward to miss the show. He hadn't been home all day and he hadn't sent her a message. He'd been so insistent she be there to watch. Mostly, she understood, so he could gloat. But she wasn't going to complain about his absence. Her hands were sweating She felt hot overall. She was nervous, almost too scared to watch. On some level she needed it. Despite the anguish and despair she felt, she couldn't turn away from it. She hoped Clay sensed her support. Then, like anvil, it hit her again; he could already be dead. Her mouth was dry and she wanted to throw up once more but, breathing deeply and holding it a beat, forced herself to calm down.

The show opened with Jose Mann's dead body hanging from the top of one of the housing units. Tight shots of the celebrating men faded in and out and then a montage of them appeared onscreen. Then the camera focused on just one of the men as Clay moved into the picture, quickly killing him then the next, surprise attacks. The image of another of the men from the montage showed on the screen and there was Clay, fighting like a man possessed, blood arced and splattered on a camera lens, a blood curdling scream. The fourth attacked Clay as the third man in the group was dropping dead to the floor. He caught Clay in the side with a chipped-rock knife, stopping Sarah's heart with fear, but Clay spun around quickly and buried a screwdriver in his chest, driving the man to the floor. The fear leapt from Sarah and turned to hope and then elation.

Clay ripped the screwdriver from the dead man's chest and stood up and looked around the room, intense and fiery eyes that told of the savageness of the place. Sarah couldn't watch any more. "Record," she said and got up to leave the room.

She was shaking all over. Her body wouldn't stop. She thought of what she had seen Clay do, the way he had killed those men, and then she realized he would likely die in the same manner. It overwhelmed her and she jumped into the bathroom off the hallway she was walking down and threw up in the toilet. She sat with her back against the sink cabinet and cried. "I'm sorry," she muttered. "I'm so sorry."

Eventually, she stopped shaking and found herself lying on the bathroom floor wondering what uncaring monster could have dreamed up Fugitive Theatre. How could she have been so wrong about Edward? How could she have married him?

She wanted it to end, all of it. Then she wailed out loud, "No!" It could only end if Clay were dead. She didn't want that. But what must he be going through, just to survive? She couldn't fathom an answer.

Then she understood, spiraling down and down in her thoughts, free falling through time without sight or a sense of ending, things could only end one way. There was only one outcome. Clay was safe, at least as far as she had been able to watch. His victory tonight, and every other night he managed to remain alive, was bittersweet. He was still stuck on the moon, a prisoner on death row. A dead man without hope.

14

A MAN SAID TO THE UNIVERSE

Whatever the process is that ushers the demented and possessed mind from its crazed state back to normality—if that really is such a thing—it left me standing just outside the housing complex at the far end of Great Cavern in awe at what I had done.

I remembered the stealth, my heart racing, time compressing. The violence flashed through my head. My screwdriver plunged to the hilt into one man's back. On another I drove it into his neck and then yanked it sideways. The final guy I met face to face.

"You're a dead man," he said. "Escobar's gonna to send everyone after you, if I don't kill you first."

Killing him felt premeditated in the aftermath. I ran at him, raising the screwdriver at the last moment, a feint, a distraction. His hands went up, panicked at the sight of the weapon. But my right foot buckled his knee, bent it backward from the force of my blow and momentum, downward and through. I heard the pop as I crashed into him. He screamed loudly and couldn't recover from the pain quickly enough as I scurried to my knees and launched myself at the body writhing on the floor and buried the screwdriver in him.

I stayed there for a few moments, considering, listening, still wanting more. In the quiet the world resolved again to its normal and placid self and my mind reorganized and congealed into its normal state. Then I got up and grabbed the dead body by the hair and pulled him outside to where I still stood.

It was all there in my head, and it wasn't. The previous few minutes were a blur one moment, crystal clear flashes of violence the next, something primal. I tried to ease my thoughts and took inventory of my body. My hands were blood covered. My side ached—when had I been hit?—and I was sweating. The adrenaline that fueled my rage was quickly siphoned out of my system and I wanted to find someplace to decompress and rest. I looked around the surrounding area for signs of danger, but saw none. I was the only killer in sight—the only one alive, anyway. Four bodies lay at my feet. I tried to view them as human, as living things and individuals, but I couldn't. They were just meat.

A landscaping bot was working nearby. I picked up one of the bodies and carried it to the bot and dropped it into the bed in the bot's back. The landscaping bots had pickup truck-like beds to cart plants and bushes and rocks around. I dropped all four of the dead in the bot. The physical work helped lessen the impact of the adrenaline come-down.

I looked up to Mann's body, still twisting at the end of the makeshift rope. It didn't feel right to leave him there. I still couldn't view Mann as the monster he had been portrayed as. He was more like a little boy from what I saw of him, always quiet and observing. I found it difficult to believe he was The Edge Knife.

Something moved down the path that led toward the center of Great Cavern. I recognized the shape and the slow lumbering movement. The Polynesian approached. He stopped several yards away and looked up to Mann's body, then he looked at the bodies in the back of the bot. I couldn't tell if he was smiling or if that was the permanent look on his face. Eventually, he shrugged and walked passed me into the housing unit. A few seconds later he was leaning out the window lowering Mann's body to the ground. I walked over and helped.

Mann was a mess. He'd been skewered from his abdomen up to his chest and then someone had cut his neck. He was even smaller and more frail with the blood drained from him, which made me view him even more as a boy. I pulled the rope—torn fabric tied together from clothes of the dead—from around his neck and carried him to the landscaping bot and laid him on top of the others. I stood looking at the bodies. I doubt I would have been able to look at them just a few weeks ago. It was a gruesome sight and it angered me to have played a part in what had happened. But I stood firm in my desire to survive and do what was necessary.

The big guy came and stood next to me, still not speaking, his pudgy hands resting on top of the bot. My crow friend landed on the top of the bot and inspected the scene as well as the two of us. The bot was assessing the additional weight it found on its back and determining its next course of action. A few sensors came out from its body. It made several clicking sounds internally and a couple beeps. It was communicating with a central control for directions, I thought.

I looked at the big guy. I was surprisingly calm given how closely we stood to one another.

"I'm getting off this fucking rock. And when I do, I'm going to hold the stupid son of a bitch responsible for all of this accountable." I could see him smile then. "Thanks for the help," I said and then turned and walked away.

I didn't want to be near anyone. I'd had enough of humanity for the moment. As I walked through the wooded area toward the lake, I questioned why I wanted to return to earth. Beyond Sarah—and revenge against Burgess—there didn't seem to be much point to it.

The crow alighted on a branch ahead of me.

"Let me ask you something, crow. Am I crazy to want to return to earth? Is that mess any better than what's here? You wouldn't know, of course. You've never been. But I have. Society there isn't so much removed from here as I might have imagined. What we've created on earth is just as ruthless, only less direct than here. That might make this place more honest, I suppose."

The bird fluttered and hopped branches.

"People starve to death on earth, adults and children, while others can't possibly spend what they have in multiple lifetimes. And the church, God's supposed emissary, could end all starvation with nothing more than their profits from a single year—my brother's keeper, indeed. But no one thinks this way. No one holds them accountable or questions their motives. Why is that?"

"Caw, tok-tok."

"Hmm. Look what we've done to our planet. The oceans that rose up and destroyed the world we had created did so because of us. We caused it. Now, after the fall, we have to deal with more disease and resource shortages than ever before. We live on algae based foodstuffs and in cheaply printed homes. But the same group who ran the world before are still running it. They've not been deposed.

No one took their money and homes and cars or businesses. We've simply continued on as before. *Thank you, sir. More of the same, please.* It doesn't make sense to me. I can't wrap my head around that. When you are directly responsible for burning down the world shouldn't there be repercussions? Instead, they've joined forces—the uber-rich Oligoi and the church. They have convinced people they are the ones to lead humanity. They'll get it right this time, I'm sure. Ha! Despite their track record—both of them—for the previous two thousand years we somehow believe them to be our best options. Laughable really, to pin the species' future on the ones who destroyed it."

The bird flew on ahead. Just as I got to the lake he was there on a rock, waiting.

"You know, I think it's more base than what I previously thought. I believe we are more averse to change than we are to walking down a road we know to be doomed. We lead such short lives and even the near future isn't something we get to see for ourselves. Most of us aren't good at putting ourselves in other's situations. So, when we view life a hundred or two hundred years from the present, we can't really fathom it, or the impact we are having on their lives. We say things like 'We made our own way. We figured it out. They can do the same.' But that doesn't really work. The world isn't as big as it once was."

I stopped by the edge of the lake. Blood was caked and dried on my hands and arms and the lower half of my body. I wasn't feeling remorseful for my actions, just a general sadness. I spent a few minutes in the lake cleaning myself then finally swam to the wall.

As I climbed the wall several poignant questions came to mind. I couldn't see the crow, but I knew he was there and decided to continue conversing with him. It kept my mind from pondering what I had done.

"Let me ask you, my multi-phasic feathered friend, what is morality? Ethics? Thinking back to what I said before, is it morally wrong that the church could end hunger and strife but chooses not to? They could purchase the resources and equipment, hire the experts and train the locals to be self-sustaining without putting even a small dent in their resources. The same is true of the Oligoi. I'm certain the Oligoi would point to The Edge and other places like it, and to the Guaranteed Living Wage, and say: But we do! But keeping others in squaller—hugging the poverty line—while you amass wealth you couldn't spend in a thousand lifetimes isn't right. Isn't that sort of wealth a social contract?"

I was suffering on the climb to my home. My side was hurting and it was getting stiffer as time passed. I stopped to catch my breath and rest for a moment. I looked down at Great Cavern. I was maybe a third of the way up the wall. There wasn't any commotion yet. The dead bodies were slowly transported by the landscaping bot. All the bots passed through the middle of the town to get into the tunnel and areas below that I had explored before. Someone would see them. All hell might break loose then.

I decided to climb some more. When I looked back I noticed the bird, just a few feet from me resting on an edge. His feathers had shifted and he looked like the surrounding rock, save for its color-shifting eyes.

"You know what I believe crow," I said as I reached for a handhold higher up and began climbing, "I believe the Oligoi are like this old poem I read when I was younger. Actually, this place, Fugitive Base, is like the poem. Stephen Crane was the author. He wrote an old book I liked. I remember the poem because I spent a lot of time in the library and it was short enough I could remember it and its meaning was straight-forward so I thought I understood it."

"'A man said to the universe:
'Sir, I exist!'
'However,' replied the universe,
'The fact has not created in me
A sense of obligation.'"

I stopped climbing and thought about it for a moment. The rock was inches from my face and smelled of chalk and dust. Something about the moon and my situation nudged my thinking along a vector slightly different from the poem.

"That's it. The universe doesn't care about human morality or ethics. Right or wrong doesn't exist in the greater scheme. What was it I had said to Sarah: 'It's a deterministic universe. Meaning doesn't exist. Cause and effect. We're always trying to create a greater purpose for humanity, to conjure something up, or act like God has a plan for us. But what if all that is just fiction?' It's only within society that morality and ethics are defined. They are ever-changing illusions, mirages. It was once legal for humans to own other humans. Can you believe that, crow? We kept other humans as pets, bought and sold them, treated them as a lower form of life. It wasn't immoral then. Neither was it immoral to commit genocide against an entire group of people, like the native Americans. All humans have to do is convince themselves that someone different is less than human—a different skin color or religion, for instance, or those who pass the Merit Analysis and those who don't. We define what is moral based upon those differences, and often upon which side of the dividing line we fall. But the universe doesn't care about any of that, does it? It's all about cause and effect. Morality plays no part. That's the base root of being human, too. Cause and effect. Survival.

Everything else is window dressing. Despite the lofty illusions we choose to live by, we are still of the universe."

The crow disagreed with me, I think, squawked loudly and flew off.

It took a while for me to complete the climb and reach my home. When I finished I grabbed some water and a food bar and sat with my legs dangling over the edge of rock. It was still quiet below but that wasn't likely to remain, not with what I had done.

The day was coming to an end on Fugitive Base, the massive skylights above were dialing down the light. There weren't any sunsets, no colors other than red, blood-red, and gray. Gray, the color of the rock beneath the lunar surface, forced its way through the living things so that they slowly turned invisible. I needed rest after the earlier events, but it might not come, too many ghosts circulating in my mind, too many haunting things. How could I go so far into my rage that I was lost to it, completely immersed? It was scary on one level. But as I sat there, gazing across Great Cavern, I sensed a truth even more scary. I hadn't really been out of control. I was aware. I knew what I was doing. I just allowed it to happen. I let it march forward, an avalanche of emotion and mounting frustrations. I chose to step aside and go along for the ride. I could have pulled back, withdrawn and walked away. But I didn't want to.

That might have been the scariest thing regarding the day. Like a dark angel, I was the harbinger of death and I had welcomed it. Somewhere I felt my soul weeping, crying out for what it had once been and what it was becoming. But all that, I tried to convince myself, was the social animal in me, the one attached to society and other humans. The thing that would get me killed if I allowed it to surface.

Total darkness arrived while I sat, except for the lights across the cavern, soft and yellow. It felt cold physically and in some ethereal way, as if it was all eggshell-tenuous and could break at any moment. I needed rest. The adrenaline come-down left me exhausted. I had to find the control room. It was still my priority. That was an unsettling thought. I had to search the area by the entrance and then, if that failed, I would have to search the main city area.

Morning would come too quickly and I wanted to be as rested as possible. I climbed into the hammock, wincing slightly at the pain in my side, just as someone let out a blood-curdling scream that traveled across Great Cavern. Even at this distance and height I knew what it signaled. The bodies had been discovered in the back of the landscaping bot. But my mind was concerned with other things. An old record was spinning round in my head, the needle stuck in the groove, repeating the same phrase over and over: A man said to the universe . . . .

15

POET OF THE MOON

Sarah couldn't sleep. She rose from bed, still nauseous, and walked downstairs. She expected Edward to be asleep on the couch or in one of the guest bedrooms, but he was nowhere to be found. Edward hadn't come home. Just as well, she thought. She wasn't certain she could deal with him at the moment.

It was two in the morning and she was tired but not sleepy. She sat down on the couch in the theater room and pulled her legs up under her. "Resume program."

The wall lit up and Fugitive Theatre started playing again. Clay piled the dead men on the bot and spoke to the Polynesian man who had developed a good following online. He was a favorite in the Fugitive Fantasy League. The cameras followed Clay as he went toward his home, recording his conversation with the crow that always seemed to be hanging around. She listened intently to his words and smiled when he recited the poem by Stephen Crane. She knew the way he thought. It was consistent with their conversations. She saw that as a good sign. He wasn't losing it. He wasn't falling into a dark place. He was coping well, she thought, at least as well as he could.

As she watched him climbing the wall and listened to him speaking to the crow she looked at the moon base, almost as if seeing it for the first time. She realized, as the cameras panned away from Clay and across Great Cavern, that the base was nicer than most places on earth, and certainly better than The Edge where she had grown up. Then she remembered who had constructed the base: the Oligoi. The camera showed a far off shot of the city center. Shops that looked like they were boarded up lined the main thoroughfare, residences rose up the wall on that side of the cavern. The forest wasn't tall or lush, but it added warmth to the surroundings. There was a chapel at the end of the main street, at the other end from where the service and maintenance bots went to recharge or get repaired. The church looked out of place, as if added on at the last minute.

It occurred to her that Clay's conversations with the crow were blasphemous. He was condemning the church and the Oligoi—the family, as Edward would say. That probably wouldn't go over well with the people Edward associated with, like his board of directors. There would be fallout from that. Maybe Clay's words and actions would doom the show. That felt like too much hope, though.

She retrieved her PED and sat in front of the wall screen again. She found herself logging onto the social networks instead of watching the show. Clay was no longer the point of interest of the show after his climb and conversation and she wasn't interested in the other men. Currently, they were replaying the murder of Jose

Mann, which looked sad and pathetic to her, with a narrator speaking over the scene. Fugitive Theatre became background noise to her online perusing.

The social networks were active. People were posting comments every few seconds or quicker. He was no longer Clay Alexander. He was given a new name by the masses and was now known as the Poet Of The Moon. Clay had become a hero to them. They were posting his words, his conversations with the crow. More importantly, they were waking up, asking questions she had never heard asked before, at least not publicly. They were Clay's questions—with an added layer of vitriol. Clay had emboldened them and become the impetus for their newfound anger and protests.

"What have you done?" She whispered, smiling the whole time. "What crazy thing have you done?" She almost giggled as she asked the question.

She cycled back to the beginning—from when the show had aired live—to get a feel for how the protests and anger had grown and proliferated. At first commenters simply parroted Clay's words. Then, as more and more of them came online, the anger built and the commenters became more brazen and emboldened. There was a clear arc to the whole conversation. The funny thing was, it wasn't slowing down. Though it was well after two in the morning, people were still posting comments at an alarming rate.

She found an interesting thread that had started several hours earlier. Someone wanted to organize a protest. That thread had thousands of comments. Somewhere down in the comments they began calling themselves The Murder Of Crows. Too bad, Sarah thought. The smart bird had always been given a collective bum wrap of a name, belying their smarts and generous demeanor. But showing up on battlefields and along the roadside to feed on the dead had its appearances and consequences.

The amount of information and chatter online went on and on, overwhelming in its breadth and depth. After a while it felt like more of the same—though still intoxicating and she found it difficult to pull away. But a glance at the clock told her she had spent an hour scouring the feeds.

"I wonder—" she said aloud. "Switch to newsfeeds, please."

There he was again, a blood-soaked Clay, fire in his eyes, muscles gleaming with sweat from his efforts. Beneath the photo it said: "Poet Of The Moon, terrorist turned agitator." The newsfeeds were recounting Clay's supposed bombing of one of Edward's factories, something she felt certain hadn't been his doing. They showed clips of the burning building. They rehashed the information regarding Clay's mother and her dissident past, the interview with Meyers, the factory manager. There was nothing verifiable, Sarah noticed, just supposition. They talked about his detachment to society, his aloofness. He was portrayed as the outsider gone bad. He was the man who hated their society because he didn't fit into it. Several pundits tried to lay the blame on Clay's inability to pass The Merit Analysis. "Cases like this are truly sad," said one of them, "they really are. But we shouldn't feel sympathy for this man. He is a terrorist, after all." His greasy smile turned Sarah's stomach.

Sarah thought they were putting an inordinate amount of energy into discrediting Clay. They knew—already they knew—he was making an impact. They were afraid and wanted to head off any protests. They wanted to get in front of it and clamp it down before it turned into something bigger.

She left the program playing in the background and refreshed the screen on her PED, scrolling back to the top of the page for the newest comments. People weren't buying what the newsfeeds were saying. They were mocking the news sites and the corporate entities that controlled them. More of the same, they were saying.

"The Murder Of Crows protest," said one of the news casters, catching Sarah's attention again, "will be dealt with harshly, this according to the authorities. Regardless of the location, officials will not stand by while these groups form and riot in our streets."

"Samantha," said the pundit with the greasy smile, "maybe the administration should look at this as an opportunity, maybe we all should. After all, we know those attending are going to be the anti-social deviants among us."

"What are you suggesting?"

"That the authorities are correct. The administration should deal quickly and harshly with these people, as harshly as possible."

Sarah was getting nauseous again and couldn't stand to listen to any more. She was tired and wanted to sleep. She voiced off the wall screen and grabbed a blanket off the back of the sofa, covered herself and curled up. There was a warrior on the moon, a killer, a supposed terrorist, a man condemned and now a poet—and she loved him. She shivered, not at the things he had done, or might do, but at the bleakness of the situation. She tried over and over to imagine a way out, a way for Clay to get home. But she couldn't envision something so fantastical. She tossed and turned for a while longer before she finally fell to sleep.

16

TO DEAD POETS

Edward Burgess felt a rising sense of panic. His insides grumbled and his head ached, the repercussions from drinking himself into a stupor sometime earlier. He had found himself at lunch at the bar just down the street from his office and drinking more than usual, far more. Desperation was circling round and round and he found it difficult to focus, or even identify why it was there. Its undertow had pulled him deeper into the bottle and more into his fears as the lunch hour turned into hours, the sun slowly faded in the windows and turned the road outside a gray mist before the lights engaged and the night awoke. Somehow, he woke the next day in one of the rooms of the adjacent hotel, parched, dry mouthed and hungover, unable to remember the previous evening.

Before getting out of bed he turned on one of the newsfeeds. His fears were confirmed, though he hadn't pinned down what those fears were while he had been drunk. But there it was before him, all in hi-def color and perfect surround sound. Clay Alexander was a rock star: The fucking Poet Of the Moon.

Edward listened carefully to what the broadcasters were saying. The biggest concerns were that Alexander was the spark that would ignite a protest. He was the ghost in the machine, moving behind the scenes and stirring up demons, demons society didn't need.

Edward knew his success with Fugitive Theatre wasn't going to last, not unless they could find another hero. The problem was, people actually liked Alexander. He could tell, lying in bed and watching the interviews of people on the streets, how much they connected with the man. Regardless of the show's success, the board were in a tight position, impossible really. They were supporting a revolution if they continued and they would prove the mob right if they squashed Alexander quickly or didn't allow him airtime at all. Besides, the crazies who watched the live feeds twenty-four hours a day would speak up, and loudly. They would pick up video of him.

Edward considered his options. Escobar, whose gang on the moon was beginning to exert some control, had a younger brother in prison serving a life sentence, if he recalled correctly. He could use that. He'd need to meet with Sam Verita, as well. They needed to cut back on the time they were giving to Alexander. Sam wouldn't like it, but there wasn't another choice. And the board was going to have to show some more patience. With a little luck, they could climb out of this with the show intact and viewership still sky high.

He rolled out of bed and fished in his pants pockets for his PED and found it. As he expected, he was in high demand. He had thirty-two new messages. None of them, he frowned, were from Sarah. He sent a message to Thomas: *Find out which prison Fernando Escobar's brother is in and set an appointment for me for late this afternoon. Also, get me all the info you can on Fernando and the entire family.* Then he messaged Verita to meet him in the evening. Finally, he read through the messages from the board and set a meeting for the following morning. After his shower he needed to meet with one of the corporate attorneys.

He was still a mess, both his head and body ached, but at least he was moving again, physically and mentally. The gears were turning and he was working through the problem. That's all Alexander was—a problem to be solved. The shower would help perk him up and some medication would get rid of the hangover. Then he'd be ready to go.

Redemption Prison Systems location 247-C was twenty miles north of the city. Sebastien Escobar was brought into one of the meeting rooms in hand- and ankle-cuffs and sat down on the chair across from Edward.

Burgess smiled. The little brother was smaller and more wiry than his older brother, Fernando. Edward sensed a lot of attitude, a chip on his shoulder.

"Know who I am?"

"Don't know and don't care, suit."

"Maybe not now, but you will." Edward smiled and leaned toward the man, elbows resting on the table between them. "Little sis shows some promise, don't you think?"

Sebastien Escobar's expression and posture didn't change. Edward probed a bit more.

"Mom and dad are getting old but I hear their health is pretty good. I'm surprised, really, that so many of your family are still alive, given the way you and Fernando turned out. You two must be an aberration, not the norm."

"What do you want?"

"To offer you a deal, Sebastien. I want to help your family, give your little sis a chance. Let mom and dad live a little better in their old age."

Burgess sat back in his chair and gave him a magnanimous smile, turned his palms up and shrugged.

"What sorta deal?"

"The kind they'd never get otherwise. The kind that means they might actually remember you fondly, despite the fact that you're murdering scumbag. That kind of deal."

"And what do I have to do for this prize?"

"That's the easy part. I just want you to deliver a message to your brother on the moon."

Escobar's eyes widened. Edward saw fear in them at first. But gradually that fear morphed into an acknowledgement that what was on offer was a way out of prison, something his sentence precluded.

"You lot watch Fugitive Theatre in here?"

Escobar nodded.

"Good! My name is Edward Burgess. I own that show. Do what I ask and you and your brother will be heroes. On top of that, I'll make your sister Cleric and find a good school for her. She seems fairly bright and a whole lot different from her brothers. She can take good ol' mom and dad along with her, out of that grime and into a better and cleaner world."

Edward could see Sebastien Escobar chewing over the deal. He thought he sensed a small amount of desperation.

"Anything else?" Escobar asked.

"You mean money? Sure, I'll throw in some retirement money

for mom and dad."

Escobar was confused. "You can make this happen? Just like that?"

"Just like that, Sebastien." Edward had to pull some strings to get everything in place, and he understood that if he moved quickly Escobar would only get one day to acclimate and train on the near earth orbital. But he didn't really care. He wanted the man to deliver a message. That was all. One that would have meaning and could be explained in a manner that would make a difference. He needed Fernando Escobar and his gang of thugs motivated and he was certain his brother could do that.

Escobar stared into Edward's eyes. "What guarantee do I have you'll follow through with this?"

Edward reached to the side of his chair and pulled several documents from the briefcase sitting on the floor. He placed the documents before Escobar and put a pen down on top of them.

"What do we need to do, my brother and I?"

"That's easy," said Edward. "I need you to murder the Poet Of The Moon."

The fear was back in Sebastien Escobar's eyes. Edward regarded him for a moment, then said, "Your brother has a group he's assembled. You know that. You've watched the show. They've taken over one of the housing structures. He has men working for him. You don't have to kill Alexander personally. It doesn't have to be you or your brother specifically, but I want you there when it happens. That's how you become stars. Gangsters order killings. They don't have to execute them."

"That's it? Kill some guy because he's talkin' too much and causing you problems? Sounds a lot like the reason I'm in here." He sighed and looked away for a moment. "This sucks, man. You put a few legal documents in front of me and that makes it okay, legal and all. You know, that Poet ain't half wrong."

Edward shrugged. "What can I say? It's the system. The deal is good. Take it. Take it for your sister and your parents."

Sebastien Escobar smiled. His gold tooth blinked and offered Edward a glimmer of hope. He sat up straight and leaned over the table.

"Where do I sign?"

"Sammy, I'm catching some heat, you brilliant bastard."

"Sorry, Edward, I never thought that would be the response to our guy."

Edward let the door to his office close behind him and put a hand on Sam Verita's shoulder. "Not to worry, my friend. I think I've got it under control, but we're going to have a storm to weather."

Verita was obviously relieved Burgess wasn't angry with him. Edward gestured toward a chair. "Sit, I'll get us a drink."

"I suppose you've seen today's report?"

"Haven't had the time," answered Edward. "Bring me up to speed, Sammy."

"That's easy," beamed Sam. "We're number one across the board. There isn't one metric we don't own."

"That good?"

"Viewership is at an all-time high by a multiple of three. Our target demographic is off the charts. The re-run of the weekend show just aired and it was number one by a landslide."

Sam took a drink as Edward sat in a chair across from him.

"I'm guessing," Sam said, "the news isn't all good, despite the numbers."

"Correct. The board is squeamish. Advertisers are buying at ridiculous rates, but some of them are leery, you know how it is. Public backlash has them nervous, but that should subside, especially with what I have planned."

Burgess leaned back in his chair and looked out the floor to ceiling windows. "This is a crazy business, Sam. The board wanted to cancel the show just a few weeks ago, poor ratings. Now, I'm sure one or two of them will want to cancel it tomorrow because it's too popular. They said there was no way the show would thrive because there wasn't a star. We gave them a star, even if it wasn't the one I expected, now he's going to be too big for them."

"That could drive a man to drink." Sam held up his glass.

"Indeed."

"Edward, what do we do with the new promos we made? There are three of them and they all feature Alexander. They are running now. Do I bring some of the old ones back and re-cut something new?"

"Gonna have to, Sam. Sorry."

The two men were quiet for a while. It wasn't an uncomfortable silence. They had known each other long enough to allow the quiet to speak for them without interrupting. Before long, Edward said, "The Poet has to die, Sam. There's no way around it. But for now, you need to cut back on covering him, not so much that we piss everyone off, just enough to lower their interest. And let me reiterate, everything I told you before is still in place: he can't use any names on air. You have edit that out."

Sam Verita wasn't fazed. He'd seen enough in his time to know what was coming. He understood the order of things and knew he couldn't test them. Arguing for Alexander was a losing proposition on several levels. He raised his glass, "To the dead poets. It's too, bad, you know. It would have been nice to have a good run with it."

Edward's inner conflict swelled. Had it been anyone but Alexander he might have fought to keep him alive. But Alexander had crushed his Fugitive Theatre dreams by just surviving, then through thriving, and now by instilling hope in the masses. He had to go.

"I know, Sam." Edward raised his glass, "To the dead poets."

Reading people was a large part of Edward's job and he had trained himself to excel at the skill. Before he entered the conference room and met with the board of directors, he closed his eyes and viewed each in turn, assessing their reactions to the current situation. There were only two he would need to worry over—Tilda Hogue and Jonathan Sterling. They were the most conservative and cautious. They also had connections that ran deep and wide through the family. He was certain they were taking calls from people who were expressed their concerns and reservations.

Sterling was a pint-sized little prick whom Edward would have no issues bullying, if it came to that. He was always and only about perception and how things appeared, surface glitter or mud, depending. But Sterling was malleable and easily influenced. He would yield to the numbers if Edward chose to go in that direction. Sterling wasn't an issue.

Tilda Hogue—the alarmist in her, anyway—wouldn't back down or be intimidated. If her convictions were strong she would stand her ground. But Edward wasn't certain where she would stand on the social unrest the show was causing. Tilda liked profits above all else. She might be swayed by the reports he had reviewed earlier in the morning. They all might be, for that matter. But if she couldn't have her mind changed by the numbers she might yield to logic and reason, something Edward felt he had on his side.

Edward ran both hands over his face and pushed back his hair. He was tired, exhausted really, and needed a break. He stood, looked at his PED, and turned to go into the meeting. Still no message from Sarah. Exasperation piggybacked on top of his exhaustion. But that had to be put aside for a while, he thought, as he opened the conference room door. The board were all present and waited for him with bated breath, agendas and opinions desperate to make themselves known.

"Edward," said Sterling immediately, "I think you know the pressure and concerns we all have right now." Sterling was working a stylus nervously with his hands, a habit that was irritating at best. Edward tried to remain calm and ignore the old, boney and effeminate hands. "We can't have this man's social commentary, not now. We just can't."

"Why not? What's happening now that would cause more strain? We aren't at war. The economy isn't depressed." Edward chuckled. "What better time could there be? You are being alarmist, Jonathan, nothing more than that. Besides, weren't you the one who said just a few weeks ago that the show needed to turn the corner and become successful? Weren't you the one who said we needed a star? Well, you're welcome. I've given you both."

Sterling started to object but retreated and sat back in his chair.

"Edward," said Tilda, "a star and profits are one thing, but this—this is too much."

Edward looked at her and thought for a moment. He was torn by this conversation. The last thing he wanted to do was defend Alexander. He hated the man and couldn't wait to see him skewered and have him fading from memory. And Edward assumed, like any reasonable man would, that Alexander was a dead man walking.

It was only a matter of time before the numbers and the law of averages would catch up to him. He couldn't live much longer, the Escobar brothers were a backup to natural law, an insurance policy.

Edward Burgess sat back in his chair and surveyed the room. Sterling was still a beaten man. Ulbright was uncharacteristically quiet. But Tilda was expectant, leaning forward in her chair and staring directly at him. He threw his hands up in the air and sighed.

"It's now become the most watched program in our history. The most profitable, too, as of this morning. But if you want to sabotage what we've accomplished, what am I supposed to do?"

"What are you talking about?" Tilda asked.

Edward reached for his PED and swiped the files up to the big screens around the room and suppressed a grin. "Just that."

The board were all quiet while they read through the reports and looked over the numbers. Ulbright glanced at Edward and smiled.

"Edward," said Tilda softly, "he has to go. The Poet Of The Moon, as they call him, has to go."

"I have a plan in place."

"What plan?" Asked Sterling.

"My plan, Jonathan."

Then Tilda asked, "Like the last one, when the show was struggling and you pulled it around?"

"Like that one."

"Ten days, Edward. That's all I can give you. I'm getting too much heat."

"I understand. Come on, now. It's like a funeral in here. The show is successful people, really successful. This is just a blip, something temporary. No one has ever done what we are doing. Remember that. Jonathan, I know your people are worried, but this won't last. The odds are against Alexander already, and they get longer and longer each day. The next meeting in two weeks most of you will have forgotten him."

The board members seemed placated and the meeting ended and they exited the room. No one was overjoyed, but Edward had bought a couple weeks freedom.

Thomas Ulbright waited for everyone to leave the room. He smiled at Edward and sat on the end of the conference table. "You know I'm a big supporter, Edward, always have been. I didn't want to voice my opinions in the meeting because, well, let me just say they aren't conventional." Ulbright smiled brightly.

"I appreciate that, Thomas. I always have."

"They are concerned," said Ulbright, tilting his head in the direction of the departing board members, "though I don't know why, really. If there is an uprising, as Tilda thinks there might be, we'll just do what we always have. We'll squash it. That's our right, isn't it?"

Edward smiled. What Ulbright wasn't saying, what he thought he understood about the man, was that he wanted an uprising. Ulbright wanted violence.

"All I'm saying Edward, is don't let them talk you out of something big because they are squeamish. They will always be squeamish. So, tell me, please, how are you going to deal with the Poet?"

"I'm going to have him killed. Fernando Escobar has a younger brother, Sebastien, who is in for life for killing a man. I made him an offer. I've given him a message to take to his brother. I made a deal with the family. Kill the Poet, I take care of their little sister and their mom and dad." Edward shrugged. "I don't care about the social aspects or the unrest. I knew the others would and at some point our advertisers might, but I doubt it. They are making money. The truth is, I was correct earlier: Clay Alexander's time is up—statistically and in other ways. We'll find or manufacture a new hero."

"That's a good incentive to get the job done. Escobar has the resources and manpower, too. Well, I knew you had it under control."

Edward took a seat after Ulbright had left the room, leaned back in the chair and looked over the reports still on the big screen opposite him. Anger rose within him. What he was looking at was an unbelievable success, yet unenjoyable given the circumstances. Clay Alexander was the cause and reason for that. Hatred wasn't a strong enough word for what he felt. He wanted to see Alexander squashed, gutted and paraded around for all to see. He needed the Escobar's to be successful. And that thought ate at him. Deep down he knew, a dead Poet was a dead show.

17

MISSION CONTROL

Who fears death when we are all dead men walking? Expectations on Fugitive Base were limited, and none of them included old age. Retirement here was removal from the game—permanently. If you desired to survive a few days you came to terms with the fact that death was around every corner, present with each step and every breath taken. Those who survived for more than a day came to terms with it, jettisoned the fear and worry and acquired a calmness that only the dead possess. We weren't immune to it, far from it. We simply understood it—death—embraced it and moved on. A line from some old song got it right, I think: Breathe in, breathe out, move on. That's all it was. You could see it in the guys who had come to terms with life here. And you could smell it on those who hadn't.

Men like Fernando Escobar tried to avoid it by building allegiances and fortifying their inner circles. But even that wasn't permanent or guaranteed. There were no certainties in the accumulation of loyalties. Bullying ownership of a piece of the city in the middle of Great Cavern wasn't going to keep you alive when others came looking for you, and they were always looking.

I suppose I was different from everyone else. I wasn't trying to survive, counting days and hours. I wanted more. I wanted off that rock and I was determined to achieve that goal. I was going to live. But death takes many guises. It comes in odd forms and sizes and some of them, I learned, are to be feared. I couldn't escape the fear or dismiss it. I accepted the notion of losing a battle or being bested in combat. That could have happened at any time. Taking on four of Escobar's men in the housing units below me, near the base of the wall, was fueled by a rage I didn't quite understand, but I knew my actions had been stupid. Surviving our own stupidity is part of the human experience. But during that foray I had been cut in the side. It wasn't deep or bad, but it hurt like hell and I was worried it would become infected. That scared me.

To die in battle was one thing. But to die from a lingering wound or illness was something entirely different. There wasn't any medical help here, even the MedBots were decommissioned.

I slept for a full day in the hammock. When I stirred I felt feverish and I ached all over. I thought rest was my best option. I had tried to get a good look at my side. It had a gash in it that was about two inches long. It was split open and wouldn't close properly. It had stopped bleeding, but it was red and tender and jagged all around. I found some material I had collected, washed some water through it, and held it tight to the wound. There wasn't any more I could do so I decided to sleep. I was exhausted.

I dreamed of the ocean, its smell and the sound of waves crashing on the shore. I dreamed of the wind and rain. At one point I dreamed of The Edge and the area known as Skin, of sirens and shouts and the cacophony of intermingled stressed lives. I missed it. It was comforting.

When I woke the sun was going down. I had slept through the day. I realized how vulnerable I had been. Anyone could have climbed the wall. I'd have never heard them or known they were there. That was my biggest fear—feeling helpless. I was lucky and vowed to not let it happen again. I subscribed to the belief that the paranoid's greatest asset is vigilance. If I were truly crazy that never-ending loop would have fed my delusion, but I was fairly certain I was sane.

I wanted to get moving and find the control room, but I still needed rest. I couldn't fight anyone in my condition. I wouldn't have been able to defend myself and it would have been difficult climbing down the wall. My range of motion was limited. It was frustrating. I even had to skip my workout for the first time since arriving.

I grabbed a food pack and looked out upon Great Cavern. I latched onto the fear again, imagining people climbing the wall searching for me while I was out cold. There was a nightmare waiting in the fear. The fear turned the food into something that tasted like dust. I knew I needed to eat so I forced it down, a drink of water with each bite to help me swallow. I was still parched, but I had plenty of supplies.

I watched through the night. It was quiet. Only once did I hear someone scream out, sharp and fleeting. The nightmares that evening weren't down below. They were in my head. My thoughts drifted to Sarah. I tried to lock them out because they were so painful. Sometimes they were overwhelming and forceful. I needed to get off that rock and back to earth, and quick. I was worried something would happen to her. I had no idea what that was or why I felt that way. I was a quarter-million miles from earth and condemned to death, but I was concerned for her safety. It didn't make sense. I was aware of that. But it was motivation for me to get moving, to overcome the injury, or move on despite it.

Night turned to day. The noises of morning in Great Cavern had become as rhythmical and familiar as those in The Edge. I found comfort in them, something signaled that all was normal, surreal as that might sound. Why do we value normalcy so highly? Fear of the unknown, the new, the different?

I watched the crows playing mid-air as the sun came through the giant skylights. They were noisy and raucous, swooping back and forth and up and down. Occasionally, one tumbled through the air before regaining control and rejoining the group. My little friend peeled away and glided toward me, a couple flaps of his wings as he landed nearby. He was boldly colored, expressing himself, I thought.

"You're not normal, you know that?"

He cocked his head and waddled a few steps.

"I need to find the control room. Might be best to do that at night. Plus, I'm still hurting and tired and can use some more rest. Check in every once in a while when I'm sleeping, eh?"

He hopped onto a rock and looked out across the cavern. I rolled into the hammock and shut my eyes. I could tell right away it wouldn't be a deep sleep. The food and water had helped alleviate the pain some and I was beginning to feel more like myself as I closed my eyes.

A fear once-mastered is something worth taunting. So I thought as I climbed down the wall at night, having slept through the day and well into the evening. Though the climbing was tricky in a few spots, it wasn't as perilous as it might have seemed. Enough light was about to create shadows on the rocks and crevices and I was pretty well versed in the climb, where the hand holds were and the tricky areas. But I would still lay odds it counted as one of those stupid things I needed to survive.

My side was getting better quickly. I spent a good half an hour before I left working out lightly, some stretching and twisting to loosen things up. Movement helped, though it caused some pain when the wound pulled apart slightly. But at least the surrounding areas were loosened up some.

Even though my side was feeling better after two day's rest, I climbed down the wall slowly. The water felt good on my side while I waited and watched and listened, as had become my practice. It was quiet, not unexpected given the time of night. I quickly moved through the forested area and then across the open area down from the housing complex where I had found Jose Mann's body hanging from the second floor. It was difficult keeping low because of my side. I crossed the road that led to the center of town and then through the scrub and rock area beyond. I felt better and stronger the more I moved.

The dividing line to the entrance area of Great Cavern and the area I had already searched was a small creek that ran from the wall toward the lake. The designers of this place had pumped water up from the aquifer below and let it run down the rocks, creating a small waterfall. It was ornamental, but a nice touch. The creek was just three or four yards across. I found a section where two larger rocks sat in the middle of the stream and I used them as a bridge.

Once on the other side I stopped and listened. Still all clear.

There were several buildings in the immediate area. One was a barn where the bots stored all kinds of things they might need. At the far end from the entrance was a compost pile of the loose things the bots picked up in the underbrush. A maintenance bot clicked into gear as I passed by and startled me. Its motion detectors must have sensed my movement. I froze, afraid someone might be sleeping there. Then I slowly pulled the screwdriver from my back. I was tense while I spent time going through the barn looking for hidden clues. It was difficult in the dark, but my eyes had adjusted and I could see well enough. Nothing was out of place or looked like it might lead somewhere else.

It still made sense to me that the control room was in Great Cavern, though my chances of finding it grew dimmer with each section I searched. Or, more likely, my anxiety rose knowing I was going to have to search in the town proper. From the place I had made home I could see the full layout of the cavern. It was similar to an amphitheater with the town and lake the closed end where a stage might have been and everything spreading out from them. I sensed the reason in the engineer's planning. The farther from the town center the more sparse the homes became. They were probably considered luxury palaces by the standards here. I guessed that most of the fun would have been in town, by the entertainment, restaurants and other people. But there were always the ultra-wealthy who wanted to separate themselves from the rest of the flock, even amongst their own kind. Most of the area away from the town was important for ecological balance. I didn't know it to be true, but guessed there were constraints on the number of people who could live here before taxing the bio systems too much.

I searched three other buildings—trying to be as meticulous

and careful as possible—and found myself by the entrance tunnel that led to the airlock and the surface. I pulled a protein bar from my bag and sat on a rock formation next to the entrance tunnel. I didn't remember anything like a door or antechamber in the rock tunnel on the way down. Searching it seemed risky, too risky, so I decided to pass on that.

Light was bleeding into Great Cavern. The gray lifted quickly and the colors awoke. I heard a few animal noises and bird calls. Morning had come, and quickly. I needed to move. I thought it best to keep to the wall. It was a longer route but free of people. I looked above the entrance and then along the wall in both directions—toward the town center and all the way back to the apartments below my home—I couldn't see anything obvious that I had missed. Nothing jutted out from the wall, nothing man-made at all, just uncompromising vertical solidity, and the section of looser rock where I made home.

When I reached the creek-head, where the water fell to the bottom of the wall, I froze. I saw noticeable tracks in the dusty floor and dirt all along the path. I couldn't hear anyone but my senses were on full alert. I crouched low and surveyed as much of the area as I could. A discernible path ran parallel to the creek for thirty yards or more. That was odd. Why a path here? Once I felt I was safe I looked in the area immediately around me. The tracks and path stopped at the wall, but not in any manner I would have expected. It was safer to say they went into the wall.

I went to where they ended. I could see it then. The wall here wasn't really stone. A printed section had been painted to match the rock. I felt along the edge. After a minute I found a seam and then a latch. Bingo. I checked my surroundings once more, nervous and excited, and then debated coming back later—under cover of darkness again—or going in now. The debate didn't last long. I had to know what I'd found.

I released the latch and pulled. A door swung open. When I stepped inside overhead lights automatically came on. I turned and pulled the door shut quickly. I didn't want company. When I turned back to the room I couldn't help but smile. I'd found the control room.

To my right a wall screen lit up, the computers booted and were showing multiple reports on the wall. In the room were a couple chairs and a table, a few shelves with supplies. An adjoining room looked like it was a break room. A coffee maker was on a counter and I could already smell the aroma without even turning it on. Coffee first, then I would look at the controls. I might as well enjoy it. I was lucky. I found a pack of coffee in a cupboard and a couple mugs. I started the coffee and then took a seat in the control room, edgy to see just how lucky I had been. It was either going to be the keys to the kingdom, or a total bust. I was almost afraid to learn which.

Two tablets were on the table. All reports were available. The tablets didn't require me to sign in. One panel on the wall showed detailed information on temperature—air and water in the cavern, and the water below in the aqueduct. Soil nitrates, oxygen, carbon dioxide levels and all sorts of readings. Sensors were spread around the cavern and the algae farm and aquifer below. One screen showed where each robot was, by category and type, and another monitored the fusion engine that was buried below in the rock.

I had no issues viewing the reports, but when I tried to search the directory and access other types of files I was scared out of my seat by the voice over the intercom. "Voice authentication and passcode required. Please state or enter your credentials."

I wouldn't be able to circumvent the security requirements. I couldn't get past the voice recognition, even if I could guess at a password. I continued to look at the reports. Something was missing but I couldn't put my finger on what. I spent hours looking over any information that was available. Multiple times I bumped up against the security protocols.

Into my second pot of coffee I realized what I wasn't seeing: Information regarding the cameras was missing. Cameras for Fugitive Theatre were all over Great Cavern, and in every room of the housing units. I was pretty certain cameras were even embedded into some of the rocks along the wall and in the stubby trees along the cavern floor. I had barely seen any of them. Actually, I hadn't really looked. They were irrelevant and more often than not I was too busy watching out for other, more dangerous, things when I was moving around.

I blurted out, talking to myself really, "I need a map of the base."

The voice from the ceiling was back. "Base overview map accessed. Specify areas to detail."

Oh. It didn't take long to figure out the system they had in place. I could view any file that wasn't deemed sensitive, but I couldn't effect any changes or see protected files unless I could login to the system.

I got up from the chair and walked to the wall to have a closer look at the map of the base. Multiple maps were displayed. One was a cut out, as if someone had sliced down through the moon. The other was an overlay from above, something a satellite would take. I saw maps of Great Cavern and the aquifer. I spent an hour looking at them and pulling apart each area, but I wasn't having any luck figuring out any areas of vulnerability. Nor could I locate the area where the camera feeds went.

I was tired and frustrated. In what I thought of as the break room was a closet. It was large, more of a storage room, though mostly empty. In the back I found several space suits hanging along the wall. The suits varied in size. They were real suits, made to be used on the surface, unlike the suits we wore when we were transported here. Ours were designed to keep us alive for a short while. These were robust.

I fished a food bar from my bag and plopped down in one of the chairs back in the control center. My mind didn't accept that this was a bust. I was missing something. I stared for a long while at the maps on the wall. Something was odd regarding the surface map, a blemish next to the solar panel farm. I thought at first it was a mark on the wall. Then I got excited and jumped from the seat to have a closer look.

"What is that?"

"Please repeat the question."

"Toward the pole, adjacent to the solar panel farm, what is that, a small building?"

"That is the entrance to the Media Communications Center. The Communications Center is approximately fifty yards under ground. Transmitters and antenna are located next to it. The Media Communications Center was constructed after this base."

"So, that's just an airlock I see?"

"Correct."

"Is there a map?"

The map appeared on the wall a second later. The center itself was small.

"There is an airlock. Does that mean it has atmosphere?"

"Correct."

"How far away is the Communications Center from the airlock of this base?"

"Point nine miles."

Less than a mile. "Is the local gravity at the Communications Center the same as here?"

"Unknown. However, given the position of the black hole generator it is likely to be less."

A plan formed in my head, something I felt certain would work. I only needed the answer to one more question, but I hesitated asking it. The wrong answer would be devastating and my position would barely be better than it had been since I'd arrived. I sat for a few minutes and thought things through. In the end, I didn't see a better way or option.

I drew in a big breath and let it out slowly. "Is it locked?"

"The Communications and Media Center is not locked."

I wanted to jump up and shout, high-five the voice from the ceiling and dance around the room. But I stayed seated and thought of Sarah. A tear fell down my right cheek. Then the emotion poured out of me and washed away the frustration, anger and futility that had built up since this all began, and I felt buoyed by a sliver of hope.

I knew how to get off the moon and, I thought, back to earth. The only problem was, I needed help. It was a two man job, at least. I thought I knew someone I could ask.

It was getting late. I had been in the control center for hours. I could have stayed there until dark, but I was too excited to get going and put my plans into motion. I exited the control center and stayed as close to the wall as I could. The light was overwhelming at first, so different from the light of the small room, and the smell of Great Cavern hit me in an odd way, powerful and richer than I had noticed before. But I quickly adjusted and forgot about it. A few places the cover was minimal along my path and I moved as quickly and quietly through them as I could.

When I reached the housing complex I stopped and waited a few minutes, but all seemed still and quiet. I ducked around behind the building and moved quickly. When I reached the far end of the building and made the turn up its side three men came around from the front. Two of them carried weapons fashioned from pieces of the printed buildings that had been torn off. One had a couple rocks in his fists. I wanted to turn and run. I looked behind the building. Three more men turned the corner and walked slowly toward me from the direction I had just come.

One of the men in front of me smiled. "Not your day, I guess, *cabrón*."

Escobar.

18

FATE

When we aren't pursuing fate, it comes to us. It was something my mother used to say. Then she would remind me that life went on whether I wanted it to or not. Might as well sit in the driver's seat, I heard her say a thousand times, if once.

My mind raced, my pulse pounded in my temples and my mouth was suddenly dry. I took a deep breath, released it, clenched and unclenched my hands, and stood a little taller. I told myself I could think of worse ways to die.

In my peripheral vision I saw Escobar's men still walking slowly down the area behind the building, the same direction I had come. I tried to convince myself I could make it to the ledge above and behind me, where I had hidden before, but the math didn't work out. I knew they would get to me before I could climb even part-way up the wall. I thought I could rush the men walking toward me, get beyond them and make a run for it, but something made me stay.

"Only six?" I asked Escobar. "I don't know if I should be disappointed or insulted."

I lifted my bag from my shoulder. The two men either side of Escobar tensed. I stopped and froze. "Testy, aren't you?"

As I completed lifting the bag off my back I reached around and palmed the screwdriver, concealing it with my hand and wrist. I tossed the bag between us, using it as a cover for my actions. I took a couple slow, small steps toward them. The men to my left had cut down a third of the distance, but were still twenty yards away. They didn't seem to be in too much of a hurry.

"When I slaughtered your men right here, all four of them, and then tossed them into the back of that landscaping bot, I figured you might be upset. But to cry and wail like a little baby in the night? Well, *cabrón*, now you've made a grave error." I angled my body to make myself look slimmer, while nearly facing the men coming from the other direction. I stared Escobar down and refused to break eye contact.

"Oh?" He finally said.

I smiled. "You're going to need more guys."

I could see doubt in his eyes, probably thinking of the four men I had killed. The man to my right took a step forward. He was carrying one of the printed pieces off a building like a baseball bat.

"Not today," he said. "The Poet dies today."

Poet?

"And," he continued, "I'm supposed to deliver a message to you from the man." He gave me a crooked smile. "The bitch is dead, *cabrón*."

That stopped me. The man? The bitch? That could only be one thing, one person. Sarah. A quarter million miles away and in that moment I never felt more connected to her. I smelled her scent, felt her touch on my skin and heard her laughter. I breathed her in standing there. But according to this guy my seeing her again was in jeopardy, snuffed out before I got the chance to get back to earth. Burgess had sent this guy to the moon with a message just to hurt me. I couldn't see straight. Anger blurred my vision. The pounding in my head was a beast waiting to burst free. Sweat poured from me. I took a step closer and cocked my head. He smiled, like he'd won a few points in the game, like I was injured beyond my ability to cope. I was certain he could see how much his statement had crushed me. But I locked it all away and sank into the anger and hatred I felt for Burgess. I let the screwdriver slip down into my hand, forced a smile, and became what I had to be in the moment. I lunged at him, bringing my right hand up under his chin and drove the screwdriver through his throat and up into his skull.

Before Escobar or the others could react I pulled the screwdriver out and jumped back. Escobar let out a scream.

"Sebastien!"

He started to kneel over the body that had fallen to the ground, then he remembered I was there.

"My brother!" He screamed.

Everyone got past their shock then and it looked like they would come at me immediately. To my left was a huge commotion. One of the guys was lifted off the ground and slammed into the corner of the building. The others were wide-eyed, staring at the Polynesian. One of the remaining two swung his stick but the Polynesian guy simply swatted it away. I had to turn back to my own little battle and missed the rest.

Escobar and his other minion attacked me. Escobar swung one of the pieces of printed material at my head and I blocked it with my left arm but dropped the screwdriver in the process. I felt the sting from the blow run down my entire left side. I kicked at his knee but missed. A rock whizzed past my head, then the guy dropped the other one he was carrying and bull-charged me. I stepped to the side at the last second and tried to put an elbow into his head, but only connected with a glancing blow. My left side was killing me and I was hit on my lower abdomen by the on rusher.

Escobar moved in and swung at my legs with his club. I jumped higher in the lower gravity than I could have on earth and kicked out with my left foot into his shoulder. He tumbled back, rolled over and got to his feet quickly. I took a step back and a quick glance at the Polynesian. He seemed to be enjoying himself. He had one guy in a headlock while he fended off the attack of the other.

Everything was so loud in my head I was having trouble concentrating. But something was wrong. Then I heard it. Up above me, wings flapping to keep it in place and squawking like a mad man, was my crow friend, his feathers vacillating between a bright and darker red. But that wasn't the noise I was hearing. There was more. I felt it as much as anything, a low rumble that was quickly turning into a roar. I turned and ran to the Polynesian who stood apart from just one of Escobar's men. The other was on the ground. I put my shoulder into him and pushed as hard and fast as I could into the wall of Great Cavern. Just as rocks and boulders plummeted down I pulled us to the cavern floor right up against the wall. The rocks bounded over us, pulverizing Escobar and his men. Escobar tried to get up and run, but a medium sized rock hurled through the air and struck his right shoulder from behind. I'm sure he screamed, but it was impossible to hear with all the noise from the falling rock.

It stopped as quickly as it started. The noise abated and we stood, covered in moon dust and a few scrapes and cuts. My ears were ringing. My left side ached and I was certain I had re-opened the injury on the other side. A huge chunk of the building on the corner was caved in and I saw six dead men strewn about.

I heard a flap and some chatter up above our position. Then I realized what had happened. My feathered friend had triggered one of my booby traps. Damn smart bird. I looked up. Standing near the edge of the roof and looking down was a murder of crows. They were brightly colored, chests puffed out, waddling back and forth from one foot to the other. They were strutting, claiming victory and clearly enjoying themselves. I couldn't help it: Despite the pain and craziness of the situation, I laughed out loud, hard. The crows joined in with that odd way they had of laughing. At least now I was certain they were laughing. The bunch of tricksters and altered things that ruled Great Cavern were having a good time.

The Polynesian looked from me to the birds and back again, smiling all the while and shaking his head.

Someone stirred amid the rubble, not quite dead. It was Escobar. I walk toward him, limping and hurting all over with the effort. But he was in a bad way, much worse than me. His shoulder was clearly broken and bleeding profusely. His right leg was at an odd angle, also broken. He tried to roll over.

"Easy, *cabrón.* I can't have you die on me yet. I need to know something first." I knelt down next to him. He was struggling to breathe, wheezing. "The first one I killed, your brother?"

I could see the answer in his eyes, and the sadness in with the anger.

"He just get here?"

He nodded slightly, affirming that was true.

"One more thing before I string you up from the second floor and gut you for all to see. Did you order your men to do that to Mann?"

I saw nothing but fear in his eyes, then resignation. He let out a puff of breath and then he died. His heart stopped. Maybe it was the injuries, or maybe the fear brought it on. We could have made a symbol out of him for everyone else in this forsaken cavern, but my heart wasn't in it. With the recognition that we had survived my mind finally registered what I had been told earlier. According to Escobar's brother, Sarah was dead. I was having trouble processing the information and facing it. I needed to be alone before I could get to that.

I stood up and looked at the Polynesian. "You okay?"

He shrugged.

"You want off this rock?"

He thought about it for a minute. I could see the gears turning inside his head. Finally, he gave me that eyes-squinting smile of his that pulled at the edges of his mouth and slowly nodded.

"Meet me right here about thirty minutes after the sun comes up tomorrow. We're leaving then."

I turned to go, picking up my bag and the screwdriver along the way. It was slow going. If anyone had attacked me then I wouldn't have been able to defend myself. But I made it to the lake and slipped under the water and stayed there for the longest time. I wanted the water to heal me, to suck the wounds and the pain from my body and restore my psyche. I tried to will it. It felt good under the surface, like a deep cleanse. But I kept seeing Sarah's face. Was she dead? I wouldn't put it past Burgess. He had no issues taking what he wanted. He was Oligoi, after all. They had a history of it. And I was on the moon, a terrorist in everyone's eyes because of him. No, I had no doubt he could do it.

The water kept reminding me of Sarah. It was silky smooth as I moved around in it, similar to our lovemaking. When I closed my eyes I felt our bodies sliding together in rhythm, connected but separate. I could feel my hand on the small of her back and see her beautiful curves. I wanted to stay underwater, just let go of everything and drift off. It was such a beautiful thought. But that siren song couldn't hold me. Another was calling louder and was more insistent. I wanted to wring Edward Burgess' neck more than I wanted peace. Visions of the men I had just killed flashed in my mind and I wondered again at what I had become.

I left the water and slowly climbed the wall toward my home. I had to stop repeatedly. Once, I saw my feathered friend, but I didn't have the strength to say anything to him, not even to thank him and his friends for their assistance.

After the long climb I reached the top and sat for a while, feet dangling over the edge again, and considered my plans. We were going to have to make an EVA of nearly a mile along the moon's surface. Then, if all went well, we were going to steal a shuttle. It was a long shot, but what wasn't here. There were a million ways to die on this moon. I was just trading one set of options for another. The difference, I reminded myself, was that survival meant a ticket home if we were successful. That ticket home was keeping me alive. With Sarah most likely dead, all I had left was revenge against Burgess. I didn't care about anything else, not any more.

I had to eat something before climbing into the hammock. The food tasted like cardboard again and was difficult to swallow. I wasn't much for sentiment, and I certainly wasn't going to miss any of the things I looked down on in Great Cavern. Change was coming and I had invited it, pursued it and welcomed it. I couldn't get excited about it. I wasn't nervous or anxious. I was numb, overloaded from everything that had taken place. It made my head ache trying to understand it. Why were we like this? I was beyond asking what was the meaning of it all, of life. Forget finding meaning, I wanted to know if there was a point to it. I even solicited God for an answer, but He was as quiet as ever, disinterested.

The sun wasn't quite set on the day, but I was exhausted and unable to stay awake any longer, too many ups and downs, and too much adrenaline flying through and disrupting my system. Deep space lingered above. Sometimes, like a filter straining reality, bits and pieces of it flowed through, riding on tiny streams of white light from distant stars, sparks of emotion filled with fury and fear that gained their own momentum. Out of the blackness leaked new forms of hatred—for the world men had created, for the Edward Burgesses and the rest of the Oligoi, and for myself and the death I had caused Sarah. The issue was I knew what waited in my dreams. I understood the visions soon to haunt me there. Sarah would be waiting and my guilt would be overwhelming. I never suspected, never dreamed, I could be the villain in my own story. Who does? But I was tired of accepting fate and what was thrown my way. It was time to control it, shape it into something I was happy with, or face the consequences of my actions. "Why fear death," I asked aloud to no one, "when you're already dead?"

I surrendered—collapsed into the hammock—and closed my eyes and wept for Sarah until sleep finally came.

19

EVERYTHING IS DOWN

"Did you miss me?"

"What do you mean?" Sarah asked.

"Well, I've been gone for a couple days. Hell, I could've been dead for all you knew. I didn't hear from you once."

Sarah regarded Edward, trying to think of an appropriate response. Finally, she said, "I knew where you were. You aren't the only one who can keep tabs on someone, you know." She got up from the couch and walked past him. "I need a drink. Want something?"

He was too happy, almost a smirk on his face. It had been a week since they'd interacted, since the last time Fugitive Theatre had aired. She never watched the mid-week re-cap show. Watching the weekend edition was painful and she didn't want to re-live any of it.

"No, I'm good, thanks."

Edward listened to her walking away, light hushed footsteps on the carpet and then down the marbled the hallway. He couldn't understand her and was beginning to think he never would. He thought by now she would come around, forget her little dalliance and see the light. Then he reminded himself what his real desire was—an heir. He wanted someone to pass the business on to, someone he could groom and turn into a Burgess. She'd come around enough for that in time, he figured. Then—he didn't really care what happened then.

He looked at his PED. A message from Sam Verita had come in, but he didn't feel like speaking to anyone at the moment. He'd call back after the show. Edward had tried to talk to him just a short while ago, but too much going on and Sam and his crew were trying pull the footage together and build the show. So much had been happening in realtime and they wanted to use the footage. Sam was frenetic and had to get off the line. Edward figured he was just calling back because their conversation had been cut short.

Sarah returned with a drink just as the show was beginning. The opening credits had changed. They weren't as impactful as what the team had put together when they featured Alexander, but it worked well enough.

There was little footage of Alexander in the first half of the show, just as they had discussed. In the last half hour Alexander was being tracked along the wall of Great Cavern. When he reached the same housing complex where Jose Mann had been killed the cameras zoomed in and followed him behind the building. Fernando and Sebastien Escobar walked around the corner of the building from the front with one other man. From behind Alexander three other men approached. He was trapped. Alexander's face, stolid and calm, was held in extreme close up for several seconds, then faded to black. Commercial break. Edward laughed out loud. He loved the tension and timing.

Sarah was tense, curled up at the end of the couch, a blanket over her legs and a cup of tea in her hand. She was staring blankly at the wall.

"You know," said Edward, "when this is over and the show settles in and things get back to normal, we should go on a trip, someplace warm, maybe."

Sarah took a sip of tea. Edward noticed she was shaking. Serves her right, he thought, placed too much hope in the wrong guy. She didn't respond.

The show returned with Alexander removing his bag from his back and tossing it to the ground.

"When I slaughtered your men right here, all four of them," said Clay to Fernando Escobar, "and then tossed them into the back of that landscaping bot, I figured you might be upset. But to cry and wail like a little baby in the night? Well, *cabrón*, now you've made a grave error."

"Oh?"

"You're going to need more guys."

"Not today," said Sebastien Escobar. "The Poet dies today. And I'm supposed to deliver a message to you from the man. The bitch is dead, *cabrón*."

Edward felt the excitement down to his bones. Sebastien Escobar had done a perfect job of delivering the message. He stole a quick glance at Sarah. She was slack jawed with a tear running down her cheek. He wanted to make a comment, but the show was riveting and he couldn't look away too long.

Alexander was surrounded and the news clearly shocked him.

This was it, the death scene that would end Edward's troubles.

Alexander took a step closer and then suddenly, with amazing speed and economy, attacked Sebastien Escobar and killed him with a weapon no one had seen. Edward was shocked. The attack had been so fast and brutal that no one else had moved. Alexander stepped back, Fernando Escobar screamed out for his brother. Escobar stopped from bending down to tend to his brother and was going to attack Alexander. But then an amazing scene unfolded. The giant Polynesian stepped forward on Alexander's behalf and was fighting Escobar's other three men. One of them went flying into the housing complex head first and landed with a thud on the ground. Another tried to hit the Polynesian with a stick but ended up in a headlock.

Escobar attacked Alexander, but Alexander was too quick, a blur of motion and anger, punctuated with violence. It looked to be a standoff. Alexander, thought Edward, would be able to hold off Escobar and the other man. Then suddenly Alexander looked up and turned and tackled the Polynesian into the base of the wall, just as rocks and boulders plummeted down, smashing into Escobar and his men. It was a gruesome scene.

Edward's heart sank. His mouth was dry and he was sitting on the front of the couch, looking on as the crows danced around on the rooftop, squawking and making lots of noise. He watched the rest of the scene and the death of Fernando Escobar. Edward was drained, robbed of energy and disbelieving of what he had just witnessed.

He staggered from the couch, forgot that Sarah was even there, and stumbled to his office. He poured himself a glass of whiskey, fell into the leather desk chair, and took a large gulp of the single malt. He was beginning to feel like the big loser in all this. He held the glass to his lips and closed his eyes. So, he thought, the fucking Poet lives to fight another day.

Sarah struggled to think straight. Her hopes swelled with the knowledge that Clay had survived. But they were wrenched downward when she realized that Edward had sent Sebastien Escobar to kill him. And what was the message Escobar had delivered? Was that about her? Did Clay now believe she was dead? So much torment and anguish, so much uncertainty. Guilt and anger rose in equal amounts, along with sorrow and futility. Only one thing was constant throughout, in the background, taunting—Edward. The feeling suffocated her. She felt trapped, isolated. She needed to break free. No more sitting on the sidelines: She had to do something.

She felt sick to her stomach again. It was an overall nauseousness. Acting would do her good, clear her head and her body. She had too much tension and anxiety built up within her. It needed to be released.

She stared at the blank wall, lost in thought. Tomorrow, she decided, she would go speak to her father. She trusted his advice and his honesty. Unlike her mother, who was an upwardly mobile social butterfly, her father was more introspective and philosophical. He saw the big picture, beyond his own little world. She could share the story with him and know he wouldn't judge her. At least she could get some of it off her chest, and devise a way forward.

Sarah staggered to her bathroom, scraped her toothbrush absentmindedly a few times across her teeth, turned out the lights, and then fell into bed. It was then she realized just how angry she was with Edward. She wanted to lash out and hurt him in the worst way possible. She couldn't even think of Clay. All her energy funneled toward Edward. With each passing moment she hated him more. Tiny details in his mannerisms—the way he laughed and the way he tilted his head back when speaking to someone—enraged her. She thrashed around in bed for some time before she was pulled under and finally slept. But the sleep was fragmented with visions of Clay, always unreachable regardless of her desperation.

Sun through the windows woke her in the morning. It was still early but she messaged her father and they agreed to meet for lunch. She still felt sick but at least she was energized and motivated, despite the lack of restful sleep. She showered, then decided to go the gym to work out.

At the gym she rode hard for an hour on one of the exercise machines, sweating and mindlessly listening to music through her PED. At least the sickness had disappeared during the workout. When she finished she showered again at the gym, grabbed a coffee in the gym cafe and found herself standing outside. A waning gibbous moon was low in the sky when she glanced peripherally, but she couldn't look at it full on and turned away, walking aimlessly down the street, keeping it to her back.

A block away was a light-rail station. She walked to it, barely noticing the people or the pigeons along the way, and then boarded a train to The Edge without even thinking about where she was going. She stared out the window of the train but the world outside passed by too quickly, the changed scenery gone in a flash, and she had trouble holding a coherent thought. The blur of the landscape swiped past: pristine downtown windows and buildings that became the grunge of industry and then suddenly something else. She felt the train slow and without conscious recognition understood she had arrived at The Edge and got up from her seat. As she stepped down from the train and onto the platform she had one thought: Home.

Sarah wasn't ready for what confronted her. Stenciled on the side of one of the printed buildings was Clay's image. THE POET DOESN'T LIE, it read below. She hadn't checked any of the social feeds in a while. She wasn't certain what was happening there, or in The Edge for that matter. But this seemed to be a sign. Clay had their attention. He had at least motivated a few to think about the conditions and social arrangements.

She walked along the outer street of The Edge. Before long she could smell and hear the area known as Skin. It was a beehive of activity when she arrived, in the road and the parking lot before the two adjacent fast food places people moved about. Sirens sounded, people shouted, tires screeched. She knew to avoid this place, years of her father's voice in her ears warning her, but she found a bench and sat. The sounds were comforting, in their rhythm was the background noise of her youth. This place was in her veins, not Skin necessarily, but The Edge and surrounding area. Even the sickly sweet grease fired smell that wafted across the street from the fast food joints was something known to her, familiar.

Sarah suddenly realized where she was. The lucid dream that had carried her this far faded and she looked down at her clothes. She felt better knowing she was wearing her workout clothes, basic sweatsuit and running shoes. She blended in well enough to go unnoticed.

Across the street, at the edge of the parking lot, two men yelled at each other. They pushed, they gesticulated, one even kicked the base of a light pole. Violence was rampant in Skin. The violence released the tension of The Edge, let it bleed off and lower the pressure. Violence. Most people, Sarah thought, would say that human's big brains enabled the ascension of man in the world. But Sarah wasn't so sure anymore. She felt Clay's view, expressed when they were naked and glistening with post-coital sweat, made more sense now than she had previously supposed. Our willingness to use violence was the force that drove us. Without it—the violence—we wouldn't have achieved so much. The machines of war unleashed innovation. Slavery used as the engine of growth. One group taking resources from others to fuel their expansion. Violence and its more subtle derivations, like greed, steered the sails of progress.

Greed drove the world and allowed humans to accomplish so much. But it had a price. The price was men like Edward, who didn't care for individual suffering, only some larger scheme.

Sarah felt shame for being a part of Edward's world. What lies did she tell herself to get to this point? That he loved her? That seemed laughable. He didn't seem capable of love now, not from her shifted perspective. Edward manipulated. He moved pieces and people around. But he didn't consider them.

Her PED buzzed. Her father saying he would see her shortly. If she left now she had just enough time to walk to the cafe. She got up and started walking back the direction she had come. She faced the sinking moon in the late-morning sky straight on and didn't fight its pull this time. More than most, she was drawn to it.

"None of this is really about what I did, dad. There's more. Before Clay and I slept together, before I ever considered it, Edward hit me."

"He what?"

"You heard me."

Her father sat back in his chair and stared down at the ground. They were at the cafe just outside The Edge, sitting outdoor. Her father swallowed hard before looking at her. "I'm so sorry, honey.

I don't know what to say. You can't stay with him. That's for sure."

"I'm not sure how to get out."

"I don't know. I'm not sure what I can do. He's a powerful man."

"I know, but I don't think it's as big an issue as it could be. I need to take time to figure it out, and I will."

He nodded his head. "I wouldn't say anything to your mother, not yet. You know how she is."

"That's why we're talking, dad. She has stars in her eyes. I know that. Being Cleric is a big deal to her. That will end, no doubt."

There was a wry smile on her father's face as he looked out to the street. Sarah asked, "What is it?"

He shrugged. "Not all it's cracked up to be, really. I was happier just down the street. We didn't have much. But we had great friends and we laughed a lot. I miss that, the laughter. Our lives are . . . antiseptic now. Hard to explain."

"No, I get it."

"Tell me about this show. What's it called?" Her father took a bite of his burrito.

"Fugitive Theatre."

She went on to tell him all about it, that Edward had dreamed it up and how Clay wasn't anything like they portrayed him, and certainly not a terrorist.

"So, he's the one, The Poet of the Moon?" He asked. "I've heard people talking about him. He's becoming quite popular. There's even graffiti here and there."

"Dad, Clay is still doomed, no matter how popular," said Sarah, then paused before continuing. "Edward sent a man to the moon to tell Clay I was dead." She wiped away a tear from her cheek.

They were quiet for some time. Finally, he asked, "Do you have a plan, or just trying to figure it out?"

"I've been so sick lately I haven't had time to think about it. I keep getting nauseous."

"Nothing serious, I hope."

"Just the stress, I think."

"All the same, you should go to the doctor, just to be safe."

"I will. I feel more clear about the way I've been thinking after our talk. I know this much, I won't let it go on. I can't. I will end it."

"Just promise me one thing, don't let our situation come into play in your decision. We'll be fine regardless."

"Thanks, dad, I won't. You know mom will be pissed at me for a while, a long while."

"Don't worry, eventually it will sink in what has happened and she'll understand. Just do what you need to."

It was late morning before Edward had woken. His hangover finally forced him up. He had several messages on his PED, including another from Sam Verita. Instead of listening to them he connected directly.

"Sam, sorry I didn't get back to you," said Edward when Verita had picked up on audio. "I saw the show and, well, I wasn't in a good place."

"Then you've at least seen what happened, that's good."

"I did. Clay Alexander has become a huge thorn in my side. I don't know what to say. It seems every time—"

"Edward," Sam interrupted, "did you listen to my message from this morning?"

"Uh, no, sorry."

"We've got a bigger problem, much bigger."

"Bigger problem? How's that?" Edward rubbed his head, tried to alleviate some of the throbbing in his temples.

"We've lost all communication."

"What do you mean, Sam?"

"With the moon. Everything is down."

20

MAINTENANCE RUN

I woke early. I felt rested but I was stiff all over. My side hurt and my right hand was bruised and swollen around the knuckles of my last two fingers. It hurt to flex the fingers on that hand. I couldn't remember injuring it, but with everything that had happened I was lucky not to be worse off than I was.

I stayed in the hammock a while longer, thinking through my plans for the day. I thought of a couple areas where the timing might be crucial, even difficult, but I couldn't figure a better way off the moon. We needed luck, sure, but I had already decided. It was worth the effort, even if it meant dying on the surface.

I trusted the Polynesian. I'm not certain why. He hadn't given me any reason not to—not surrounding Mann's death nor Escobar's, or even as far back as our meeting in the tunnels by the algae farm. It was a risk to trust anyone, but so far he had come through.

He had saved my life in the fight with Escobar. I owed him. If he wanted off this rock then I wasn't going to question his motives. I couldn't figure him out though. He was like a giant kid. I think he was having fun, no other way to look at it. He was enjoying himself. He might be the only one on Fugitive Base who did, but that's the impression I got.

There was an eerie quiet to Great Cavern. Just before the day broke everything slipped into a deep sleep. The background noise of the cavern was soft and filtered, almost purring. That's when I realized how close I was—to Sarah, to home. If the day went as planned, if we survived and made it through, I was hours from seeing Sarah again, or confirming her death. Either way that coin landed, dead or alive, one thing was certain: I was hours from killing Burgess. Or I was myself dead.

I tamped down the excitement and was reminded that it was still a long shot.

I rolled out of the hammock and sat on the edge of the rock wall again. Sunlight began slowly filtering into the cavern. Down below one of the landscaping bots was collecting the dead. I had begun thinking of them more as carrion bots. Every time I had seen one recently they were picking up or carrying the dead. They had a lot in common with my winged friends.

"Are you there bird?"

A few seconds later I heard the flap of wings and in the low light the bird alighted on a nearby rock.

"Thank you for yesterday. That was a slick move. I'm glad you and your friends enjoyed yourselves."

The bird's feathers switched colors, like a gradient washing over him, dark to a lighter gray then a deep red.

"I'm leaving today. I won't be coming back. I would appreciate it if you kept an eye on us. We're heading to the main entrance shortly."

The crow ruffled his wings, cocked his head. I had lots of thoughts sitting there looking at him. Maybe I was wrong before. Maybe the question wasn't what does it mean to be human. Perhaps that had already been answered and it was simply that the answer left me wanting. Maybe I wanted there to be more to us than there really was. What if the real question was: What does post-humanity look like? These birds that had been adapted and allowed free rein of the place might be a clue. They might be the answer, or part of it. They might be the future. The Oligoi had to know how successful the birds were. They had to peer into the future and envision a way to sculpt humanity. The first thing they would do is separate themselves from the rest of us. Longer lives, more robust health, better senses, skills and abilities; they'd take it all for themselves. They'd lie, call it evolution, proof they were meant to be our overlords. Then, create a few docile worker bees here—just add some bovine traits or maybe pull some loyalty from the family dog. Over there create a few soldiers, with aggression programmed in and enhanced with some adaptive camouflage from a chameleon, and the stealthiness of a tiger. It's only information, after all, DNA. All it takes is the knowledge to map it and manipulate it. We contain our pasts, not just the human past, but all those species we evolved from. Their genes are still there, not useless, dormant maybe but not discarded—just waiting to be expressed in some novel way. There's no telling how far along things were. Maybe places like The Edge were laboratories. The moon was certainly a laboratory. I hadn't been able to look at any of the other living things here, no time. There's no telling what I might have found.

Conspiracy theories, I chided myself. But then I looked at the crow, and thought of men like Burgess, and couldn't convince myself it was all lunacy.

"Time to go. Thanks, again, crow."

He squawked and flew off. I grabbed my bag and began the descent.

I ran through my protocols, waiting in the water and moving slowly and as silently as possible through the small wooded area. I didn't want to end up dead before I had the chance to get off that rock because of carelessness. The Polynesian was waiting for me.

"Ready?"

He nodded.

"Good. I think we should stay along the base of the wall," I pointed along the route. "Over there, just before the main entrance, I need to show you what I found."

He smiled and began walking. We were quiet and moved quickly. He was quite agile. He was also very alert. At one point he stopped and froze. I could tell he was listening for something. I couldn't hear anything and nothing felt out of place. After a few moments we moved again. It didn't take long to reach the creek that started from the waterfall.

I put a hand on his shoulder and he stopped. We walked down the path to the mid-stream rocks and crossed. Where the path ended at the wall I stopped and waited and listened, making certain we were alone. Then I found the release, pulled out the fake section of the wall, and opened the door.

"Control center," I said to him, once we were inside. "Coffee?"

He beamed a great big smile and I walked to the break room and started a pot. A few minutes later we both were drinking a cup and leaning against the wall of the main room.

"Show me a map of the base, please."

"Base overview map accessed. Specify area to detail."

He shook his head at the voice from the ceiling and walked over to the map on the wall.

"Here's the plan," I said. "We need to make an EVA to this point here," I pointed. "It's the Media and Communications Center. It's not quite a mile away. Suits are in the back. One should fit you."

He was frowning and taking it all in.

"It's pretty simple, really. We're all on a big reality show. If we cut off the camera feeds and access—controlled there—they have to come and fix it. Then we hijack the shuttle and go back to Olympus."

He started laughing.

"Right. I can't see any way they would expect someone outside the base. We should be a complete surprise. My guess is they will land the shuttle right here," I pointed again to the map, "where they dropped us off. It's a landing pad of sorts and they know it. I don't expect more than three men, maybe four, but that's doubtful. The shuttles are auto-piloted. Once we're onboard we can instruct it to take us back. From Olympus, I'm going home. I have a score to even."

He sat down in a chair and leaned back, his head bobbing up and down.

I had one other concern. "I'm not certain how long before they come. We know how long the ride is from Olympus, but they may not launch immediately. They'll try to figure it out from earth. They can even try to reboot the system. When none of that works they'll have to send a crew. My biggest question is how long can we make the oxygen in the suits last. If we start to run out of air and have to go inside we do that quickly. The suits take up air and process it almost immediately we'd only need a few minutes. It might take longer to recharge the suit batteries, but not too long."

I walked back to the map. "I think we should wait here, inside the solar farm. We would be hidden well enough and we'd be able to see in both directions, in case they touchdown someplace other than the landing pad."

I thought about what I had just said. "Control, is there another landing pad here?"

"There is not."

I shrugged my shoulders. "There you go. The Media and Communications Center was built after the base, just for the show."

The Polynesian leaned forward on his chair and studied the map some more.

I said, "We need to pack food and water. I don't know what is over there."

He finished his coffee and got up to get another cup.

"Leave in a few?"

He just smiled and shrugged—why not.

I stood outside the airlock on the landing pad in awe. Nothing is so beautiful as looking back toward earth. The colors are so deep and saturated, so beautiful, it is impossible to explain. But that wasn't what caused my awe. The blackness of space cannot be described. The stars are still out there, but the eye can't detect them with so much light reflecting from the lunar surface. The darkness was so deep it was disconcerting. It was an odd feeling, for me, anyway. The Polynesian didn't have much to say on the matter, but I could tell he was as dumbstruck as I was.

It had taken us several minutes to get into the suits. It was an easier fit for the big guy than I thought it would be. His suit adjusted nicely. They were easier to get around in than the suits we wore to the moon. Both suits had side pouches for carrying whatever was needed. We grabbed water and some food from my pack. It might all freeze, unless the pocket was heated, but we still might be able to use it. We left the control room and walked to the entrance after suiting up.

The crow was waiting above the tunnel, perched on a rock. I stopped and saluted. Others joined him. The murder of crows gave us a sending off party. It took quite a long while to walk up the tunnel. The airlock was automatic. Once we snapped our helmets into place a heads up display powered on. It recognized where we were and we could call up an overlay map at any time. It had been a nervous feeling stepping outside the airlock.

The big guy turned and started walking a few moments later and I followed. Gravity was still close to what it had been in Great Cavern. I wondered if it would change as we moved on. We moved through the fine lunar dust, up and down hills and around boulders. Earth was above the horizon to our right, above the solar field. Sarah felt closer than she had in a long while. I wondered then how long I had been gone. I couldn't remember. Counting days didn't seem to be relevant to life in Great Cavern, a waste of energy and focus.

It was scary along the surface of the moon. I realized how small I was, a single living creature out in the vastness of space. I felt more alone than at any point in my life. Yet, simultaneously, I felt more connected than ever to the blue dot hanging in the darkness. Space, and the level of aloneness and the mirrored feelings of oneness, opened new areas of thought, far beyond my tiny self and the struggles I had experienced. It was difficult to process or come to terms with and I could tell I was going to ponder it for a long while.

After we had walked for a while, the Polynesian stopped and pointed to the solar farm.

"Let's go look," I said.

As we veered off path I noticed the change in gravity. It was getting much more difficult to walk. We found it easier to hop the farther we got away from the cavern airlock. A structure stood partway out in the solar field. It looked like a relay station or maybe a service station. It was the perfect place to wait. We could see the landing pad and I thought I spied the Media and Communications Center. I climbed up on the edge of the relay station to get a better look. I could definitely see the antenna array.

"This is perfect."

We walked back the way we had come and then moved on toward the Communications Center. Gravity was definitely lower as we approached. We were hopping along. It was near impossible to walk normally. The big guy was definitely more agile than I might have supposed. I'd seen him fight and move around in Great Cavern and I'd seen him traverse the moon's surface. He'd definitely kick my ass in a fight. I was glad he'd become an ally.

The airlock had a big button next to the door. I pushed and it cycled itself through the process. It was big enough for both of us. Once we were inside our helmets let us know the air pressure and atmosphere were good. Before I removed my helmet it said: Ten minutes to full recharge of oxygen and battery.

The airlock led to another tunnel. We followed it down. This one was just a third of the depth of the tunnel to Great Cavern. Gravity still wasn't good, but the tunnel had handrails all the way down to the control room and they made it easier to move.

The room's door slid open as we approached. One thing the designers clearly never anticipated was the need for much security. Once inside the door slid shut behind us. It took a few seconds for the lighting to come up to full power. The room was smaller than the control room in Great Cavern, but it, too, had a secondary break area and a storage room. We made some more coffee and grabbed a food pack from our pockets.

"Computer, show me the camera feeds from Great Cavern, please."

"There are thousands of cameras. Please be more specific."

"Oh, how about the town center, then. Main feeds, especially if there are people around."

It was still pretty early and there wasn't much going on. I looked inside some of the buildings. It was boring and felt voyeuristic spying on people's lives that way. "Cameras off. Is there a schematic of this center?"

"Schematic of the Media and Communications Center accessed."

I studied the images on the wall. It was pretty simple really, surprisingly so. But then, as I said before, they hadn't thought they would need much security.

I looked at the big guy. "Ready for some fun?"

He grinned.

"There's a panel right over there. Open it and rip out the wiring and cables."

It wasn't as easy as that. Getting the panel off was no problem. Killing the wiring and cables took a little more. But it didn't take him long.

"Replace that panel, will you. That way they'll have to look to find the issues."

He did then we both sat back down at the central table. I looked at the Polynesian. "Computer, display the camera feeds from the main part of town."

"Camera feeds are offline."

"How about from the algae farm?"

"Camera feeds are offline."

"All of them?"

"That is correct."

"I think I'll nap," I said.

The Polynesian nodded is head and got up and walked into the break room.

"Computer, alert us in eight hours, please."

"Alert set for eight hours from now."

I had trouble falling to sleep, too much on my mind. A couple hours into our wait the screens began closing and the entire system shut itself down. Earth. A few minutes later the system rebooted.

"Computer, are there any camera feeds available?"

"Camera feeds are still offline."

"Are there any cameras in here?"

"There are three cameras in the Media and Communications Center, all are offline."

I calculated we had at least ten hours. It would take eight to get here and at least a couple to pull together a team. Most likely, they would grab some of the engineers from Olympus. If not, it would take longer to reach us. Knowing the timing of things quieted my mind and I nodded off to sleep.

When I woke the wall screens had been restored. The screens showed open windows everywhere. Earth had tried to go trough the files and software scripts to find the issue with the cameras. It was clear they were frustrated. Physically damaging the wiring was a good decision. They couldn't actually see the issue or look into. They only knew what the problem wasn't.

I walked into the break room. The Polynesian was leaned back in his chair, mouth agape, out cold. I hated to wake him and figured we had a couple hours before we needed to get into position. I let him sleep. The bathroom had a shower next to the storage room so I decided to jump in it. First, I looked through the storage area but couldn't find anything we could use for weapons if they left someone to guard the shuttle. I didn't want to leave anything to chance, but I was oddly calm about facing any security detail that might be along with the engineers.

When I finished showering I found the Polynesian sipping a cup of coffee in the control room, watching the screens.

"Anything moving there, opened or closed?"

He shook his head.

"Good. I think that means we've got around an hour before they arrive, if they've sent a team from Olympus. One last job for you, if you're up for it." I smiled. "We need to destroy the system here, including the screens. If the team gets in here we can't have them communicating with earth in any manner. We took their camera feeds out. But there is still something in the hardware connecting with earth."

It didn't take him long. He liked working with his hands, I could tell, and he was clever. They had a transmitter and systems in place to communicate with the satellites around earth, and a back-up.

"Do we need to figure out how to take the antenna offline?"

The Polynesian looked around the room at the mess he had

made and shook his head.

"Computer, can you contact earth?"

"All communications are down."

"You can't contact earth, at all?"

"The transmitter and the back-up are not functioning."

I got something to eat and the big guy jumped in the shower. Time had moved slowly since we had entered the communications center, but now it flew by. We were suited up and walking up the tunnel in no time and things came at me in a rush.

"Hey, I just thought of something," I said. "We need to keep radio silence when they get here. Their suits are like ours, I think, and they may be on the same communication channel. Hand signals only, besides, you talk too much and I could use some quiet."

He stopped walking and laughed out loud. We were standing next to the airlock and I pressed the button.

We hopped out to the solar field and took up a position by the relay station. I tried to get used to the blackness of space, but all I could think of was how vast it was and how insignificant we were. All the local light blocked out the stars that were so far away. My mind told me they were still present, but my senses were squirrelly, disoriented. Behind me was earth and beyond earth the sun. I had spent a couple weeks on the moon—or was it more?—but this place was foreign to me.

I looked down and saw lunar dust all over our feet and lower legs. Something reflected light and caught my eye. One of the maintenance bots was moving down a row of solar panels not far away, quietly because of the lack of atmosphere. Up above the bot, several miles away, I detected movement and saw the shuttle coming into land.

I tapped the big guy's suit and pointed toward the shuttle.

We lost sight of it for a few moments, then it slowly descended over the landing pad. A couple minutes later the bay doors opened and three men got out. We watched as they made their way toward the Media and Communication Center. It was more tiring than I would have supposed making the trek. That might have been from the strange environment more than the effort, but I could tell at least one of them wasn't accustomed to it. It looked like the guy in front was security, even in a suit he had that demeanor. He slowed and stopped when the group was across from us, waiting for the straggler to catch up.

When they stopped I got a good look at their suits. They were the same as ours. At least that part of the plan would work.

We let them get a few yards farther on then headed out toward the shuttle. We had agreed to move quickly as possible so they couldn't double back or reach us quickly enough in case they figured out what was going on.

As we neared the shuttle we saw the other man. He was outside but didn't notice us until we were right on top of him. I gestured to my helmet indicating that communications were down. The Polynesian was behind me to hide his bulk, though the suit covered it pretty well. The man raised his hands. I shrugged as best I could and then reached into my pocket and pulled out the screwdriver. The Polynesian walked around to the left by the shuttle. I could see the man was confused as he watched the big guy lumber by. That made it easy to run the screwdriver into his side before he knew what was happening. He started venting air and buckled over from the pain and panic. The big guy had worked his way around behind him and suddenly smashed a rock into his helmet. The glass didn't break but the helmet buckled from the blow and the seal broke.

I looked the guy over. He wasn't security, just the guy told to stay with the shuttle. I felt bad about killing him, but I wanted off that rock more. He didn't have a chance, really. Who would expect a couple mass murderers to be walking around on the surface of the moon?

We entered the shuttle. It was old like the one we had transported in, but it was in better shape. The seats were nice, the interior almost comfortable.

"Shuttle," I said, taking wild guess, "shut the doors and pressurize the cabin."

The doors closed. A few seconds later my heads up informed me it was safe to take my helmet off.

We entered the flight deck and took a seat. "Shuttle, plot a course to Olympus and take off when ready."

"Course plotted. Take off in sixty-seconds. Please secure all items."

The lack of security was almost comical. Under normal circumstances only authorized personnel were ever near the shuttles. I was concerned security might be an issue and we would have to work around it. Most likely that would mean taking someone with us. But my first assumption had turned out to be accurate. Some things seemed so unlikely they had never been anticipated: things like poets and pirates on the moon.

There was no way to quickly repair the communications center and get word back to earth. The raw materials they needed weren't there. The supplies they brought with them were in the back of the shuttle, our shuttle. It seems they were on a recon mission to discern what the problem was first. Now they were in a difficult situation. They couldn't go into Great Cavern or Fugitive Base, which meant they'd be locked in a small room together for a long time. Eventually, someone might figure it out, or they would be able to make the repairs and communicate with earth. Either way, we had time.

The engines fired, we rocked about a minor amount, then the fusion engine engaged and we said goodbye to the moon.

21

CONQUERING OLYMPUS

Earth grew larger every hour, and my hopes with it. It was difficult to remain guarded, or to quell the anticipation. Olympus was ahead, home of the Gods, the Oligoi. Was it wrong to want to rip it to shreds, to watch it tumble to earth in a blaze of fire? Maybe, but I wasn't certain. Even though there would be satisfaction in its destruction, it wasn't my mission or my intent. I couldn't be certain about the big guy, though. His plans were unknown to me. And he didn't feel the need to share them.

What would happen, I wondered, if the Oligoi fell, if their reign came to an end? I found it hard to imagine. Entire social structures and ways of thinking about the world had been woven and melded into our lives centered on their power, assumptions and illusions so old that they went unquestioned. It may not have been possible, that much change. Humans keep to the path because it is known and comfortable, even if they hate the thorns in their legs and the rocks that cut their heels. Alleviate the pressure for a while, take away the thorns and rocks for a few minutes, give them something else to focus on, and they forget the pain and discomfort. Wars were often more a distraction than a necessity. Inventing an evil to overcome was just a game. Misdirection was the Oligoi's best strategy. Watch the bauble, follow the shiny thing, fear it, capture it, destroy it. Now, relax, you've earned it. But nothing much changed, a few freedoms here, a little extra cash there. But the same order was maintained.

I was reminded that the ancient gods of Olympus died long ago when Emperor Julian of Constantinople was killed in battle against the Persians. All that library time when I was young came in handy occasionally. Perhaps the gods could fall again.

Heading toward earth and angled toward the sun, it was still impossible to see the stars. Earth was suspended in the darkness, afloat in the void, a grand and isolated experiment. I wondered, was money the only way forward for intelligent species? It drove human society and heralded our advancements, including science, but was there a different path? With money, greed, as the root driving force we were bound to the Oligoi and all their iterations back through time—the monarchs, the kings and queens, the feudal lords, and the more modern day bankers and corporate heads. They were the winners in a money-based system. It was their game. They wrote the rules.

Those thoughts were just a mind game to occupy the time between the moon and the home of gods. Then reality snapped into view—Olympus was gleaming and flickering in its geosynchronous orbit. It seemed a lifetime ago that we had been there. During that trip we hadn't been able to see the station on our approach. It was nothing special on the outside, a bunch of boxes and cables and a central hub that was spinning. The central hub was the older section, if I recalled correctly. What I didn't understand at that moment, was how immense it was. We were still a long way out. As we vectored in its size became more apparent.

I expected us to dock at one of the external stations but we were directed into a hangar. The doors to the bay slowly opened and the computer managed a perfect approach and touchdown. There weren't any other shuttles in the bay.

"Are we clear on the plan?"

The Polynesian smiled and pulled his helmet over his head. I looked out the windows as we entered the shuttle bay. Only one man in a suit was in the bay.

"Computer, which way to the communications center?"

"Communications is through the holding area and then thirty yards dead ahead. You will find it clearly marked."

"Thank you." I snapped my helmet into place.

"Shuttle doors opening in thirty-seconds. The shuttle and cargo bay will not be pressurized. Gravity is high enough for stability and your suit shoes are charged."

"Understood. Computer, is there a roster of personnel currently on Olympus?" I asked through my heads up.

"Currently there are only fourteen guests, twenty-three crew, including construction, and seven security."

"Construction?"

"Olympus is currently under construction and closed to guests. Those remaining are here by special remit."

"What about the Fugitive Theatre crew?"

"That section is currently closed until tomorrow when the next guests are expected."

The shuttle doors opened. In the shuttle bay lights were flashing red and the bay doors were already closing. The man in the suit walked toward us. The Polynesian jumped down and began walking away, toward the holding area. He passed the man walking toward me without recognizing him, striding with purpose and intent. I waved the man over.

The Polynesian doubled back and quickly overtook the approaching man. He put a foot into the back of the man's knees and knocked him to the ground and whacked him across the back of his helmet with something hard. Then he grabbed him by the back of the suit and picked him up. As the doors to the shuttle and cargo bay came down, the Polynesian threw the man under them and off into space. He stood and watched as the doors closed.

Once we got to the holding area, the computer gave the all clear and pressurized notice. We quickly stripped out of our suits and stood at the far door that lead to the interior of Olympus, both in our cut off pants and t-shirts. The Polynesian smiled and hit the release button on the door. Two security were waiting on the other side, but they weren't expecting trouble and were unprepared. Their weapons were still in their holsters. I jumped the man nearest me. We wrestled and twisted down the hallway. I heard a weapon discharge, though no idea what type it had been. I wasn't familiar with the weapons used here, but it may have been a charge round similar to the one I had been hit with in The Edge, when Burgess' men came for me.

I got my man in a headlock, raised up and adjusted my grip into a chokehold and then fell to the floor with my back to a wall. He strained and tried to elbow me, caught me once in my injured side and sent jolts of pain up and down my right side, but eventually succumbed.

I looked down the hallway. The big guy's left side had been hit by a charge round, I could tell. I knew that pain. But he wasn't having any problem, and just seconds after I looked he ripped the man's gun from him and smashed it in his face.

I stood and walked to him. "You'll recover quick enough. I was hit by one of them once." I looked behind me. "Think we should clean up?"

He picked up the guard he had been fighting by his shirt collar and practically flung the man into the holding area. I understood his intent and grabbed the man I had fought and dragged him next to the other, my side complaining the entire time. Then we closed the door. They weren't out of the way, just hidden somewhat, but it wouldn't matter.

I pocketed the guard's weapon and walked toward the communications center. Security was right next to it. We stopped outside and I asked, "Need a hand?"

The Polynesian frowned, almost as if I had insulted him, and shook his head. He didn't hesitate and walked into the security offices. Three officers were down. That meant four remained. It was unlikely they were all in the offices. At least a couple had to be out around Olympus somewhere. Two against the Polynesian wasn't fair, but neither was condemning us to the moon.

I debated taking one of the security team's uniforms for myself, but that only meant giving the team more time to discover what was happening and respond. So far, we were unexpected and that was a huge advantage.

I entered communications and looked the place over. A man with thin with white hair, and a woman, taller and younger than him, stood in a glassed in conference room. The room was large and had several cubicles. There was one office door, open, and a door leading elsewhere. I put my head down and started walking toward the man and woman.

As I got close to the door of the conference room I looked up. The woman looked at me again and squinted, then she was overcome with emotion. She had recognized me. I thought I could use that to my advantage. She started to react and lunge for a comm button that was several feet away.

"Don't. You know who I am. What do you think I will do if you try to alert someone?"

She pulled back and I could see her tremble.

"Who is this?" The man next to her asked.

The woman just stared and didn't answer.

"Who are you?" He asked me.

"I need your help. I need to get back to earth on the shuttle I just came in on. And I need it to be done on automatic pilot."

"Who are you?"

"It doesn't matter who I am. Help me, or I kill you."

"I'm calling security!"

"Your security are all dead."

"Computer—"

"No," exclaimed the woman. "Don't. We'll help."

"We certainly will not!"

The man puffed out his chest and tried throw his authority at me. I closed the distance immediately and hit him in the throat, quickly and precisely, with the side of my right hand.

"Don't ever speak to me like that again," I said, as calmly as possible. He grabbed his neck and stumbled, choking. "Next time I kill you, no more warnings." Then I remembered I had the weapon on me. I had spent so long on the moon without any real weapons that I forgot I was in possession of one. It didn't matter. So much of the fight, any fight, came down to acting swiftly and decisively.

I grabbed the man and pushed him into a chair. He was recovering quickly. I hadn't hit him hard. I motioned for the woman to take a seat.

"Settled now? Good." I looked at the woman. "I need the shuttle to take me to earth. Obviously, I can't fly it, but I know it can return on auto pilot."

"It can, but you have to have clearance," she said.

"Is one scheduled to return?"

"No, we have few guests right now."

"I understand. What goes wrong with them, the shuttles? Why do they have to go for repairs?"

"A lot goes wrong," she laughed, "they're old." The man looked at her disdainfully. "Nothing serious, mind you, but we have to send them down on occasion for repairs."

"I need you to arrange that now, with two passengers. No names. Tell them we wish to be anonymous, just a ride along."

"As I said, there aren't many people here now."

"I know, fourteen who are not crew, seven security, and twenty-three construction. If anonymity is an issue, I have no problem choosing one or two and tossing them out an airlock."

The man looked at me in disbelief.

The woman looked at him. "John, this is the Poet of the Moon."

"Poet! Animal is more like it."

I back-handed him across the face. He flew out of the chair and hit the wall behind him. I got up and moved to him. "Maybe I should throw you out an airlock and pretend to return as you."

He held his hands up to his face for protection, blood trickling out of the side of his mouth. I grabbed him by the hair on the back of his head and forced him into the chair. "Hands on the table.

Don't move them."

In the back of my mind I wondered: What were we going to do with the employees? To be safe, I knew we should kill them. But that seemed harsh. This guy, sure. But I wasn't certain I wanted more blood on my hands. I pushed that aside for the moment. I'd have to come back to it after the plans were in place.

I addressed the woman. "Can you make it happen?"

"Yes, actually, it would be easier now because there are so few people here. It's an obvious time to send it down."

"Is that the shuttle," asked the man, "sent to the moon for repairs?"

I smiled at him.

"Oh, my God, what have you done?"

"Nothing worse than was done to me."

The woman asked, "Are you not the terrorist?"

"I am the guy who was set up and turned into a terrorist. But I didn't blow up a factory. Edward Burgess blew his own factory up to frame me."

The man was incredulous. "Why would he do that?"

"Why would I? And where would I get the materials necessary to blow up a building?"

"I saw the interview with the priest, the Merit Analysis," the man practically spit. "You hate the system."

I looked at him and realized nothing I said really mattered. He believed what he was told to believe. "I do hate the system. Does that make me a terrorist? Or a bomber? Bombing a building wouldn't change the system—not now, not ever."

He just stared at his hands.

The Polynesian burst through the door to communications. I waved and he walked to the conference room. "Need help?"

He shook his head.

"Are there more security?"

No, again.

"I'm arranging a shuttle home."

He cocked his head to the side and smiled. "I think I'll stay."

I laughed so hard I thought I would fall off the chair. "Okay, any other revelations?"

He shook his head.

I looked at the woman who seemed confused and awed by the big guy. "I need clothes, nice clothes, so I look the part."

"I can help with that, I'm sure."

"Can you find somewhere for this guy?" I asked the Polynesian. "He isn't to be trusted even a little bit."

He shrugged. The woman and I started walking to the door. "Back in a few minutes."

We walked to one of the apartments on the other side of an entertainment area. She opened the door to the apartment.

"The . . . guest isn't around. And he won't miss anything."

I made her come with me to the bedroom. I didn't trust her either and wasn't willing to let her out of my sight. She was a keen observer. The man's clothes, whoever he was, fit me well, except the shoes, too small.

"I can open one of the retail stores on the way back and get you some shoes."

"That would be good. Think we can get me a PED and a couple smaller items?"

She confirmed she could. As we walked, I asked her, "Who are you?"

"My name is Celia Jackson. I'm the second in command here at Olympus."

"The old gut your boss?"

"No, my boss is home right now."

"You've been helpful, Ms. Jackson, too helpful, almost."

"I've seen what you've endured. I know what you are capable of and I know my own limits. Besides, this is just stuff." She looked around her. "No matter how expensive or rare, just stuff, including the shuttle. There is a great deal of truth in the things you said on that show."

"I don't even know what I said, to be honest. I just talked to keep from going crazy."

She had opened the door to a shop and I pulled a box with my size from a shelf. I slid my left foot into a pair of burgundy colored shoes that matched the suit I was wearing.

"I don't believe you. You were true to who you are. Tell me, were you really set up?"

I shrugged, "I was."

"Answer one question for me Celia. Why do they call me the Poet of the Moon?"

"You don't know? Of course, you wouldn't." The corners of her mouth stretched across her face in a big smile. "One of your talks with the bird, you recited an old Stephen Crane poem. I think it got to people, started them thinking. After that you became the Poet."

I frowned and shrugged my shoulders. "I spent so much time alone and in the library when I was a kid. I was an orphan from age twelve. My mother died in an accident and I didn't have any other family."

We walked along the corridor. It was eerie with the place so empty. "How many people are normally on Olympus?"

"On average, over 350 people are here, but it can go way higher with big events, ten times more. This is unusual. The renovations are necessary and complex. It's been a decade since this place closed down for repairs and renovations. We are only closed for a few weeks, so the timing of your visit is impeccable."

"Do you know Edward Burgess?"

She shook her head. "Not really. I met him once when he negotiated use of the original section for his show. As far as I know, it was the only time he has visited. Are you going to kill him?"

I stopped walking and looked at her. "You are asking dangerous questions, Ms. Jackson. Please stop. I don't want to be forced to do something regretful."

She gave me a wry smile and walked on. She knew I was half joking, at least. But I couldn't answer for the Polynesian.

Now that I was dressed the part it was time to phone home. John, the man with the white hair, was sitting at a cubicle looking uneasily at the big guy.

"Wait here, please," I said to Ms. Jackson and pulled the big guy aside.

"Are you sure about staying?"

He nodded.

"What should we do with these people?"

He looked at the two of them and squinted and puckered his lips. I could tell he had no issues dealing with the older man, but he had reservations regarding the woman.

"We could," I offered, "take out communications after I leave. I think everything is relayed through the main antenna array. I'm going to need a few hours once I get down the gravity well, maybe a day. I don't want anyone to learn about us for a while."

"I saw the access to the antenna array. I can take it offline," he said. It still shocked me that he spoke. "The construction crew might have their own system, though. But I don't care about them. I might even join their crew. I like building things." He shrugged and gave me a smile that was all eyes. "These are the only two people who know that I came with you from the moon."

"Yeah, but I'm guessing you're recognizable."

He laughed. "Not so much with the construction guys. I fit right in. Can we get the woman to assign me to them, or ask them to find work for me?"

"Let me get this straight. We escaped the moon so you can get a construction job here on Olympus?"

He looked at me seriously. "There's nothing for me on earth. So, yes."

"Fine by me. And I think she will do it. Just explain what you want. What about the guy, John?"

"He won't make it. No choice. Don't feel bad. He is part of the problem and why we're here." He looked around. "Olympus—sometimes the gods need to fall. Might as well be us. Just finish the job." He gave me that big smile and we returned to Ms. Jackson and the man.

"I'm ready," I said to them.

"You'll never get away with this," said the man.

I looked at the Polynesian who nodded his head almost imperceptibly.

"What's the procedure, Ms. Jackson?"

"We call it in. The shuttle can automatically exit the shuttle bay and then go to a predetermined point. From there, earth takes over. It's really simple."

"When your guests return to earth do they wear a suit?"

"Not usually, no. It's been more than a decade since we've had an accident. Even the older shuttle you came in on is quite safe."

We made the call. Things went smoothly with earth. They were busy—two other shuttles were in for repairs—but they understood it made sense for the shuttle to go now while Olympus was shut down.

The Polynesian locked the older man in a closet while he and I and Ms. Jackson went to the shuttle bay. He picked up the two men in the holding area and pulled them into the bay with us.

"You certain you don't want to come?"

He smiled, flipped his hands palms up and waved. Once I was on the shuttle they returned through the holding area doors, shut them, and stood watching on the other side through the slit windows. The shuttle bay doors lifted and a bot grabbed the front wheel of the shuttle, maneuvered it around and pulled it to the open doors. The shuttle lifted off. It felt like the thing was moving in slow motion as it exited the shuttle bay.

The moon and Olympus were behind me, earth ahead. Burgess was there, and too, I hoped, was Sarah.

22

INSURRECTION

Sarah had a thought about Clay that made her smile, something all too foreign since he had been sent to the moon. She was sitting outdoor at the same cafe where she had met her father for lunch. Something about the place felt comfortable, familiar even, and she had been drawn back to it. Perhaps because it was so close to The Edge, so close to home.

She thought again about Clay and considered what she knew of him, not the superficial statistics, but the things that defined him. He was fit and athletic, something she liked. He was strong willed and thought deeply about questions most never considered. And when he expressed his thoughts a great deal of confidence was behind them. He was rational almost to a fault and when he cared for something or someone it was deep and unwavering. In that way he might be a poet, she thought. He saw past the surface and peered into the core. She didn't know anyone else like him and his uniqueness attracted her.

The thought was still there, lingering. She flipped through more of the comments on the social networks. Poets inspire lovers and dreamers, they don't insight revolts, she thought. Then she asked herself again: When was the last time a poet led a revolution? It felt good to smile, despite the limited and doomed nature of his situation, their situation. He was a quarter-million miles away but he was making a difference, having an impact. The Murder of Crows revolt was gaining momentum.

There were a myriad number of conspiracy theories circulating regarding the last day. The feeds from Fugitive Theatre were down, something she just learned. The official report was that communications had been lost and the network was working to fix the issue. But few people believed the official report. They saw something more sinister. Several alternate theories had gained momentum and garnered attention. Two caught Sarah's eye and made her think. The first wasn't so far fetched given her closeness to Edward and the lengths he had already gone to eliminate Clay. According the conspiracists, the network was purposely cutting off the feeds because they were afraid of the Poet.

It wasn't really a reach, Sarah thought. If Edward were under pressure from the board of directors it might be a move he would make. Cutting the feeds for a few days might quiet the talk around Clay and the things he had been saying. Clay dying meanwhile might snuff out the revolt before it got much traction. People couldn't rally around the Poet if he were dead. Sarah didn't think he was enough of a threat or hero yet to be turned into a martyr, though she conceded she could be wrong.

The other theory floating around was that the network had sent a team to the moon to hunt down Clay and kill him. When the job was finished the show would resume. Sarah wouldn't put anything past Edward, but that felt too extreme to her, and costly, something he wouldn't do lightly.

The social feeds quickly felt like more of the same, a monotonous drone that never seemed to get anywhere. She flipped to the news feeds and was surprised to find a lot of heated debate centered on Clay and the Murder of Crows protests. Even they were simply rehashing what had been said in the past. They portrayed Clay as someone outside the system, a loner, angry because he couldn't pass the Merit Analysis. He was an orphan who never fit in and it turned him into a terrorist. Rehashed and overplayed, Sarah thought. But the networks were protecting the corporations and church that supported them. Of course they would say that. A few of the hosts softened their response and perspective somewhat, saying Clay never had a chance. He became a terrorist because the system failed him, and ultimately it made him. "Maybe," said one of the hosts, thinking he was making a clever comment, "we all made Clay Alexander. Maybe we are all responsible."

A new thought occurred to her then. Something she hadn't considered before. She could come forward, confess everything, including Clay's innocence and the belief that Edward was behind the bombing. That would damage Edward, and the show, assuming anyone believed her. That was a very real obstacle. The networks could turn the confession against her—The Edge girl made good who couldn't overcome her guilt for leaving her friends behind. It would add legitimacy to anything Edward wanted to do with her and their relationship. They could easily portray her as being out of her mind. And none of them would attempt to look at the evidence. She was sure the evidence, whatever had existed, had already been buried or twisted in ways that would cause her to seem crazy.

As Sarah watched people walking down the street in the late-morning sun she latched onto the thought that leaving Edward, moving out, might be the only option she could pursue. But what if he wouldn't allow it? What if it angered him to the point of acting again?

The thought nagged and persisted, but something in it jolted her memory and she pulled up the doctor's office on her PED and logged in to make an appointment.

How does the trapped man escape? By what magic, or influence, or daring does he turn the tables and slink away the victor? Is there a scenario where he comes off the hero and sheds the outside guilt and buries his own complicity in whatever mistakes have been made? Edward Burgess had no clue but he relaxed somewhat as he entertained those questions and thoughts. Born a Burgess had many redeeming and attractive qualities. The most important, he reminded himself, was that he was one the few who wrote the rules. Regardless of the ruckus caused by the damn Poet—Alexander—the worst thing he would have to endure was the loss of Fugitive Theatre, nothing more.

Any social turmoil caused by Alexander was temporary, easily managed, and ultimately so far below him that its impact would hardly be noticed. There might be some noise from others in the family regarding the changes—the slimmer profits would be seen as a point of irritation, the social freedoms surrendered annoying—but they would only be minor inconveniences in the long run. He could easily make the argument they had been brewing under the surface for some time and that Fugitive Theatre had forced them to be dealt with now and saved them more trouble over the long haul.

He thought of the paintings hanging in the halls of his office building, of the men who had led the company through their own difficult eras. This would look like a minor event to the future. Some might even view it as an important and progressive moment that worked to the benefit of society. Basically, because of his position and resources, this would blow over and pass without any real struggle or disappointment. The thought relaxed him. So what if they raised the Guaranteed Minimum Income a minor amount. Even if they announced a few programs to allow greater mobility into the Cleric class it wouldn't impact him or those in the family. The trivial victories would placate the masses, give them a false sense of victory, and quiet their discontent. Did anything else really matter?

In the meantime, he might just salvage his Fugitive Theatre. It wasn't likely, but stranger things had happened before. Still, it wasn't likely he would ever find another hero like Alexander. He hated the man for that. It wasn't enough that he had slept with his wife. Now the show's success was built around the Poet—who had to die. It was infuriating on too many levels. The only sanity-saving grace in the entire affair was that no one else was aware of the relationship between Alexander, Sarah and himself.

"Sir, Thomas Ulbright would like to speak to you," said Thomas through his PED. "I told him you might not be available."

"It's okay, Thomas. Thanks."

"Thomas, how are you?"

"I'm well, Edward. How is your situation?"

"I'm still uncertain," said Edward. "we have't received a report yet regarding the communications breakdown." Despite his earlier thoughts, Edwards felt a twinge of nervousness when he asked, "How is everyone viewing this?"

"Oh, you know, everyone is true to form. Some are angry because they think it's going to cost them, others don't seem to mind. Quite a few have asked me to speak to you, since they know I'm on the board. They want to know what you are going to do to right the situation."

"How big is the Murder of Crows Protest?"

"It's becoming bigger, but right now it's only an irritation. Personally, I'm not yet worried about it. Truth is, we could snuff it out tomorrow, I think. We know who some of the leaders are. We could turn them into terrorists and lock them all away, if needed. Right now, though, I don't think they have clear goals on what they want. I don't think it will take a lot to keep them happy."

"That's good to hear," said Edward.

"What about the Poet, what can be done about him?"

"I tried to hire someone to solve that issue but it didn't work out how I thought it would. If we have to, I can have Sam fake his death and then not film him any longer. But that would mean taking the twenty-four hour cams offline permanently. The show has a large group of addicted followers. They will have a fit without all day access, and so will the conspiracists. To be honest, I thought Alexander would be dead by now—law of averages."

Ulbright sighed heavily. "As much as I hate to say it, that might be the best solution for us. We might have to take him off air. Can Sam do that?"

Edward thought about it. "He might be able to do it, yes. We can take the cameras offline, that's easy. We control them from here. Faking Alexander's death is more tricky, but Sam can handle it. It'll have to be top-notch. That video will be picked apart."

"Any timeline for the communications to come back online? I don't have to tell you, we look bad no matter what at this point.

Some people are arguing the studio purposely took the show offline because of Alexander. Others are even saying a hit squad was sent to the moon. No one believes there was a mechanical issue, or that it was out of the show's control."

"I know," said Edward. "I can't say when we will be back online without the report and it's overdue now." Edward laughed, "Who knew making the show this successful would cause so many problems?"

"I wouldn't get too down about it. The solutions aren't too painful. The people who will complain are the ones expected, but they always complain. I think they only care for the money they might lose. Let me know what Sam says, will you? And I'll communicate to everyone else where things stand. That's the best we can do at the moment."

"Will do. Thanks, Thomas."

Edward thought about making himself a drink after disconnecting from Ulbright, but decided it wasn't the time and pulled up Sam Verita's information and connected.

There weren't any greetings from Verita. He went directly into the conversation. "No information yet, Edward, sorry."

"Have you heard anything, Sam?"

Verita just shook his head.

"When did you expect to?"

"They are past due. Could be they are struggling with the issue, but they should have contacted me by now. I don't have a clue what is going on. There may be something that has knocked out communications entirely and the shuttle and base are not able to get through. At this time, that's the best guess."

"I take it you have some experts trying to figure it out?"

"They don't understand it either. They say something has to

have happened to the base. We can't access any of the communication logs from here anymore. Everything is offline."

Edward was exasperated. "Okay, Sam. I have something else to discuss. We need to plan ahead a little, just in case. How difficult would it be to fake Alexander's death?"

"I knew you were going to ask me this. Dammit! My biggest concern is the rabid fans pouring over everything we do and discovering it's a fake. They are already trying to invent conspiracies around this."

"I know."

"We can do it. I asked some of the techs about using older footage that we haven't used in the show. We need to make it look like the data came through damaged and spotty, corrupted. That will track with our current problems. We can scrub the footage we use from the database when we're through. If we start on it now we can just barely make it for this week's show, which will be mostly highlights at this point."

"Let's move forward with that. Also, we need to put together a Best-Of highlight pitch for the next couple weeks, just in case."

Verita hesitated, "That would be a lot more believable with the Poet in there."

"If he's dead I don't think it will be too much of a risk. Just don't overdo it, and take out any of the conversations he had with the bird, just the action. Let me know when you hear anything."

Edward disconnected the call and tapped his fingers on the desk. He considered calling Thomas Ulbright again and informing him of the plans but decided to give Sam time to figure out the communications issues.

What was the worst-case scenario? He wondered, but not for long. They could always say complications with the base meant everything was a complete loss. It was space, after all. The show would end, and money would stop rolling in, a temporary loss, but it was always a possibility.

23

ANGRY GOD

The view of the gods invited contemplation. It was a quiet and solitary view. Against the blackness was a blue and green sphere with wisps of uniquely shaped white clouds. The colors exploded against the darkness. And the quiet was deafening, except for the persistent thoughts rattling around in my head, and the occasional ping and knock of the hull of the shuttle. Those thoughts wouldn't subside or recede into the background. I was forced to deal with them.

As the shuttle appeared to float in space in geosynchronous orbit above earth, I asked myself if it was worth it, what I was about to do, what I wanted. I had survived the moon and Fugitive Theatre, something I had no right to expect. Fugitive Theatre wasn't meant to be survived. There were no winners and no one was expected to thrive. It was a death sentence to be executed on earth's lone satellite. The moon had long been inspiration for humanity's fables and lore, including extensive ties to its horror stories. Fugitive Theatre was just another iteration in a long line.

I had played my part. I was done with it, but I had trouble shaking free of it. I was up against its creator, Edward Burgess, and one of the questions I tried to answer was: What type of person makes real something as grotesque as Fugitive Theatre? He was Oligoi. I understood that. They viewed themselves as apart from humanity, our overlords by birth right. But that was just so much bullshit, a lie repeated so many times and in various ways for decades that it had become accepted as truth, so much so that no one ever examined its veracity. It was one of the inevitable downfalls of a civilization built upon money, the rise of the overlord. Those with all the money—all of the resources—were held up high as examples of all we could be, even when that money had been inherited, not earned. But no man got rich by his own devices. An inherent social contract accompanied the accumulation of wealth, or should have. We paid for his products and bought his services. Society played a part in making him rich. Should he also get to write the rules to his advantage regardless of the harm to others? When commerce is the true God, I thought, there is no question who will sit at His right hand.

What of their failures? I still wondered how the same group, the Oligoi, who had led us to such a horrendous outcome—climate change, rising seas, spillover zoonotic diseases, crop failure and disappearance—were allowed to continue leading humanity. I supposed it all came back to the one true god, commerce and money. But how does one group fail so miserably and still retain power, and for such a long time? Was the species so invested in the illusion that wealth equates to "special" that we were unable to see it had become delusion?

And what should be made of their skewed rules? The Merit Analysis was nothing more than a loyalty test, yet so many vested everything they had in hopes of passing it. Becoming Cleric had its perks, but those who passed the test didn't seem any happier to me, and I had been in a position to judge given I had a foot in both worlds. I don't believe the Clerics enjoyed life any more than most.

I pondered what I wanted in returning to that world. What was there for me? Was I looking for a quiet corner somewhere just to pass my days? Or was it only revenge and the chance to bite off the head of the snake that enticed me? And revenge against whom? Edward Burgess, sure, but all the Oligoi? The man who created Fugitive Theatre didn't value human life. He played with it, toyed with it. What of the others? Were all Oligoi like Burgess, so far removed from humanity that they forgot they were a part of it?

Celia Jackson told me on Olympus that my ramblings and conversations with the crow had gotten people riled up. If they were asking questions now—about their positions, about the life we had dreamed into existence—then good, but I wasn't sure I wanted any part of it. Their protests might be real and justified but that didn't mean I had to participate, even if I was the impetus. I knew them. History had always been repetitive. Cut off the head of one snake and replace it with another. Nothing really changed. We don't have the imagination or the desire as a species to effect that much change. I believe I came to that conclusion on the moon. We would rather walk the path with thorns and sharp rocks because it's the path we know. In a maudlin way it was comfortable. I didn't want to be a part of that.

I missed the vibe of human hustle and bustle, the subtle vibrations we made upon the world that moved in our psychic undertow. I missed the connection. I realized I had felt disconnected on the moon, unattached and singular. Even if I was anti-social I still felt the rest of humanity around me. I wanted to feel that again.

Returning to The Edge was impossible, assuming I survived what was to come. I liked my place, the warehouse, but I could find another like it in a new and different area, even in our homogenized world. Miyamoto, my cat, would be fine regardless. He could fend for himself. I liked the neighborhood kid, Tabitha, but I probably wouldn't see her again, either. Whatever was back on earth was going to be a new experience for me. Nothing of my past existed any longer.

I could travel around, I supposed, find odd jobs here and there. It wasn't the worst thing to live that way, an orphan's life, blend in and disappear, listen to the stories told of the Poet of the Moon. How different would the legend become from what I was? Or would the legend stutter and stall and just disappear?

It wasn't appealing, none of it. I found nothing attractive in it, but that was due to my thoughts constantly returning to the one reason I had for returning, beyond revenge against Burgess: Sarah. I had avoided hoping she was still alive. Escobar's brother had said, before I killed him, "The bitch is dead." That might have been talk, Burgess trying to rile me up before I was supposed to die, but I could only say for certain by returning and learning first-hand. I had to find out. I was scared, I had to admit it. I didn't want to learn the truth. The truth held too much pain if the answer was that she was dead. What of the world would be left for me then? I worried for what I would become if that were the case. Who would save me if Sarah were gone?

So, I told myself a story as I sat there looking out upon earth. It went like this.

I met a woman in The Edge as I walked toward home one

day. We got to know each other and I fell in love with her. She was beautiful and smart and engaging. She was everything I thought I would never find or experience, yet there she was, welcoming. She changed my world, colored it in, brightened it and added meaning I didn't understand had been missing until then. And then one day we found ourselves entwined in bed and making love as if we were the last two people on the planet. Did our actions merit my doom? Had I, in that moment, become a terrorist willing to bomb a building and possibly murder innocent people? I admit I was wrong—we were wrong. She wasn't my wife. She belonged to someone else. But was it justified for Edward Burgess to blow up a building and railroad me to the moon for our indiscretion? That answer might depend upon perspective and world view. Once Burgess made the choice and took action, the consequences of his actions had to be accepted. Edward Burgess tried to kill me in his own demented and, ultimately, cowardly way. But he failed. He had laid down the ground rules and named the game. So far, despite his best efforts, I had won. I was still alive—and I was angry.

My turn now.

I folded up my feelings for Sarah and the need to get down the gravity well and set foot again on earth and take a deep breath of its fertile air. I put them away. They weren't needed yet. What I needed to be, still, was the man who survived Fugitive Theatre. I needed to be the mass murderer who took no prisoners and who didn't hesitate to kill when necessary. I had to be as cold as the universe and as calculating as the math that sculpted it.

I had to abandon my humanity, slough it off again, like a piece of dead skin, and emerge as a horror only the moon could conjure. I had to descend from Olympus and exact a harsh toll, even if it was only toward one man. I was an angry god and I had to kill the thing that created me, Edward Burgess. And if Sarah were dead, as I feared, his death would be slow and painful. I was a dead man walking, anyway. What did I have to lose? I had already lost everything.

The shuttle lurched and I felt the engines kick in. Olympus disappeared off to my right, receding away and disappearing beyond the view of the windows. It was only earth ahead now. Nothing else mattered.

24

AFTER THE LOVE

Sarah worked hard all day long to avoid thinking about the awkward and uncomfortable situation that loomed in her evening. She was expected to be home to watch Fugitive Theatre with Edward. It brought on too much anger and frustration when she attempted to view it head on.

Early a.m. she threw on her workout clothes, packed a bag of items she needed for the day, including a fresh set of clothes, and bounced out the door. Security stepped from behind the stone entranceway as she pulled out the driveway. It always angered her to see them. This day was no different. Exasperated, she thought, *Why should anyone need men with guns roaming their property?* "The real question," she said aloud to no one, "is why did I allow myself to get into this situation?"

She turned up the radio, hoping to find some distraction in the pop music or even a retro channel over the satellite network. But every channel was more talk about the tragedy of Fugitive Theatre being down and the talking radio heads wondering when it would all be fixed. She wanted it all to go away, if only for a few minutes.

She voiced the radio off but the quiet was no better. An angry portion of her conscience emerged and belittled her every thought. Apparently, a part of her mind was certain she was useless and to blame for everything it found wrong with the world. *She had done too much. She wasn't doing enough. Clay was just roustabout from The Edge who would have never amounted to much. She was blowing it—everything, with Edward, with her opportunity. Her parents, even her father, would be ashamed of her eventually. And why haven't you left him yet!* She was conflicted. Each indictment had its counterpart, its polar opposite, equally true and powerful.

When she finally got to the gym she put on her favorite playlist, turned her earbuds up louder than normal, and pushed herself as hard as she could during her workout, weights first, then some light stretching before jumping on one of the machines. A few awkward gazes were cast her direction, but she ignored them and pressed harder. The self-inflicted pain felt good, cleansing. An hour after she had started on the machine—shirt drenched with sweat and breathing hard—she plopped down onto the floor to stretch and calm down.

The conflicted thoughts were gone, siphoned off with the effort and the sweat that poured from her. Then, before her mind had time to torment and strangle her again, she found she was angry at the world. She raised up after a few moments, wiped down the machine she had been using, and marched with purpose toward the women's locker room. She wasn't aware of it at the time, but a plan was forming. She didn't accept that she could do nothing.

She sat by the large window overlooking the street in a deli just outside The Edge less than an hour later. Menache's Deli had long been one of her favorite places, especially when she wanted to get away from everyone and find a quiet place to think. That was odd, really, the deli was busy with people coming and going, like the street before it. But the sounds and smells and quality of light through the window blurred together and wrapped her in a cocoon of isolation. The world wrapped its fingers around her here and made her feel safe. Besides, the food was better than most places—even if it was algae-based—and John, the big, fat owner, greeted everyone with a warm and friendly smile in his white smock that was stained with his efforts on their behalf. She was certain he recognized her and knew who she was, but he always treated her the same as anyone else.

She viewed her problems as two-fold: she had to deal with Clay's situation, or rather her view of it, and she had to figure out how to extricate herself from Edward. Clay's situation was impossible. She knew that. But she had to determine how to deal with it so that it didn't rip her apart. Edward was different. Somewhere her mind had churned through the gears and processed their relationship and determined she was out, leaving him. She didn't remember thinking it through, only that it had been decided. She could get out quietly. Or she could make a lot of noise. She wasn't certain she could live with herself if she surrendered quietly. That would feel like a betrayal of Clay. Besides, having an affair was far less of a crime than framing a man and sending him off to the moon to die. But there lay the conundrum. She needed evidence.

The hard workout had left her ravenous and thirsty. She finished the sandwich, soup and iced tea quickly, then pulled a bottle of water from her bag. She pushed the dishes back and logged onto her PED. She had messages from friends and from her father, but she didn't want to look at them. Instead, she logged onto the social networks and flipped through the hot topics. The Poet and Fugitive Theatre were all over the feeds. The longer the cameras were down the more traction the conspiracists garnered. Today's specialty was that the Oligoi had sent a strike team to the moon and that Clay was still holding them off and the cameras would be down until they finally caught and executed him. It was an interesting thought. But she didn't believe there was enough unrest to warrant it, or that Clay had that big of a following, though she wasn't certain of that. Plus, the potential exposure was too high. Edward and the family valued privacy too much for something so rash.

As she scrolled through more of the comments she was surprised how openly some people were expressing themselves. Some brave soul even quoted from the banned book The Oligoi Wars: Give them just enough to believe they own their freedom, no less and certainly no more.

Freedom was a great illusion, Sarah thought. We are all trapped and tied to so many weights and pegs in the ground that freedom was nothing more than vapor. Her own situation was the perfect example. As a member of the "family" she should have more freedom than any of the people walking down the street, or living in The Edge. Yet, she sat there feeling trapped and the one thing that was missing, that she longed for, was freedom. She sighed and reminded herself she was there to remedy her circumstance, to whatever degree she could.

Another headline caught her attention. Tonight's episode promised to be a blockbuster. Thousands of comments that swirled around the most predictable outcomes. What, wondered Sarah, was Edward up to? Edward had to have a hand in leaking the information about the evening's show. She thought there would be a rerun from previous footage. With the cameras down that made sense. But she knew Edward well enough. He had to have something planned. Her anxiety raised a few levels. She felt flushed and stared out the window and watched the glitter of sunlight on the shiny moving things on the wrists of passersby, and the glinting chrome on scooters as they moved up the road, and the flash from doors that opened and closed. Shiny objects, bait, like little freedoms that spoke of bigger things never realized.

Then she thought of Clay again and the awkward and uncomfortable situation to come in the evening. Perhaps she should just not show up, leave now, find somewhere to stay for a few days and get her thoughts straight and her plans clear. But that would be an alert to Edward and he had already proven he had no issues hunting her down.

No, her path was clear, she realized. It was to confront him, lay it all out there and demand they split up and go their separate ways. He would fight it, she was sure. But eventually he would give in. She could already hear him talking to some of the other Oligoi: "You can take the girl out of The Edge, but you just can't take The Edge out of the girl." So be it, she thought.

"Everyone has worked hard and fast to meet this deadline, Edward. I can't tell you how great the team has been, even the guys I had to pull in from outside worked well with everyone. It cost us, a lot, but it was worth it."

"Very good, Sam." Edward was confirming with Sam Verita that Alexander had been killed off. They had just been able to finish in time for the evening's show. He didn't want to leave anything to chance this time. He wanted advance confirmation that the job was done. He felt relieved to hear Sam say it.

"About the other problem," continued Verita, "we still haven't had any contact with the team that was sent to the moon. Now, something else has popped up."

"Something else?"

"Yeah, we've lost contact with Olympus. Olympus is closed right now, as you know, and only a skeleton crew is working up there. But we haven't been able to reach them. It worries me. I put some feelers out to the guys I know who might have other information, but haven't heard anything back yet. No one seems worried, but it feels odd to me. One of the guys here thinks there may have been a solar event or something similar that caused the outages."

"Solar event, like a sun spot? Wouldn't we notice that here, on earth?"

"I don't know, maybe. Our atmosphere protects us from a lot, but I'm no expert. I'm trying to get answers, but so far nothing."

"Okay, keep me informed as soon as you hear anything."

Sam sighed and paused a beat, then asked. "What are we going to do with the property when all this is done?"

"Fugitive Theatre—I'm not sure, Sam. If we can keep a chunk of the audience, and I think we will, it might worth continuing. Otherwise, we need to regroup and figure an alternate plan. I'd love to hear any ideas you have."

"I just want the cameras back online. If we can get them back I think we can salvage the show. It's still a good brand."

"I don't disagree, but you are correct, we have to get the cameras back. Tilda Hogue wants to shut it all down, but she always wants that until the money rolls in."

"Well, I'm just glad you get to deal with that." Sam laughed.

"The team are combing through the archives already to put together the next show. We'll have a good plan over the next couple days."

"Sounds good. Talk to you soon."

Edward sat back in his office at home and twirled the small amount of liquor in his glass. Too many unanswered questions occupied his mind. He had to be patient and wait for the answers. If they got the cameras back online and things were normal Fugitive Theatre would move forward. If not, if something serious had happened, then they would need an alternate plan. That was a quarter-million miles away. The only certain thing was that he had killed the Poet of the Moon. Alexander had been an unsolvable paradox in his life. He was responsible for the show's success. And Edward hated him for that. By killing him he could have just killed the show. Record viewers gone. Record profits gone. Too bad it couldn't have been Mann, he thought. He could have worked with Mann.

He lifted his drink and watched the caramel colored liquid swirl around the glass. "To forgotten poets," he said, then finished off the drink.

Sarah was watching the wall screen and sitting on the edge of the couch with a blanket over her legs when Edward entered the room. He hadn't heard her come home. She looked beautiful to him. He hoped they could get past this time and move forward again. His deep need for an heir flared up in his stomach again, causing him to flinch and think twice about the drink he had poured.

Fugitive Theatre was just beginning. Sam had stuck with the same opening graphics as the show before, the credits and intro without Alexander. But that was as far as he went. Alexander was in the show quite often in first half, usually from a distance. It was a recap, The Rise Of The Poet, almost. Alexander had been in a few minor scuffles that hadn't been shown before and they were used in the first half of the episode. The second half was different. A story had been built with some of Escobar's men, pieced together segments that made it look as though they were hunting down the Poet or waiting to see the outcome of the fight with the Escobars. Edward was certain most of it had to be computer generated, but he couldn't detect anything that would lead to that conclusion. By the midway point of the second half the Poet was being stalked, that much was clear. Sam had rehashed the fight with Escobar and shown Alexander leaving by himself, footage no one had seen before.

The last part of the show couldn't have gone better. Alexander was known to use the lake to get to and from his home. Verita's team had put together a great battle between two of Escobar's men and Alexander just he was trying to enter the lake and then swim to the wall. Escobar's men had been waiting in ambush after the fight by the housing unit. The men battled fiercely. Bloodshed was everywhere. One of Escobar's men was seriously hurt. Alexander had caught him across the temple with a rock.

The other man was wearing down, but he wasn't quitting. The two men hit and wrestled and grabbed anything they could in the small wooded area before the lake. Alexander pulled a low hanging branch from one of the trees and wrapped it around the other's neck. It looked as though he would choke the man to death. Somehow, with blood and sweat and the sounds of the battle flying around, he slipped free and swiped at Alexander as he got away. Alexander's side was cut and bleeding badly. Nice touch, thought

Edward. His side cut had been known. That added a degree of authenticity to the fight.

The fight was a standoff, the two men face to face ten yards apart, both breathing hard and bent over at the waist. Alexander was close to the water. "Not today," he said, and dove in the lake and swam to the wall of rock.

At first Edward was confused, almost angry. The show was about to end and Alexander was still alive. Then the video started going haywire, interference caused the picture to jump, the images pixilated and lost definition. Alexander was climbing the wall, as he always did. The cameras tried to follow him but the picture cut in and out and the quality slipped. A few moments were grainy and then black and white.

It appeared as though the feed was degrading as Alexander traversed the wall. One hundred feet up something fell toward him. It bounced and spun and caused rocks to begin flowing downward. Alexander saw it too late. One of the rocks careened straight into his head, knocked him from the wall while the camera tracked his fall. His unconscious body hit the wall toward the bottom and then skipped out into the lake. The dead body bobbed in the water in the low resolution footage. The camera feed was getting worse, but Alexander's fate was clear. The show ended with him face down in the water as the scrambled video faded into a commercial.

Edward had to hand it to Sammy. It was brilliant work and they had told a plausible story. Unless the geeks found mistakes in the video, the Poet was dead.

"Damn," said Edward, softly.

Sarah got up and walked past him.

Sarah was beside herself. She couldn't breathe, short rasps of breath in and out. Her chest tightened and her hands were clammy. She made her way to the bedroom and then collapsed on the bathroom floor, kicking the door shut. Then she started crying.

She wanted to believe that Edward had somehow faked it, created Clay's death just to kill him off the show, but she wasn't able to convince herself that was true. Clay had become too important to the show. Edward had always put money and profit first. She knew he had to hate Clay for becoming the show's driving force. Maybe he had had enough and put an end to it. Or maybe, she thought—and the tears started flowing again—Clay had actually been killed.

She didn't want to face that. She thought she was prepared for it. His death was inevitable. Still, none of that had lessened its impact. She felt nauseous again and reached for the toilet.

Some time later she considered killing Edward. It wasn't in her and she didn't think she could will it. She might hire someone to do it, but then realized she wouldn't even know where to start. Then she started dismantling the events of Clay's arrest, the bombing and its aftermath. Was there any evidence she could uncover to use against Edward? He didn't do the work himself. He had to hire someone. She might find information in his personal cloud or on his PED. But even if she did, he was Oligoi and would be protected. That's what they did. They didn't play by the same rules. They wrote whatever rules they wanted.

She realized he would bury her. But, she figured, she was already dead with the way things stood. Maybe the best approach was a long game. Collect as much evidence as she could and find a way to release it.

Sarah thought of Clay and the first time they met. She knew right then he was different. They were connected. She didn't want to admit it at the time, but it was there. Then she curled up on the floor in the bathroom and replayed the events after they had met, including the time in his home and the afternoon of lovemaking. Eventually, she cried herself to sleep.

25

AND THEN I WAS DEAD

The descent from Olympus was long. The near-earth orbital wasn't as close to earth as most would expect or believe. Given how large it can appear in the night sky that made me realize just how big it was. It was built to house the Oligoi if another major pandemic struck, a backup to all their protections on earth, at least in part. I also believed it was a reminder to the rest of us living in places like The Edge that we weren't like them, that they were different from us, hanging like diamonds against the darkness, humanity's jewels. I've seen two small sections of it—one impressive, the other not so much. But as Ms Jackson had said, it was all just stuff.

The same could be said for Fugitive Base on the moon. It was an impressive feat and the areas under Great Cavern were a marvel, as were the autonomous robots that managed the base and my crow friends. But then again, I had escaped and disabled and disrupted the whole thing without much effort. I put that down to the hubris and arrogance of its builders. I also chalked it up as another proof that the Oligoi were still bleeders and members of the human family. My opinion was that they were a bastard step-child, but I was bent like that. They could have just been the poor third cousin most of us never met or missed. They were barely part of the average person's life as individuals, most were part of a group of abstract things.

How much longer would they remain human? I wondered. The crow was clearly an experiment in genetic expression and enhancement. I was certain they had bigger plans. Maybe they would adapt to be able to survive on Mars where they could rule us from afar as Gods.

As the shuttle approached earth it moved into orbit. I saw satellites and bits of space junk as the shuttle angled toward entry. For the first time since I had initially been shot into space I was nervous. Things were getting real.

A rumble preceded the onboard computer announcing: "Fasten your safety harnesses and prepare for re-entry in sixty-seconds."

I strapped in and took a quick look around. It felt odd not to have a suit and helmet on, but Ms Jackson was almost indignant when I had asked her about it. A vibration ran from the front of the shuttle to the back. The cockpit heated up a minor, but noticeable, amount. Earth grew large through the cockpit windows.

My mouth was dry and I felt like peeing. Nerves. I wondered if it mattered if the shuttle burned up on re-entry. No one would ever know then what had happened to me. I would be more forgotten space junk. Then I focused on Burgess, gripped the sides of the chair a little tighter and held on. The shuttle went through several maneuvers that were the scariest part of the descent.

The view below was remarkable, what I could see of it. The

old North American continent loomed, vastly redefined from the old maps I had studied as a kid in the library. Later, as the shuttle dropped from the sky, I could see remnants of one of the cities that had been swallowed by the rising seas. Then, like it was nothing more than a commercial flight from New Philly to New Houston, the shuttle emerged from the clouds and glided downward.

I started to worry about readjusting to earth's gravity. Gravity on Fugitive Base was near that of earth, but I was worried—even with the workout regimen I had maintained—that I was going to have trouble adjusting to the added weight.

The shuttle glided into New Houston and touched down without any issues. Before anyone opened the doors I scrambled to the passenger area and took a seat. The shuttle came to rest, then lurched and began moving again. It was being towed.

I straightened my tie and brushed off my suit. I told myself I was one of them, an Oligoi, returning from a quick trip. I had grabbed a briefcase before leaving Olympus. I thought it would be good cover. I knew some of the Oligoi liked to carry them around. It gave them a retro look they liked. I had seen it in photos and advertisements.

When the shuttle stopped the bay doors lifted. I was ready. A set of stairs was wheeled up to the edge of the opening doors. I stood and waited. The shuttle popped and pinged. The sunlight was brilliant and I was unaccustomed to the glare.

"Sir," said the man who had wheeled the stairs into place.

I nodded and walked down. I felt a minor amount of weakness, but overall I was good. I was happy I had kept up the exercises when I was on the moon. The sun was really difficult to handle and I squinted even when looking away from it. The light on the moon had been filtered in Great Cavern and I hadn't spent time looking out the windows in the section of Olympus I had been on. Thinking back, I realized the windows I had seen were probably just cameras and wall screens to protect against radiation.

I knew if they wanted they could make portions of Olympus appear to be a platform in space. They didn't need actual windows.

I started to walk to the large hangar but stopped and asked the man if there was a locker room. He pointed without looking back to me and said, "Door to the right. Locker room is just down the hall."

As I walked down the hall another man came toward me. I was afraid he might question me. I put my finger to my ear and tapped. "I don't really give a damn what you think," I said angrily. "I'm not doing it. Is that clear?"

I stormed past the man as if I had more important things to deal with. No one is more afraid of the Oligoi than Clerics, always so worried about losing the meager things they have. They'd do anything to avoid confrontation. I stopped several feet after passing the man and turned around. "One moment, please," I said to the unidentified person I had been speaking to and addressed the man behind me. "Thank you for the lift. I appreciate it. What is your name?"

"Um, Charles, sir."

"Well, Charles, nice job and thanks, again." I nodded my head started back up with my imaginary conversation and walked away.

I wasn't certain what I was looking for in the locker room. My plan had been to find a ride across the interior of the country, probably in one of the self-drive semi trucks. They were required to have a human rider along with them. What I needed for that was another set of clothes or a reason to be there. I searched several lockers but didn't find anything I thought I could use. I was considering a different mode of travel when I finally came across a locker whose contents fit my needs. I was going to pose as security.

I pocketed what I needed and then snuck out of the locker room. It was a slow day with very few people around. That made sense with Olympus officially closed. Security was focused on incoming traffic, not someone leaving. Cameras were everywhere, though. I didn't want to leave an easy trail if it wasn't necessary. I laughed to myself about that, knowing what I was about to do. I found an empty conference room with a window that looked out toward the front entrance and reassessed the situation. My choices were limited.

I always knew there were some risks I would be forced to take. Using any of my bank funds could tip off Burgess or the authorities. I thought it would be a long shot that they were monitoring my accounts. I also didn't think they would drain any of my accounts—not yet, anyway. It hadn't been that long since I had been just another guy from The Edge.

With security and the cameras I couldn't wear a hat, that would look wrong with the way I was dressed and draw attention to me. So, I donned the sunglasses I stole from the locker and pulled out the PED I had acquired on Olympus and strode confidently out the front door, the briefcase in my other hand. Act like you own the place, I told myself as I looked at the blank screen on the PED. I needed to get away from there as quickly as possible.

The two men at the security station nodded as I approached, but they didn't pay close attention otherwise. I stopped before them and asked, "My ride is delayed. Is there a coffee shop nearby?"

"How long delayed, sir?"

"Can't say. I'm tired of staying here and just want to sit somewhere. I can re-direct them to pick me up anywhere." I smiled.

"Take the train," he pointed across the road, "the northbound one. Second exit is a really nice shopping area. You'll find everything you want there."

"Thank you, gentlemen."

"Sir," asked the second man, "I don't remember you coming in earlier?"

I grinned, "Just came down from Olympus."

"Yes, sir," he said. "Good day."

As I crossed the street I saw the train coming and hurried to catch it. Once aboard, I stared out the window and watched the guards. This felt like the weakest part of my plan, but it appeared to pass as routine. Nothing was amiss with the guards. The train lurched and began moving and I felt a huge weight lift off my chest.

I looked around. I was back on earth. I felt the gravity drain on me some, but that could just as easily have been nerves. The place looked different, older, worn and tired. It had lost some of its appeal. Civilization tasted stale, smelled rotten and sounded like a wail against the darkness. Only a couple people were on the train. They, and those I had interacted with earlier, were blind, deaf and living inside their own heads. Nothing would change their world. I wasn't certain if I had been like them before I was shot into space or not, but I didn't want to be them now. I wanted to be more aware.

The shopping area came up quickly. I waited and watched until the last second, then hopped off the train. This was a nice area and I fit right in with the way I was dressed. I may have been too well dressed, but that had always been the case when I lived in The Edge, too. I felt comfortable.

I walked toward the station entrance and looked for a map. Another stop similar to this one was a block over. It ran east and west. In case my accounts were compromised I needed to get away quickly.

I found a bench on the periphery of a large courtyard before the multi-level shopping and dining area, took a seat and started up the PED. It was new so I had to go through several start up protocols but finally signed in. I used an alternate login. I had two. The one I was using on this PED was old. There wasn't really any protection in it, but it felt safer. I downloaded the banking app I used and opened it. Then I thumbed the screen and entered my passcode. It took a second to access my personal files.

My accounts were all there and none of the money had been touched. Still, they could have a flag on it. I turned off the PED immediately. Again, they could easily monitor where I had logged onto the system from and trace the address. But it was still safer than leaving the PED on. That would have given them a definite location down to a few feet. Now I had to act quickly. I found a men's store and bought some casual clothes, including a hat. Across the way was a quick mart and I purchased a drink and a few items to eat. I pushed the food and drink into my briefcase. It was empty, anyway, just a prop for disguise when I left the shuttle. Then I marched across the courtyard and up an escalator and took an outdoor table at a restaurant on the mezzanine, somewhat hidden behind a tree but with a clear view to the places I had just shopped. I ordered something to eat and drink and then waited.

Nothing happened. I was nervous and pretended to read something on the PED as I waited, just a guy having a meal by himself, something I was accustomed to doing. The waitbot stopped coming by after a while, only showed up to refill my drink when it got low. People came and went, shoppers and others with jobs in the area. After an hour of quiet I called it. I was confident my accounts weren't monitored. It wasn't likely they would have been. My case was closed and the police had never really opened an investigation on me. They didn't need to. Burgess gave them everything they needed. But Burgess could have monitored my accounts if he suspected anything. But why would he do that when I was on the moon? It did surprise me, though, that my accounts hadn't been frozen or seized. That would have been on Burgess, too. He had other things to worry over. I was just a prop to him.

I paid for the meal and walked to the eastbound train platform. It felt good to walk in the sunshine and feel the breeze on my face. The train was due in a couple minutes so I sat on a small wall near the platform and took out the PED and turned it on. I was looking for an industrial area where I could find a ride. Specifically, I wanted a refueling stop, someplace the big trucks had to plugin for a few minutes, or allow their human drivers time to relax. The rules required the trucks to be off the road, inspected and down for several hours each day, a remnant from days when men actually drove the trucks.

I was feeling better about my prospects, but still guarded. My nerves didn't relent and my stomach turned, possibly from the food. It was different from anything I had had in a while.

It was only a twenty minute ride so I turned off the PED and looked out the windows. I wanted to do several things on the PED but it would have to wait. The homogenized landscape could have been anywhere. I was heading to the fringe of New Houston, but it could have been anywhere else. The topography might change somewhat, but the human-built things were carbon copies, machine stamped or printed for efficiency. The world seemed void of art or inspiration. I hoped, as I sat there on the train leaving the gray cityscape, that there would be areas of nature along the journey east, trees and grass and water without human encroachment.

It was a long-shot, but still I hoped. Something in my soul longed for it.

Shortly before my stop I logged onto the PED and pulled up TRANSEC and looked for any information that might be useful. Transportation Security wasn't a well known agency but the truckers would be aware of it. Whenever there were shortages of medicine for the new spillover pandemics a TRANSEC rep would pop up and talk about fending off attacks on the truckers. Somehow the terrorists wanted to keep the cure from the people who might suffer from the new disease of the month. I thought it was a bunch of hot air, lies and subterfuge. Now, I thought I could use it. They listed a couple recent attacks, but nothing serious. I had time to invent a backstory.

The train stop wasn't too far from the refueling center so I walked and enjoyed the chance to be out in the open. The sun's glare wasn't as intense and the glasses helped a lot. I was tired and figured it had to be a mixture of nerves and the effects of gravity.

It was a typical refueling center with trucks lined up alongside each other and the plugin chargers, a building with retail, a restaurant and bathroom facilities, including showers. I entered the restaurant and took a seat so I could see people coming in and leaving, as well as those at the retail checkout. People came and went. Some of them were characters and I found it entertaining. I decided I wanted to avoid well known people. They were easy to identify because lots of people would wave and say hello to them.

The first guy I targeted was going the wrong way. I thanked him for his time and then left him to get on with his trip.

I found a younger guy traveling alone who hadn't said a word to anyone the entire time he had been there. When he got up to leave I followed him. "Excuse me," I called out when he neared his truck. Then I flashed the identification I had stolen from the locker. "My name is Stan Brandt. I'm with TRANSEC."

His eyes lit up, worried, a good sign for me. "Yeah?"

"No need to worry. In fact, I'd like your help."

"How can I help you guys?"

"Where are you heading?"

"East—all the way east, I'm going up to New York."

"Upstate?"

"Yes, sir."

"Long trip," I grinned.

"Pays the best and I don't mind."

"I understand," I said. "Are you familiar with the reports of terrorism against some of the trucks recently?"

He frowned and tilted his head. "Always something going on. I haven't seen any myself."

"Well, that's good," I said. "We are worried something might happen along your route. TRANSEC has assigned several guys like me to ride along with drivers like yourself to observe. I'm not going as far as you, but would you mind if I tag along for a while?"

"Um, no, I don't care." He looked a bit perplexed. "You sure you're going to be comfortable like that."

I laughed and held up the bag. "I have other clothes."

He was a nice guy, trying to figure out his place in the world. He didn't have anywhere to live, other than on the road in his truck and the occasional hotel. He wasn't close with his family and didn't have many good friends, said he wanted to see the world before finding some place to call home. It worked perfectly for me and I could relate to him.

We settled into the long drive and the conversation petered

out and became a comfortable quiet. I decided to login to the PED then and do some research. The first thing I discovered, quite to my surprise, was that I was dead.

26

THE HORNETS NEST

It isn't easy overcoming the shock at being dead. Words can't describe the way reality warps and bends before you. One minute your heart is beating, you can feel sweat trickle down your back against the hot seat, and you sense the energy of the person next to you, then it all disappears and you feel like a discarded paper wrapper, human detritus. But, but, but, I wanted to say. The brain knows the rational truth, but emotions come into play and knock everything askew. Rationality, I found, eventually wins out. Stick with it long enough and other qualities blossom, including a new sense of freedom. For the second time in a very short while, I was going to re-invent myself, become something different to survive. I really wanted to choose a name for myself and I wanted that name to be Anonymous. But something told me it would attract too much attention.

It dawned on me gradually, the ramifications of being dead. I could move freely about as long as no one recognized me. All I needed to do was let my hair grow longer and change where I lived and no one would be the wiser. As far as Edward Burgess was concerned, I could move freely toward him. Without the communications from the moon, he wouldn't suspect I had returned. I felt confident the Polynesian would take care of Olympus. People only talk to the dead. They never go looking for them. With Burgess responsible for my fake death he couldn't tell anyone. And by the time it was discovered what had happened on the moon and Olympus it would all be over. Either he would be dead, or I would.

I watched the death scene on Fugitive Theatre several times. It wouldn't register. I knew what they had done. It was all computer generated, but it felt almost real to me. The graphics were good, too good. I couldn't tell they had been faked.

I looked at the guy I was hitching a ride from. "You ever watch this—Fugitive Theatre?" I flashed the PED toward him.

"Sometimes, not really my thing, though."

"Mine either. What do think about this guy, the Poet? Think he's dead from a fight, or did the Oligoi go after him? Helluva lot of people are angry about it on social media. Might just be a bunch of conspiracy theorists, though."

"We never get the truth, you know. We only know what they want us to think. Doesn't matter if he's dead or alive, really. Look what he's done—a lot of sleeping people are waking up. I'm not sure if that's good or bad, but he definitely has stirred the hornets nest, if you know what I mean."

"Yeah, right."

"Of course, they could have turned him into something bigger by killing him. People don't like it when their heroes die."

I sat back and thought for a few minutes. Latent rage can be volatile when someone kicks at it. In its eddies are festering wounds and ideas that haven't been able to germinate and flower before. They were things that stayed just beneath the surface. Social change was often like that. It simmered under the surface waiting for the right time to boil over and express itself. Perhaps that's part of what I had done, unintentionally, of course. I still believed what I had thought earlier. That no matter how hard and far that hornets nest was kicked, the changes would result in more of the same. A few extra freedoms might be won, more jobs and pay, but nothing really new. We weren't built that way. We liked keeping to the path. We were good at placating and convincing ourselves we had won a larger victory when reality was different. In the end, we wouldn't destroy the hornets nest. We'd only kick it a little farther along the path.

That led me to the social networks. I had never participated in them, but I had an account. I was shocked by what I found there. I didn't remember a time when people were as outspoken against the Oligoi and the church as they were now. Suppressed anger surfaced in the online comments. Maybe the driver was right, the hornets nest had been kicked and people were speaking out.

The truck rumbled down the highway. We moved from the fringes of New Houston to the country. The countryside didn't change much, smaller towns and communities that were extensions of the city, so many people packed into the smaller landmass. Nothing had its own character, only the land differed. When the seas rose and the old coastlines disappeared many people reappraised where they wanted to live. They moved in massive numbers to places like Cincinnati and Wichita and Des Moines, away from the coasts and the fear of volatility, toward something more solid and permanent.

Places that had once been smaller cities became burgeoning metropolises in the new world. And they acquired old problems like over-crowding, resource shortages and increased crime rates. It appeared to me, traveling through it now and observing from a distance, as if humanity were desperately trying to survive. We weren't creating the world any longer. We lacked style and flair. Confidence was missing. It was easy to understand how the Oligoi and church could step in and offer a future with structure that seemed appealing. It was stable and familiar enough for most, another step along the path. That was all most wanted from life—safety and stability.

Hours passed monotonously, sunshine then rain and back to sunshine. At dusk I felt like we were riding in place with a background looping over and over around us, a cheap old cartoon with low budget and forgettable art. The new neighborhoods were cheaply printed homes, row after row of them. As the sun sunk in the sky and the color drained from the landscape I withdrew from the scenery. "Where is art in this modern world?" I asked absent-mindedly.

"Eh?" My ride looked up from what he'd been reading, then out the window along my gaze. "We gave up our right to it, or lost the energy for it."

"You think the Clerics have it any better?"

"I think art is a perspective more than a thing, you know. It's an attitude toward life and an appreciation for it."

I was really beginning to like this guy. "You think we lost that right when we changed the earth?"

"We didn't change the earth. We disrespected it. And no, we didn't lose it. I'm not talking about paintings and sculpture. I'm talking about the art of living, elevating the species. That's what we've lost, everyday inspiration. You're seeing the same landscape I am. Each new community mimics the last, only the names change. Customs and culture aren't any different."

The miles plodded on and darkness settled. I was avoiding something I knew might be painful. I looked at the dark screen on the PED. My reflection ghosted back at me in the glare. I activated the device again and searched for Sarah Burgess. If her death had been reported I was certain I would have lost it right there. If it didn't turn up anywhere it wasn't a guarantee she was alive, either. The Oligoi were notoriously quiet on such things. I'm certain they had their own network for those sorts of announcements.

I scrolled down through the news. There wasn't anything about a death. Again, I wasn't reading too much into that. Then I tapped to view the images. My heart pounded in my chest. I was sweating. I realized I hadn't taken a breath in some time and inhaled a lung-full of air. She wasn't overly photographed and she clearly didn't post a lot on the networks because none of the photos were from them. Her images sifted to the top of the results because of her public profile as a member of the Oligoi. She was breathtaking—beauty and smarts—and somehow she had found herself inside my world and seemed to like it, found it a fit. I thought again of our afternoon of lovemaking, of the conversations we had had in the warehouse. Even Miyamoto liked her. That cat was indifferent to everyone, but somehow he liked curling up with her.

Then guilt and shame slammed me back into the seat in the cab of the truck. I felt weak and tired again. The weight of earth and my actions pressed down on me. I felt at some level I had betrayed her, that I was responsible for our situation. But, I reminded myself, while I might have killed others on the moon—and I was definitely going to kill Burgess—I would never strike her as he had. I wanted to believe Burgess' act had absolved me of our indiscretion but I had trouble making that hold up. Doubt crept over me again. Was I strong enough to move forward and finish the job, as the Polynesian had said?

I had caused her so much harm and trouble. Now I had become a killer to survive Fugitive Theatre. How could she ever see me as the same person she knew? Especially after I'd murdered Burgess. To atone I might have to walk away when this was all done, leave everything, including her, behind. All the same, I wasn't backing down. My resolve held. And looking out upon the dreary lives as the truck rolled on I felt that conviction deep down. It was my way of hitting out at the system and all its inequities wrong-headedness.

I was tired. I closed my eyes and recounted the day. I had started on Olympus, up among our would-be gods, and now I traveled across the country in a semi-truck—a dead man on his way to a funeral. The hours and minutes of the recounted day stretched into a haze in my mind and then I fell asleep.

"You were out of it."

"I was," I said, groggily. "Where are we?"

"Not far from where you wanted to be dropped, I think."

The sun was coming up. East was a salmon-colored sky. The truck barreled down the highway tirelessly.

"What's next for you?"

I didn't want to blow my cover so I made up a story. "On the outskirts of town I need to get off. My orders are to find a ride back the way we just came."

"That sucks. I always take a couple days after long trips like this. I started in Arizona the day before we met. Takes them a day, sometimes two, to get to the truck and unload it and get me something new. Every once in a while they have something ready to go, but not often."

"Lucky for you. My bosses want us on the road, especially with this Murder Of Crows Protest. They're worried they might do something."

"Lot of BS, that."

"I agree."

The PED showed a light-rail station close to the refueling center outside Philly, my destination. We pulled into it and said our goodbyes. I liked the guy and couldn't have picked someone better to travel with. Most importantly, I had made it across the country without incident. I checked my accounts again but nothing had changed. No one was aware of me.

I thanked the trucker for the lift and he motored silently away, only the tires on the pavement making noise. It was a ten minute walk to the light-rail station. The day was warm and welcoming and I felt refreshed after the long sleep. I had gotten so used to sleeping in strange places—on the ground at Fugitive Base and then the hammock I had cobbled together, then the cockpit of the shuttle heading toward Olympus—the truck cabin felt like a luxury.

As the sun climbed higher in the sky I could tell a change in the weather was coming. I could feel it. The humidity on my skin felt wonderful, something I hadn't thought about in a while. The birds were awake, chirping and singing good morning, but not much else moved. A stray car or truck motored along the roads. The people in the cabins of the their vehicles stared vacantly down the road, a cup of coffee in one hand, some still near sleep.

According to the PED I had to take the train all the way through town and then a short way south, where I would have to switch trains. I tried to plan my approach to the Burgess estate and realized I would pass close to The Edge and considered stopping and going to the warehouse, but someone would surely see me.

I needed to acquire supplies at some point. I had gotten used to fighting without a weapon—aside from the screwdriver I had picked up in the bot maintenance area—that I couldn't envision using one for what was ahead of me. I had lost the fear of facing someone face to face. Besides, I had the element of surprise. And there was added satisfaction to be found in tearing Burgess apart with only my hands. I decided to get to the Burgess place and recon the area and then decide on tactics. There would be plenty of time because I didn't want to attack until late at night.

After stopping for something to eat and purchasing water and some food bars, I found a surplus store and picked up a knife and a used pair of binoculars. I still felt more comfortable keeping things lightweight and simple. Then I took the train as close as I could get to the Burgess estate. From there it was a good walk, but there were a couple parks along the way and much of the distance I covered by using a bike path that snaked between and behind properties.

The area was wooded and I got through a neighboring property to the back of Burgess' estate without detection. By dinner I had created an observation post in a clump of trees and learned that four guards were on duty—two at the main gate that led up the main drive, two who others stayed close to the house and made rounds once an hour. Burgess' property was on seven to ten acres, mostly wooded like the rest of his neighbors. Concealment wasn't an issue. And access was easy. I made a trip around the property looking for security cameras and anything else I might need to deal with, but didn't find anything. The fence was easily crossed at several points because of the over-hanging trees.

The light faded from the day and the temperature cooled off. It was comfortable in the trees. My vantage point was toward a back corner of the property. I hadn't seen anyone come or go throughout the day, but I hadn't paid too close attention. From where I was it was difficult to see the front section of the house, but I could easily see anyone coming up the long drive.

As night settled I waited and tried to keep my nerves and wits from getting away from me. I kept coming back to the same thoughts. Sarah, if she were alive, was only yards away.

27

A LACK OF COMMUNICATION

Once the decision was made a weight lifted and the world was a little brighter. The new sense of freedom found her smiling as she walked down the street, something she hadn't experienced for some time. She wasn't trapped inside her own thoughts any longer, oblivious to the people or events taking shape around her. The world was open again. What came next didn't matter. She was in control and it felt right, as if something missing in her life had been found again.

Sarah pulled her PED from her purse and messaged her dad: *I can't do it any longer. It's not worth it. I'm leaving him.* She was certain he understood. He had been right regarding her mother, too. She would come around eventually. She might need a little time, but she would understand.

Sarah looked at the time on her PED and realized it had been stuck for days in a meaningless and undefined loop. Ever since Clay had been sent to the moon she had been living in a vacuum, a gray, drab nothingness. That was no longer true. The world was in motion again, even if duller because of Clay's absence. Color was leaking in at the seams, sounds and smells, too.

She felt some trepidation about confronting Edward, worried he might lash out again, but she was determined and she wanted to get beyond this—especially if Clay were dead. But she didn't trust Edward or that Clay was dead. Edward could have faked his death, or even the blackout of the camera feeds from the moon. She couldn't estimate how much pressure Edward was under from the board of directors. But if the walk from the park—a few blocks from the doctor's office—was any indication he might be feeling a lot of pressure. Clay was everywhere, or at least The Poet was.

She was early for her appointment and decided to walk from the park, the fresh air might do her good. The park was near The Edge and the doctor's office was just a few short blocks away. Someone had graffitied more of Clay's words on the sides of the buildings she could see in The Edge and a couple in the surrounding area. She overheard one conversation as she passed through the small park—a group of teens—about the blackout of the camera feeds. No one believed the official report. Conspiracy was everywhere. She nearly dismissed the conspiracies until she thought of her own opinions. Even with her inside view she couldn't be certain Edward hadn't been behind the events transpiring on the moon. She wasn't much different from the teens—guessing at the truth.

And that wasn't all: she shared their anger, as well. They were right to question the official line. That thought gave her pause: how many times throughout history had the conspiracists been correct? History is written by the victors, someone had written that long ago. She knew it to be true. The Oligoi version of history was just that; a version of it. There wasn't anything definitive or authoritative about what they said. The events and perspectives commonly taught in schools and passed along through the media and down generations wasn't necessarily objective or final. The world—human history—no matter how one tried to analyze it, was slanted and biased.

All of that brought her to one thought, something Clay had tried to convey to her, and it helped her understand life more clearly. Her journey—anyone's, for that matter—was unique and self-defined. History was just an illusion to provide cohesiveness and a way to navigate forward. Despite her efforts to view the world objectively, at best life and history were just illusions, and at worst a delusion. The only thing that mattered was to make the most of it, deal honestly with the things before her and shield her eyes from the glare of others' motives. With those thoughts in mind, she felt better about her decision to leave Edward.

It was already late afternoon and Sarah was feeling the pressure mounting from the coming confrontation with Edward. She dreaded going home. She got to the top of the stairs leading to the doctor's office and was short of breath and feeling ill again. The only respite she'd found these past several days was during and immediately after she had worked out and sometimes after she had eaten. She paused a moment at the door, gathered herself, then entered the office.

Edward ate a late dinner by himself at the kitchen island, wondering where Sarah was and when she would be home. The dinner was bland and uninspiring. He checked his PED but there weren't any messages so he flipped through some of the news items. There was chatter about The Poet Of The Moon, but most of it centered on the protests cropping up throughout the land.

When he finished dinner he entered his office and decided to finish a few things for work. He sat at his desk distractedly for quite some time, never really able to concentrate enough to finish anything. Eventually, he stood up and walked to the bar and poured himself a drink, hopeful it would help him think more clearly. What came next? That was the tough question. He needed more data. Sam had to come through with news soon. Even though it was late he considered calling him. As he finished his drink his PED chimed. It was Thomas Ulbright.

"Thomas, how are things?"

"Getting fun now, Edward. Nothing really new, though. It has been decided that the protests are becoming too widespread and important. Your poet has made too many allies."

Edward didn't say anything, but he did reach and pour another drink.

"Nice work, by the way, killing him off," continued Ulbright. "But it has been decided something more needs to be done. I'm sure you've seen the protests forming in several cities. The media have framed them as terrorist groups. We also informed the media the protestors will be dealt with harshly."

"What does that mean?" Asked Edward.

"It means there will be arrests and if anyone gets out of line they may be shot. The family doesn't want to mess with this. They want it nipped in the bud. Too much bother for something that isn't too dangerous, if you ask me, but that's what they want."

"Even with Alexander dead they're still worried?"

Ulbright sighed, "Like I said, more bother than I think is necessary at this point. But you know how some of the members are: they see change everywhere and don't like it. Any progress on getting back online?"

"Not yet, no. I'm still waiting to hear from the maintenance crew we sent."

"That's odd, isn't it? I mean, it's been a while."

"It's really odd, worrisome" said Edward. "Oh, and Olympus is down, too."

"I heard communications are down, but there isn't anyone there right now, anyway."

"A skeleton crew and some construction guys, I think," said Edward.

"Do you think it means anything?"

"I can't tell, Tom. It's exasperating. Sam Verita thought it might have been a solar event that caused the communications malfunctions between the moon and Olympus, but I don't know anything about that. I'm still waiting to hear back from him."

"Keep me apprised of the situation, will you?"

"Will do."

Edward poured another drink and sat down at his desk. It was getting late. He shuffled files on his PED and felt the alcohol filter into his system. For a long while he sat there, staring ahead, lost in his thoughts.

Close to midnight his PED lit up. It was Sam.

"Sam, any news?"

"Nothing good, Edward. We can't reach the moon at all. Can't access the files on the system and we haven't had any contact with the team that was sent there. I'd suggest sending another team, but I know how expensive it is."

Edward ran his fingers through his hair and squeezed his head. "Christ! This just doesn't get any better."

"I spoke with my science friends and they said there haven't been any events that would cause the communications blackout, nothing solar and no rocks banging into the moon."

"Any luck reaching Olympus?"

"No," answered Verita. "But something is strange there, as well."

"What do you mean 'strange'?"

"Can't say for sure, again, but it looks like a construction accident."

Edward put his head on the desk. He heard the garage door open as Sarah entered the house, but he wasn't in a place to deal with her. He had had too much to drink and he was already struggling to process everything Sam was telling him.

"Jesus, Sam, we need to get eyes on this right away. We have to figure out what is going on, both on the moon and on Olympus. Find any experts you can and bring them in. Look, we need an all hands on deck meeting first thing in the morning. I want everyone there. Eight o'clock in the conference room."

"Understood. Edward, have you seen the protests forming?"

"I have, some, anyway. Plans are in effect to mitigate any damage and to keep things from escalating. Media will be framing them as terrorists and a police crackdown will hit any of the protests."

"Okay, see you in the morning," Verita signed off.

Edward had heard Sarah come to the office. He knew she had stood in the doorway for a short while as he spoke with Sam. But, thankfully, she turned and left. He couldn't handle speaking with her at the moment. He also knew how much she hated it when he drank.

He poured a new drink then stayed at his desk with his head resting in his hands and arms for some time, eventually falling asleep for a couple hours. Something startled him from his sleep. He rose and staggered to the bedroom. Sarah was curled up on the far side of the bed. He wanted to slide over to her and put an arm around her but, despite the alcohol in his system, knew it was a bad idea. Besides, he was still tired—the weight of the day's events and the alcohol had taken a toll—and he fell asleep almost as soon as his head hit the pillow, still dressed in what he had worn earlier.

28

SOMETIMES, JUST MAYHEM

The early evening was crisp. The stars blinked one by one into view for a while, then in groups appeared as night fell and the area quieted. I waited in my hideout at the back of the Burgess estate and watched the guards make their rounds. They were methodical and their tracks worn. But they weren't too alert. They had become familiar with the repetition of their work and embraced its mundane nature. They clearly weren't expecting trouble.

Lights from the sparsely spaced homes throughout the area slowly went out. Around midnight the outdoor lighting around the perimeter of the Burgess estate turned off, leaving only the home lit. The darkness became all edges and splinters of light where I was. But that was all good for me. I wanted the guards complacent and I needed the cover of darkness.

Just before midnight a car had pulled into the driveway. I wasn't certain who it was. It wasn't clear if someone was already in the house and I didn't want to risk moving about until later at night. An upstairs light came on for a brief while and then went out. Someone could have gone to bed or just used the bathroom. A light was on in a downstairs room so once the guards had made their rounds just after midnight I climbed the fence and snuck around the side of the house. I wanted to observe from a different angle.

The sensation of prowling about the Burgess property was strange. It felt all wrong. Something about returning to earth made me feel queasy over what I was about to do. I had killed a lot on the moon and hadn't really thought much about it. It was kill or be killed there. I was surviving. But this was different. This felt like murder, a different sensation from what I had experienced before. I stood in the darkness under a tree that overhung the fence and reviewed the past few weeks. Edward Burgess deserved to die. I hated him for what he had done. I was comfortable as the blade that sliced through him. Still, here rules and laws mattered. Here was judgement. I was in society again, with all its written and unwritten rules. I couldn't entirely slough off my societal connections, despite everything I had been through. But I thought again about Burgess sending me to the moon to die and the anger and hatred sent bile to the back of my throat.

The guards made their rounds again, still lax in their attentiveness, guns in their holsters and one of them played music in at least one ear. When they passed I followed one around the property, keeping to the shadows along the fence where it came close to the back of the house. I was fifty or more yards away from the house. They stopped on either side of the front of the house and stood quietly in the shadows. I couldn't hear the guard closest to me say anything across the distance, but assumed they had to communicate with the others.

Burgess must not have had any electronic security around the property, which seemed odd, but I had checked upon arrival and looked over the perimeter really well. He trusted the guards more than technology, but why not both? That said, crime against the Oligoi was non-existent, or near to it. Perhaps he thought it wasn't necessary. The only thing of note I had found were a few cameras in the neighboring property. They all pointed toward the house and I had done my best to avoid them.

I waited a while but nothing changed so I slowly slipped deeper into the shadows and made my way to the front of the property. It was a pretty good trek. I could see the winding driveway into the estate and was thankful the surrounding area was wooded. It provided plenty of cover.

I camped behind some bushes until the next rounds were made. This time the guards switched positions when the rounds were complete. A small wooden kiosk blended in perfectly with the surroundings next to some bushes toward the road entrance. One of the men walked to it and stayed briefly, then took a position behind a tree several yards away. The other crossed over the driveway and took up a similar position.

I pulled the PED out of my bag, dimmed the screen as low as possible, and activated the camera. It had a night vision mode that worked pretty well and I could clearly see the guards.

I needed to take out the guards closest to the road first, then I could make my way to the house. I wasn't certain what the guard did at the kiosk, but I would have to trust I could figure it out, if needed, but I didn't think it would be necessary. It would all be over before that mattered. The same was true for any in-home security alarms. By the time the police arrived it would all be done and I would either be long gone or dead.

I had a plan, now it was time to execute it.

Something made me nervous so I waited another hour and watched as the guards walked up the drive and made their rounds. I slipped quietly across the driveway and waited where the guard had been stationed. When I saw them coming back down the driveway I packed the PED away and left my bag near the entrance to the property behind a bush. Then I climbed up into the tree the man had stood under and pulled the knife I had purchased earlier from the back of my belt.

The guards went through the same routine. I waited until the man was below me. He was carrying one of the new short, semi-automatic rifles that used charge rounds and he placed it at the base of the tree, then leaned against the tree himself. Next he pulled something out of a pocket, unwrapped it, and placed it in his mouth. I lowered my self slowly and quietly from the tree, knife between my teeth, ready to drop on top of him if I suspected he'd heard me.

The guard put his head back against the tree and raised up his right knee and rested his foot on the trunk. I was squatting on a lower limb just above him and I put the knife in my right hand, grabbed the branch with my left and swung down and drove the knife into his throat.

He reached for his neck, tried to scream but couldn't as blood rushed down my hand and arm. I stood right against him and drove the knife in harder. He slumped over and I gently lowered him.

I made a quick check of the guard across the driveway but couldn't see him. That put me on alert. I didn't hear anyone coming near, just the normal night sounds. Then I heard a low chirping coming from the dead guard and I pulled the small device out of his ear and placed it in mine. The other guard was telling him to keep quiet. The guard I had killed was dressed similarly to me, so I stepped out from the tree and raised a hand and gave a quick nod, then stepped back.

I wiped the blade on the guard's pants and searched his body for anything else I might be able to use. He had a knife and the gun with the charge rounds. But the gun was designed to incapacitate someone, not kill them. I couldn't leave any of the guard's alive. They might be able to identify something about me. If I got away I wanted it to be clean. As far as I knew I was still considered dead. I wanted to keep it that way. The charge rounds also made a noise similar to a pistol shot, so that wasn't going to work with the two at the front of the house.

The property sloped down to a small bridge and the driveway curved up and around toward the house. I grabbed my bag and snuck through the woods down the hill toward the bridge. It was low enough there to hide me from the two guards at the house, though they were quite far away. Once I reached the bridge I saw a small creek that must have run underground from the edge of the property where I had circled around to get to the front. I pulled out the PED again and activated the camera. I could see the remaining guard at the front of the property well enough to know he was facing away from me. I crouched past the base of the bridge and moved up the hill on the other side of the driveway.

It felt like it had taken me forever because I was cautious, but I wasn't really certain how long it had been. There wasn't a clear path to the guard that would provide me cover. Just as I was kneeling down to crawl as close as possible, he walked a few feet away to the kiosk and pulled out a large PED. The screen flipped on and I could see a couple camera feeds coming from the house. Burgess had cameras on his roof and they were pointing out on his property.

The guard enlarged each window frame and flipped through the different camera angles. I used the time to move closer and dropped my bag next to a tree. By the time he finished I was in the perfect position. I wanted to slice his throat like I had the other guard to avoid any communication or emergency call to the guards at the house.

He returned to the same position he had been in before. I was close enough then to reach out and touch him. I took a deep breath, tried to still my pounding heart and quiet my nerves. With a quick step I grabbed the hair at the back of his head and pulled, bringing my left hand around to finish the job.

Like the other guard, he didn't have anything on him I could use except the charge round gun. I slung it over my shoulder and then went to the kiosk and pulled out the PED. I counted five cameras in all. They surrounded the house and looked out on the property, just as I thought before. That explained why there weren't any trees or bushes for the last fifty yards leading up to the house in the front. It was near impossible to sneak up. The back of the property was shorter and more heavily wooded, as I already knew. I confirmed the cameras along the back fence line were for the neighboring property. Burgess really wasn't worried about security. But, as I said earlier, crimes against the Oligoi were almost non-existent. He didn't need to be worried for the most part.

I couldn't see any other way to get to the guards by the house except by my original plan. I tossed the PED from the kiosk, grabbed my bag, and made my way around the property the same as I had come earlier. I got to the back of the house and snuck up the side and hid in some bushes near the back corner. Then I waited.

It wasn't a long wait. The guards made their rounds on schedule. I let the guard pass by me and walk around the back of the house. I closed my eyes and tried to stop the pounding in my head. Every little thing sounded so loud, including the blood rushing through my veins. I imagined the guards stopping and surveying the back of the property, nodding to each other—there was radio silence—and then going off in opposite directions.

I had decided to use the gun I had acquired. I pulled it out, checked the ammo, and switched off the safety. A few moments later the guard passed before me. They had changed sides of the house. This guard was wearing a hat. Just as he passed I stepped out from the building and shot him as he was going by. The sound from the gun wasn't as loud as I thought it would be. But the other guard heard something and made radio contact.

"Mm teth shilta, cot," I mumbled aloud, barely above a whisper, trying to confuse him.

Then I pulled out the knife and finished off the guard I had shot. I grabbed his hat, put it on, and quickly pulled him off the walkway away from the house and into the grass where he could easily be seen in case the other guy came around. Then I walked toward the front of the house. My adrenaline levels bordered on uncontrollable. I could see and hear everything far better than normal. I breathed in a strong metallic smell from the blood I had spilled. I tried slowing down some to seem normal, but wasn't sure I was pulling it off.

The final guard came to the corner of the house as I approached. It was dark enough that he was unable to see me clearly and recognize I wasn't his partner. I was several yards away and made a sign to be quiet, then pointed back at the dead man. He peeked around his raised gun and saw the man. I lowered my gun which caused him to relax a slight bit, dropping the barrel of his gun toward the ground.

"What the fuck?"

I raised my gun quickly and shot him, before he had time to react and figure it out. It wasn't a clean hit. He tumbled backward and screamed out. I dropped the gun and pulled out my knife and raced toward him. His gun was a few feet away. He reached for it with his left hand and fired a shot just as I got there. The shot nicked my shoulder and sent a jolt of electricity through me. But it only slowed me down. It didn't stop me. His right side was shaking and he was too weak to get off another shot.

I drove the knife in deep.

I rolled off the man and lay there in the grass for a few moments. My shoulder ached. I tried to catch my breath but was having difficulties. I couldn't hear anything around me, but I didn't trust my senses. Eventually, I rolled over and worked and stretched my left shoulder. I had been lucky to only take a glancing blow. But it still hurt like hell and my arm felt like it had had the circulation cut off and fallen to sleep. I took the pins and needles feeling as a good sign—that the feeling was coming back.

I was reasonably certain I was safe. All guards were eliminated. I took a few minutes to walk around the house and look for a way to gain entry. As expected, there wasn't an unlocked door anywhere or an open window. I realized I was feeling more comfortable with what I was doing, and more relaxed about my position. I took a seat on the patio in back and relaxed for a minute, letting my shoulder and arm work their way back to normal.

The moon was low on the horizon, partially obscured by trees. Men were dying there—for sport, but mostly for profit. They weren't good men and they weren't heroes. But I couldn't find a way to turn them into something as evil as the one who put them there, or the ones who supported the cause.

I was grinning. I had escaped that tomb, stolen a shuttle, taken over Olympus and found my way back to earth. Now it was time to make revenge my own, to finish the deal.

There was no sense worrying over the alarms when I broke into the house. I guessed it would be a silent alarm, but it was possible that wasn't the case. In the event an alarm sounded, I would have to hurry to get to Burgess before he could get prepared and arm himself.

I identified a window at ground level that would work as my ingress point, located the release handle through the glass and wrapped the butt end of the knife in a t-shirt that was in my bag. I hit hard one time with the knife and broke the window enough to get my hand through. It was, thankfully, a relatively quiet break. The floor inside this room had to be carpeted, I thought. I carefully reached inside and flipped the latch. No alarms so far. Silent alarm, then, I figured. I dropped the shirt and bag outside and lifted the window and crawled through.

I was in a small room that felt musty and unused, like a storage room. It was too dark to tell, though a small amount of light filtered in under the door. The door led to a hallway. I could hear a PED buzzing in an adjacent room. The hall wound around to a set of stairs toward the front of the house. I climbed them as quickly and silently as I could. I stopped at the top and listened for any signs that Burgess might have been roused from bed. I didn't detect any signs of movement or noise, just my heart pounding in my chest and ears.

It was easy to see from the layout where the master bedroom was—straight ahead and at the back of the house. The darkness was different inside, more complete and blurry. But my eyes were adjusting quickly. The door to the room was slightly ajar. I pulled the knife from its sheath and pushed the door open.

There were two people in the bed. Burgess was sprawled out on top of the bedspread, clothes still on. I could smell alcohol. It looked like a woman on the other side, smaller, curled up under the covers on the edge of the king size bed.

Sarah.

I froze. Then I fought off tears and my racing heart.

29

THE PRICE OF REVENGE

I hadn't prepared myself for the possibility that Sarah was alive. Looking back, I realized it was too painful to consider, especially had it not been true. But there she was. I could see her blonde hair, even in the low light, and the shape of her body showed through the covers. My mouth went dry, my heart pounded in my ears, and in a rough and whispered voice I muttered her name, "Sarah?"

I hadn't meant to waken her but as I stumbled toward her side of the bed she roused from sleep. Tears clouded my vision as I rounded the corner of the bed and pulled up to her side.

"Clay? Oh, my God! Clay! How—?"

She pushed herself up on one arm and wiped her eyes with the other. I traced the outline of her face with my left hand, overcome with emotion. "I, I never thought I would see you again."

I was stammering and shaking. Something deep and insistent

had taken over and I found it nearly impossible to control. I pulled her close and held her tightly. She was clearly as moved as I was. I felt her shaking as we embraced. No words could express what I felt.

On the moon, and the journey there, I had wondered what it meant to be human. I was focused on humans as a species, as big brained sentient monkeys living in complex systems and twisted societies. I had never considered the question from an individual perspective, not really. Society isn't the individual and often what defines one—or what is good and necessary for one—is wrong for the other. They don't mesh, at least not nearly enough. Sometimes they can barely coexist. In all my ramblings I never considered that the lives of two people might vary drastically from the collective. Yet, there I was, holding Sarah and thinking life had more to offer than I had ever imagined.

Burgess had woken from his drunken stupor. I hadn't heard him or noticed. He jumped up from the bed and pulled open a table drawer next to the bed. He turned and stumbled momentarily, tipsy still from the alcohol. I saw the gun as he turned. I jumped on the bed as he raised the gun and drove toward him, my anger and hatred swelled as I remembered why I was there. A shot rang out and the bullet whizzed past me. I dove on top of him and punched him in the face and then batted the gun away as another shot hit the ceiling fan.

Burgess crashed into the wall and screamed out. I kept pounding his face with my fist. I couldn't hit him hard enough. I wanted knock his head off, make him pay for sending me to the moon and for what he had done to Sarah. He raised his arms in defense but I didn't care. I beat them with the same force and anger and then lowered my aim and hit his ribs and stomach. Eventually, I saw the gun a few feet away, picked it up and aimed it at him.

His face was bloodied and cut and swollen, one eye shut already. His nose was off to the side, clearly broken, and his left shoulder looked dislocated. Blood was splattered against the wall behind his head. He slumped against the wall and slowly sank down to the floor like something pitiful that needed to be put down.

"Fucking Alexander," he said, voice gravelly. His breathing was coarse and raspy. "You'll never be like me—not in a million years. Not in your genes."

"Not anything I would ever want, Burgess. You're everything that's wrong with humanity. You—and others like you—destroyed the world through your greed and avarice and small-minded delusional thinking. You think you're better because you were born into wealth and given everything your whole life. But you aren't any different from me, just privileged because of what others before you did. All anyone will remember you for is being a drunken, wife-beating prick of a person. Nothing more than that."

He looked beaten and torn up. I also sensed guilt coming through his one open eye. But some fire inside him recovered and reasserted itself. "Still better than you," he said.

I knelt down to be at eye level with him and grinned.

"You're just a flash in the pan, Alexander, fifteen minutes of fame, that's all," he said.

"Says the dead man."

His eye widened and I sensed fear in him. Then I shot him in the stomach with his own gun. He barely moved, but his eyes were shut and his body shook.

"I hear," I said, "it's a painful way to die. And look at that, you still bleed like the rest of us."

I had been lost in the anger and intensity of the moment. Suddenly, I came to my senses and an uneasy awareness came over me.

I heard Sarah whimpering behind me. She was in the middle of the bed, bleeding. I dropped the gun and hurried to her. She didn't look good. I rolled her over slowly and saw she had been shot. One of Burgess' bullets had found her chest. Her eyes were weak and she was taking short breaths.

"You came back," she said, just a whisper of her normal voice.

"For you, of course I came back. He told me you were dead. He sent someone to the moon with that message."

"I know," Sarah said. "I saw."

I crossed my legs and lifted her up and held her. She was bleeding badly and I tried to put pressure on the wound.

"Not going to do any good, Clay."

"Don't say that. We need to get you to a hospital. I'll call now. Hang in there."

I was getting frantic and wanted to reach for a PED next to the bed but I didn't want to let go of her. But she had an eerie calm and she smiled softly at me.

"No, really, too late. Not going to make it."

"Please don't. No! Hold on. We can get someone here." I pulled her close to me. I had a million things I wanted to say to her, to tell her. But all I really wanted in that moment was to switch positions with her.

She glanced over at Burgess who watched as he slowly bled out.

"It's okay," said Sarah. "If it's going to end this way then it's okay."

"Don't say that. How could it ever be okay?"

She looked back to me. "I'm pregnant, Clay—not ours. Happened weeks before we met. I just found out."

She looked at Burgess again and spoke, her voice a little louder now: "The stupid son-of-a-bitch just killed his only child, his heir.

The one thing he wanted and needed."

Her eyes closed then. "Sarah," I said, "Sarah, stay with me."

She opened her eyes again. "You came back for me Clay. I felt like I was letting you down, not doing enough."

"Of course I came back. But I didn't think you would want me after what I did on the moon."

"Always. You did what you had to. You're a hero now."

"I'm not the hero. The Poet Of The Moon is. I don't think I want anything to do with it. I'll take a quiet life with you, see where it goes, answer all those questions we used to ask."

"Yeah, that. Sounds wonderful. Tell me about it, Clay, that life. I'm cold. Hold me, don't let go."

I squeezed her a little tighter.

"Have a good life, Clay. Live well. Don't forget I love you."

"Never," I said. "I love you, too."

"Tell me the story, Clay. Start with the moon and how you escaped."

"I'll tell you how I escaped from the moon. Then I'll tell you about our future, the life we'll build."

But she was fading fast. I could feel it. She died while I was holding her. I didn't want it to be true so I kept my arms wrapped around her as I told her the story of how I had escaped the moon, of the control room and the Polynesian and our trek along the surface. I told her of the communications center and Olympus and hitching a ride across country just to get back to her. I told her everything, and of the dreams I had for us, the things we would do and see together, the places we would explore.

Edward Burgess was dead. I looked at him from the bed, slumped against the wall and blood pooling beneath him. I still felt hatred toward him. But I felt something else, too. I felt guilt. Sarah was dead because of me—because of Burgess and myself. I wanted to blame him for everything, but I had played a part. My return hadn't protected her or freed her. I wanted to cry, to just sit there and weep. But off in the distance I could hear sirens. Time was up. I either left then or faced worse things.

I brushed Sarah's hair away from her face and laid her gently down on the bed. I'd have traded places in a heartbeat, but that wasn't my fate. I was doomed to live.

I took her PED from the nightstand. I considered what I had done in the house and the things I had touched and thought I might be in a good position. There wasn't much direct evidence I had been there, mostly on Burgess but that might be covered by his own blood. I didn't care at that point.

I wiped my prints from the gun and placed it next to Burgess. Who knew what the authorities would make of the incident. The dead guards would point to intruders from outside the Burgess household. It would definitely be murder. But they would look a long time for viable suspects and find little. The cameras might have recorded something outside the house, but that wasn't certain. And the darkness may have offered enough cover to hide my identity. Or, maybe Burgess had some bad relationships with people in his business, enemies with motive, and they would make assumptions and look down a different path. It didn't matter to me. Nothing much mattered in the moment. I had murdered Burgess just as I had wanted.

But the price of revenge was too high, far too high.

30

GOODBYES

The police pulled up the drive as I left the Burgess estate, sirens blaring and lights flashing. I climbed out through the same window I had entered, noting to myself that I had used a t-shirt to break the glass and hadn't left any prints. The shirt was in my bag and the bag over my shoulder. I kept to the exact same route as I had taken when arriving: over the fence at the back of the property to the neighboring estate, skirting along the wooded perimeter until I reached a road. But then what? I didn't know. I stood for a few moments contemplating, but couldn't clear my head. Too much static and conflicting thoughts prevented me from thinking clearly. I wanted to stop but thought it a bad idea. I had to keep moving.

I walked along the side of the road for a long while, down side streets and through a park I hadn't seen before. I was exposed in these neighborhoods. Anyone walking here at this time of night was definitely out of place so I was wary of every little noise. A while later I came upon another park I didn't remember—or perhaps an unfenced estate—and crossed through it, keeping to the trees and brush. Sirens came and went, usually quite distant, but because of the quiet hour their sound carried a long way and I tensed each time I heard a new one, expecting it to turn toward me.

Eventually, the houses changed from the massive estates to nice neighborhoods as I made my way back to the light rail station. I can't say how I got there or how long it took, but it felt like a long while. I was moving in a fog composed of grief and guilt and a sense of great loss. The light rail station was something I knew and my broken mind probably connected a familiar thing or place to safety.

A homeless man was sleeping under a bench. He didn't move when I sat down several feet away. I was cold and couldn't get warm, but that was caused by something other than the temperature. I leaned against a post and stared into the night, haunted by the sound of Burgess' gun. My mind messed with me. Red was everywhere—blood—whether it was an object's color or not. It poured out of crevices and from joints in the station roofing. It jumped from the packages in a nearby vending machine. I couldn't keep from seeing red. I closed my eyes but Sarah was there, her beautiful face and those piercing blues eyes, and I couldn't bare it. The darkness made things worse, less to distract my vision and occupy my thoughts. The paucity of people and moving things was an indictment against what had happened and an accusation for my having played a part. The universe shined a spotlight on me and I was wilting.

A train arrived and I watched in a disconnected manner as it came into the station. One of the cars toward the back was darker than the rest. It had a burned out light so I entered it and took a seat. The train lurched forward and I melted into the chair. Outside the car was dark, objects and places blurred out the windows and inside the car became a gray fog. I fell into my own myopic world and barely existed outside my thoughts. I was numb. The world and all its sensory stimulants receded before me and pain replaced it.

The train barreled toward its stops and through the night-covered neighborhoods and sleeping sections of town. I was oblivious to them. At one point I roused enough to look out the window, but all I saw was my own reflection. I wasn't ready to deal with it, make friends again or recognize what I had done or been a part of. That would take time. So I looked away, back to the floor and the rubber mat and chaotic grime.

The sun slowly came up. The world became more clearly defined. I was exhausted and feeling exposed in the color and light. I got off the train in the northern part of town and walked to a nearby all night fast food restaurant. I wasn't hungry so I ordered a drink and sat in a booth and watched as the area slowly came to life. People moved about silently in the early morning. Some workers moved along the street, but in this part of town there weren't many Clergy heading to jobs. Mostly, a few lost souls like me drifted about in the early sunshine. Others were disconnected in their own way from the realities of the modern world. Some worked out or walked dogs. A few of the homeless ambled past. Where do they go, I wondered? What is on their agenda?

I wondered then if anything had been made of the Burgess murders. I pulled the two PEDs from my bag. I had forgotten that I had Sarah's. I turned it off. They could trace it if they noticed it was missing.

There wasn't yet any news of the murders on the networks.

I sat in the restaurant for a couple hours. The world fully woke and became noisy. Sunshine glittered off shiny surfaces and the shadows added definition and depth as more people moved about. I didn't have the energy for it. Just observing tired me out.

Another small group of the homeless sauntered by. They moved slowly but were in good spirits. I needed to leave the restaurant. It felt important to keep moving. I was too exposed sitting in one place. I was beginning to feel more human but I was in no position to face things, and certainly didn't want to ponder the future.

I packed up my bag and left the restaurant. I decided to follow the small group of homeless people that had passed a few minutes before, something about them intrigued me. The group made its way to a shallow but wide creek that ran for miles through this part of town. There they brushed teeth, washed their faces and hands and chatted with each other. A few washed clothing and hung the pieces on nearby branches to dry.

I found a seat against the base of a large tree that was hidden from the roads and surrounding area and spent the day there. The homeless left after an hour. A couple came and went later, using the creek to wash. A silver fox ran about and drank from the creek, ever wary, then raced off. Mostly I listened to the sounds of cars and trucks on the nearby roads and rested in the sunshine. My mind was blank. I wasn't hungry or thirsty but remembered I had a protein bar or two in my bag for later if I wanted.

Eventually, the day dimmed and I fell asleep with my arms crossed, holding the bag to my chest, still thoroughly defeated.

When I woke the sun was just coming up again. I was stiff and sore and my hands were badly bruised from where I had beaten Burgess. A sense of panic surrounded my thoughts. I needed a plan, some way to navigate forward. Leaving the warehouse and this city behind was the only choice that made sense. Establish a new identity, find a way to work again and build a life away from anything familiar. There wasn't much else to consider. I had few friends to worry over. I was used to being alone in the world. Starting over wouldn't be too much trouble. As an orphan since twelve years old I possessed the mindset.

The warehouse contained a few items I wanted so I caught the light rail to The Edge. It was early in the morning and few people were out. While on the train I checked the news feeds. The Burgess murders were mentioned. Police didn't have any clues yet, or none they were releasing. They intimated they had some suspects they were pursuing but wouldn't expand.

"I understand you want answers," said a Chief Detective on the case. "So do we. Mr Burgess and his wife were valued and important members of our society. But right now this is an ongoing investigation. I can't say any more than that at this time. Things are fluid and I will inform you as they develop."

Several journalists made the ties to Burgess and Fugitive Theatre and speculated the murders might be retaliation for the downed communication lines and cameras from the moon. One reached out to Sam Verita.

"We spoke every day," said Verita. "My heart and hopes and prayers go out to Edward's family and all the community. He never mentioned any threats on his life, but a man in his position had to be wary of many things."

Another journalist asked if the Murder Of Crows protest were involved. Everyone believed the killings were the work of several people given the number of dead bodies around the estate. If anyone knew anything more they weren't saying.

I disembarked from the train at the same spot where I had overheard two police talking about me as if I weren't there just a few weeks before. It had an odd feel about it. I wasn't dressed so nicely now and I didn't feel like the same person. Had the same police been there I might have confronted them.

The Edge was dirty. It looked old and weather beaten now. The cheaply printed buildings were tired things that had witnessed and endured too much. There weren't many people about at this hour so I didn't feel threatened I would be discovered. Some of the buildings had the Poet's image graffitied on the side. It wasn't me, I reminded myself. It was the icon they had created. But I wondered what their reaction might be if they had known I was the one who killed Edward Burgess.

The Edge never pretended to be a nice place before I went to the moon. I didn't harbor any unrealistic or sentimental views toward it. But somehow it looked far worse than I had ever imagined in the past. An old question surfaced again; what does it mean to be human? Looking around at the squaller and grime was depressing. It couldn't be this.

Sarah had shown me something different for a short time. She was beauty and grace. She made me realize that two people could build a life together that was different from society, something unique to them, something precious. But places like The Edge—where the bulk of humanity existed—threatened to turn that into a lie, as well.

The lights glowed inside the convenience store. Dom probably still worked there. What would he think of Fugitive Theatre now? I would find it strange and surreal now, I'm sure. The middle school was still quiet, but Tabitha and the other kids would be yelling and jostling about the place soon.

I passed the place where Sarah and I first met. I pulled my bag tighter around my shoulders and tried to scoot on by, but the brain can be a cruel instrument. It wouldn't let me forget that meeting and served it up in full color and rich detail. The accompanying sadness quickened my step and my heart skipped a few beats.

The warehouse was as I had left it. The security protocols were still in place. The heavy door opened and I stepped inside. I was home—but I wasn't. Something was off, out of kilter. I dropped the bag and stood there for a few minutes. It wasn't the warehouse that was out of whack. It was me. Nothing in it had changed. Everything in me had.

I knew then I could never stay. I had to move on, create something new. My home, the place I loved, had become tainted. I walked into the living area. Something scuffed the floor under my right foot. I looked down and saw one of the casings from the charge bullets that had been fired. I reached down and picked it up. As I raised up Myiamoto strolled over and rubbed against my legs. I knelt down and picked up the big scraggily cat.

"You don't look any worse for wear."

I had left the door partly open and someone burst through it.

"Who are you? Why are you here?"

I turned and smiled and dropped Myiamoto. "You ought to be in school, kid."

Tabitha's jaw dropped to the floor. "Clay!" She raced to me and gave me a big hug.

"I don't understand. You're dead. I saw it. We all did."

"Don't believe everything they tell you, Tabitha. I see you're still out getting dirty."

I smiled and rubbed at the dirt marks on her shoulder.

"What happened?"

"Let's just say I escaped."

She looked at me with expectant eyes and a tilted head. "So, you're back now?"

"No, can't stay. But I'm glad you came. We need to talk."

"I saw you just before you got to the warehouse. I thought someone was breaking in."

"Awfully early for you to be out, isn't it?"

"Ah, you know me, Clay, always out doing something." She grinned.

"Look, I have to leave," I told her. "For good. I wish I didn't but things would get real ugly if anyone knew I was alive."

I could see she was upset and confused.

"Don't worry, I'll find a way to keep in touch. It may take a while, but I will."

"Where will you go? What will you do?"

I shrugged. "Dunno."

"You're just going to leave?"

"In a few minutes. This place, the warehouse," I looked around at everything, "it's all yours. I will show you how to get in."

"I figured that out, Clay."

"The security system? No way!"

"No. I climbed up to the roof and came in that way. There wasn't any security there."

"Smart kid. I will give you the codes anyway. You have to keep everything a secret, Tab. I mean, no one can know anything. They can't know about this place and they can't know I'm alive. Understand?"

"I understand."

Myiamoto rubbed up against her legs. "Do I get this crazy guy, too?"

"Of course, he's part of this place."

I spent a few minutes teaching Tab the security protocols and programming them to work for her. We walked up to the roof and looked out upon The Edge. The city was waking up and it had gotten noisy while we had talked.

Eventually, we walked back downstairs and I packed a few things I wanted into my bag.

"There is one other thing, Tab. In the safe is a copy of a book: The Oligoi Wars. It's illegal to own it. You would be in big trouble if anyone found it here. That's another reason to keep this place secret. Also, there is some money in the safe."

I showed her where the safe was hidden and how to open it. Then I took a little of the money.

"Who uses that anymore?"

"No one does," I answered. "But it hasn't been made illegal to have it yet. After a while, take some to the bank and change it to credit. Tell them some really old person paid you with it to do some work around her house. They'll believe that. Use it to take care of Myiamoto and the warehouse. It's not a lot, but it will help."

"Myiamoto doesn't need a lot. He's pretty good on his own. But, thanks. I will remember if I need it."

It was time to leave. I got a little choked up saying goodbye. The warehouse had meant a lot to me. And I liked Tabitha a lot. I gave her another hug and promised to contact her soon.

"I can't believe you came back. You have to tell me about it later."

"Sometime later I will. Don't be late for school," I said, and walked out the door.

31

ONLY HUMAN

When our gods fall they do so quickly and often violently. Myths and legends become frail and brittle and their facade fragile and all too human. Their weakness, now perceived, angers men to violence. A mob mentality replaces awe and respect in those who feel they have been duped. That same group, of course, had elevated the man to a god in the first place. It is an unstable platform given the fickle nature of human emotions.

I spent the day on the light rail after leaving Tabitha and the warehouse and then found a ride north with a couple in a truck. I had no idea where I was going, only that I needed to leave. It felt good to be traveling. I felt safe moving. Mostly, I used the time to unspool from the emotional rollercoaster I had been on and to find an equilibrium between the despair of the recent past and the future and whatever it held.

In the evening I found a cheap motel and lay on the bed, exhausted but unable to sleep. I opened the PED—which I had avoided all day—and looked at the news feeds. The headlines spoke of fallen gods and protests. It seemed my Polynesian friend had been busy. Apparently, part of Olympus had come loose and was careening toward earth. Communications were still out with the near-earth orbital and foul play was suspected with the falling debris, though a few of the more cautious news sites allowed for the possibility of an accident given the ongoing construction. Things were unravelling for our once tightly knit societal structure. Communications still hadn't been restored with the moon, either, causing more supposition and concern.

As part of the near earth orbital made its way toward the atmosphere people viewed the events with a twist toward anger. Some believed it was the True God taking his vengeance against our would-be overlords. Others didn't care for that. They saw the weakness—fueled by the Poet's rantings and his death and the protests that had been building—and began frothing at the mouth. Regardless of the source of their questions and frustrations, those angered were growing in number.

The police had already come down hard on two of the protests in the larger cities. Forces—ideologies—clashed, people died, some searching for freedoms, real or perceived, others, fewer in number, to maintain the status quo. The violence, according to the news feeds, wasn't lessening or receding as the day wore on, simply recoiling and striking out with renewed vigor once recharged. But the Murder Of Crows protest was suffering great losses. Though, apparently, the police weren't discriminating. It had become hunting season and anyone near a problem area was fair game, member of the protest or not.

Sometime in the late afternoon new information from the Burgess murders had been released. Several of the leaders of the protests were implicated and arrested. According to sources, they blamed Burgess for the death of the Poet and for the show going offline. The murders were supposed to be seen as a quid pro quo—you take ours, we'll take yours, an eye for an eye.

I knew the truth, of course. The Oligoi were taking a stand, rewriting history—same old same old. They took the opportunity to create a villain and justify their actions, just as Burgess had done when he bombed one of his own factories and blamed me. But the Oligoi provided me with cover. Their desire to end the protests was my lucky break. They couldn't claim the murders were the product of an angry group of protestors and still implicate me. It also meant that the police investigation would be closed. They wouldn't continue looking into Edward Burgess' death if they had already captured and tried someone in the media for it. That would lead to too many questions. No doubt they believed this would quell the resistance and quiet things down. That worked in my favor.

The more I read the more my mood lightened. The world's chaos provided cover for me. I could create a future without always looking over my shoulder. I fell asleep then, thinking of the Polynesian and fallen gods and feeling more comfortable with my situation.

I woke the following day, showered and had breakfast, then took the train to one of the northern cities on the current coast. It felt comfortable walking about. I liked the place and its vibe.

I had come to a decision during my sleep; I was certain I didn't want anything to do with the protests. I was moving on. I hadn't even bothered to check the news feeds when I got up. I was content to disappear into the multitudes and find my own way. It wasn't that I believed the protesters were wrong. Their cause was justified. But I believed one outcome existed, which didn't interest me. Minor changes were the only result I could see coming from the protests, the same group of people, the Oligoi, would remain in control. Humanity had its patterns and we weren't about to break the mold now, despite all the ramblings I had made as the Poet.

Sarah had shown me what two people could have, what they could create, even if it was only a brief glimpse. I had tasted the possibilities and knew the wonder. I also knew the opposite, trapped on the moon and forced to transform myself. But that was only part of the answer to the deeper questions that haunted me. I still couldn't answer what it meant to be human. Society wasn't the individual. They could be vastly separate entities. So, what did it mean to be human? That wasn't necessarily the same as what it meant to be me. Whatever definition I decided on, I knew it had to include pain.

I found a seat at an outdoor cafe along the ocean and ordered some food. I was suddenly ravenous. A couple large ships were a mile or so out from the shore and an old man walked the beach below me, combing for small treasures and lost items. As I watched the man and the ships I reflected upon the previous few weeks.

A seagull swooped down and glided toward the beach. It reminded me of my winged friends from the moon. What of the experiments I witnessed there? Clearly, the Oligoi were experimenting with genetic expression and probably modification. Also, Burgess was always so intent on pointing out how different he and I were. It might not have been our backgrounds that were so different. There may have been more to it. The bigger question, of course, was what future plans did they, the Oligoi, hide?

Those thoughts couldn't hold my interest. I didn't really care any longer. It was in my past and I needed to focus forward.

The food was served and I ate quietly and watched the people around me as the restaurant filled up with patrons. The buzz of quiet conversation was something I missed when I was on the moon. I didn't need to participate to soak it in and feel it. I found it soothing. When I finished my late lunch—early dinner?—I sat back in my chair and let the thoughts I had previously pondered sift through my subconscious and reveal something more enlightening. When Edward Burgess condemned me to die on the moon I believed I had to abandon my humanity to survive, to become a killing machine and lose all sense of community and compassion and jettison morality and ethics. But humans are the most violent creatures on earth. We kill other adults of our own species at unprecedented rates, far greater than any other species does. Violence is our nature whether we like to admit it or not. It has to be part of our species' definition.

On some level I was wrong, I realized, when I said I had to abandon my humanity to survive the moon and Fugitive Theatre. The truth was, I had to embrace it.

ABOUT JACK MCDANIEL

Jack McDaniel lives in Colorado. Several of his short stories are in The Future Is Short, volumes 3 and 4, a collection of short science fiction stories. His writing has also been featured on the "A Creative Mind" fiction podcast. His previous novels include: *Agents Of The Undertow*, *Agents Of Hope* and *Agents Of Change* in the Pan21 series, and *Purple Hearted Man*. You can learn more at his website:

www.JackMcDaniel.net

Twitter

@jackmcdaniel

www.ingramcontent.com/pod-product-compliance
Lightning Source LLC
Chambersburg PA
CBHW030810310726
48980CB00006B/450/J

* 9 7 8 0 5 7 8 3 3 1 6 3 8 *